Tiponi

by

Evelyn Timidaiski

Tiponi

Cover Art by *Debbie Taylor*

The Wild Rose Press, Inc.
PO Box 708
Adams Basin, NY 14410-0708
Visit us at www.thewildrosepress.com

Publishing History
First Edition, 2021
Trade Paperback ISBN 978-1-5092-3600-8
Digital ISBN 978-1-5092-3601-5

Published in the United States of America

Dedication

To Jamesy with love

Acknowledgements

Authors rarely complete their novels without a support group. I'd like to thank my friends and family for their continued support.

I'd like to thank my editor, Kaycee John, for her generous patience and support with all the updates and changes that were made to make Tiponi a quality novel. Thanks also to Amanda Barnett, Senior Editor for the Fantasy Rose line at TWRP, for her support and help.

Thanks to my cover artist, Debbie Taylor, who did a fantastic job on the cover art.

Thanks also to you, my readers, for your interest and following my book.

The chilling cry of a wolf sounded on the night breeze.

Powaqa stilled. The sound resonated with her body as if played by a master musician's fingers, plucking a finely tuned instrument. "I recognize his voice." She gasped. Her mind filled with warmth, and her senses tingled. "I feel him in my mind." Excitement burst through her body. Every cell of her being aligned itself with the animal's call. Quickly, she turned to the one person she trusted to explain this unexpected occurrence. "I've heard this voice before, haven't I?" She knew the answer without asking. All through her childhood she'd been aware of a presence. Even when she'd felt alienated by her differences, the being had been there. Not until she heard the chilling call from the hilltop, did she realize—they were the same.

Chapter One

Kahoti Reservation, 2224 A.D.; Powaqa''s Coming of Age

Waves of shimmering heat moved like silent wraiths across the distant horizon. The cerulean blue sky hung over the parched, red terrain and wind etched monoliths and plateaus. Thousands of millennia of Kahoti had lived and died in this desert. Wars, famine, and persecution had ravaged their numbers, but not their traditions.

For the Kahoti this place was spiritual—a place of discovery. From their point of emergence in the Grand Canyon, her ancestors journeyed in all four directions, and then settled in their chosen place, Black Mesa. Here they had lived simple lives according to the edicts taught by the Katsinas.

"I love the desert." Powaqa placed the medicinal herbs she'd collected in her basket and looked around. Dark glasses protected her weak albino eyes from the harsh light, but they also enhanced the colors. "It feels so free and alive." She turned to Kaya, her Earth mother. "Don't you feel it?"

The old woman gave their surroundings a quick glance. "I feel the pull, but not as strongly as you, child. You and the desert have a special connection. It will always call to you."

She watched the sun glint off the colorful rock formations and felt a sense of yearning, though was unsure for what. "You said my mother was in the desert when I was born. Why? Did she mean for me to die?"

"No, she wanted you to live. It was she who wished to die."

She stood and paced the sandy area of their campsite, her steps jerky. Her mind buzzed with questions, needing to know so many things. "Was she ashamed? Didn't she want me?"

Growing up, Kaya had called her *special*. She'd been born an albino among a people of red skin. Wasn't that special enough? Did the Great Spirit have more planned for her? Anger and angst warred in her chest. With an effort, she curbed her painful thoughts. She must push those things behind her and move on, but at twelve, how could she show such wisdom?

She looked over at Kaya, whose silver-streaked hair encircled her head in a tight braid. Her Earth mother sat near the tent, weaving sweetgrass into long ropes and bundling herbs for drying. Her chocolate eyes were open but held a faraway look as if she saw things only a shaman or waken woman would see. Powaqa's heart skittered a few beats as her bitter questions hung between them like a noxious gas in the air.

Kaya turned a hard stare on her. "It is time. The story must be told—but know this, the knowledge will change you forever."

She stopped pacing and joined Kaya, sitting cross-legged on the ground. She forced herself to remain still as she waited long minutes for the old woman to speak. Anxious to hear the story—yet fearful of what it might mean, she drew in several long, slow breaths to calm her spirit. Kaya had worked for years to teach her the art of controlling her thoughts and emotions. So far, she'd have to admit, her Earth mother still had her work cut out for her.

Kaya's voice startled her with its intensity. "Your mother was Kahoti, but not from the reservation. She did not have tradition to guide her, and your father was never named."

Hurt squeezed her chest. "So, in addition to being a mutant, I'm also a bastard?"

Kaya's face lit with emotion as she grabbed her hands in a steely grip. "Where have you heard such things? You must never speak those words again. "You are so young, and what I am about to tell you is complicated, even in the adult world. Know this child: I am here to help you." A weathered hand ran down her cheek. "You know about the Christian faith?"

She nodded. "Yes."

"Do you think the world believes ill of The Virgin Mary? Would anyone dare call Jesus a bastard, though his father was not of this earth?"

Powaqa pulled her hands free and stood to resume her pacing. "No, but I can't be compared to such exalted people. I'm not a saint, nor am I…" She paused, searching for words to explain. "I'm not sure *what* I am or why I'm here."

"You were born for a special purpose. This might be hard to believe, but you are not of this world." Kaya paused a moment, then in a strong voice added, "You are spirit, not human."

Powaqa froze. Fear, uncertainty, and anger warred within her. "What do you mean? I'm as human as you, or any other Kahoti. I may have albino eyes, but I bleed red and I feel pain." Terror raced down her spine at the implications of Kaya's words. She was already different from her people, and now to discover she wasn't human? "I don't understand. How can this be?"

The old woman placed another braid of sweetgrass into her sack. "The spirits sent you to us through your mother. At the appropriate time, you must return to them and help save our people. The Great Spirit promised to send someone to save our world. In the beginning, White Mesa Woman saved the emerging people from starvation and taught them how to live."

"I know the legend," she stated impertinently. "How does it pertain to me?"

"Do not sass your elders, child. You would do well to listen more and talk less."

She stopped pacing and knelt before the old woman. "Forgive me, Earth mother. I still have much to learn from you." Easing to the ground, she sat with her legs crossed once more.

Kaya remained silent for several long moments.

Powaqa suspected she tested her patience to see if she had learned.

Kaya placed the herbs she had woven aside. When she continued, her voice bore an eerie solemnness. "The Earth is experiencing great quakes and storms. Time is running out. The Blue Katsina will return to dance in the square. If he removes his mask before the people, the world will suffer great catastrophes." She paused as if to give weight to what she was about to say. "You are destined to be our savior. You will be the next White Mesa Woman. Grandfather has shown this to me in a vision."

Agitated, she sprang to her feet. Her mouth opened,

then closed. What could she say? From the dawn of awareness, the legend of the Blue Katsina had passed from the lips of the first Kahoti to emerge from the sacred sipapu to the ear of every elder born to her people. Foolishly, at six she had smeared her face with blue paint, angry at her classmates for teasing her. She'd been determined to teach the jackals a lesson. In her wisdom Kaya had used the incident to teach rather than scold. The legend now held special significance to her. Holy Grandfather, would she be asked to fight the Blue Katsina?

Kaya patted the ground beside her. "Come, child. Do not fear what has been foretold."

Powaqa dropped to her knees, head bowed, waiting for Kaya to impart more wisdom. "You have been chosen to save not just Kahoti, but all people."

She peered into the face of her Earth mother. The old woman's eyes glowed with pride, yet the corners of her mouth turned down. Something about her revelations made Kaya sad.

This wasn't the coming-of-age ceremony she had expected. She'd thought she'd get the traditional sex talk all girls her age received along with oral traditions and family stories mothers passed to their daughters.Talk of marriage and other rites her people held secret and sacred. Not this. As unbelievable as it sounded, she didn't doubt what the old woman had told her. Kaya was *waken*, holy. She spoke only the truth, and her visions always came true.

Her mind spiraled with the implications of what she'd learned about her future.

Instead of answering her questions, Kaya created more. A cool breeze touched her cheeks bringing the scent of Saguaro blossoms. Sweet followed by a tangy twist. Her hands trembled, and she clasped them together, allowing herself a moment to think. The hoot of an owl gave her pause. "Does this mean I can't marry and have children or…?"

"Or what, child?"

The owl called again.

She brought one of the herbs to her nose and sniffed. Normally, its pungent odor would bring a smile to her face. Her voice faded as sadness descended. "I don't suppose any Kahoti man would want to marry someone like me."

"I don't have all the answers, but who can say what the Great Spirit has planned for you? You must be patient and learn as much about our ways as possible. I will teach you about medicines and train you with meditation exercises." Kaya paused. "You know I have visions?"

"Everyone knows."

"You will have them, too. Your powers are starting to grow. Soon, you will experience flashes of insight into others and may even pick up their thoughts."

Her voice rose, then cracked. "I'll be able to read minds?"

"Don't make light of it. With power comes responsibility. You must learn to either tune out the thoughts or use discretion with what you hear. Do you understand what I'm saying?"

She ignored the excited yip of a coyote. "I hear what you're saying. I don't understand it, but I'll do my best to deal with it. What you've revealed is frightening. How will I ever be normal?"

"It has nothing to do with normal, child," Kaya

answered with heat. "You were born different for a purpose. You must live with what the Great Spirit provides. He made you white, so you must live with white and move on. He also gave you great power. You must learn to use and control it. The fate of your people will rest in your hands."

Uncertainty and a need for reassurance filled her voice. "What powers will I have, and when will they begin to show?"

"Your gift will manifest itself soon. Your body is tuned to the psi energy found in all natural things. You must be open and allow yourself to explore the energy you feel around you. I have much to teach you before the Great Spirit will summon you. Don't be afraid, Powaqa. I am here for you and will see you through this."

Staring off into the near darkness she bowed her head. "Somehow," her voice turned wistful, almost yearning, "I always thought I'd take your place one day and become the next medicine woman."

Her Earth mother stared back at her with fathomless dark eyes, now glistening with moisture. "You are destined to become so much more." She wrapped her arms around Powaqa's shoulders and squeezed. After a few brief moments, she sat back and began to weave the flowers with nimble fingers.

The smell of wild herbs teased her senses as the last rays of the sun burned the sky like fire. Powaqa crossed her arms, trying to feel safe in her now uncertain world. "How much time do I have?"

Kaya worked with nimble fingers, stopping only to answer. "Not even I can say that, but when the time comes, a message will be sent."

As she listened to the words of the only mother she'd known, her chest constricted with love and pain. She didn't want to leave, but she would if it meant saving her people.

"Do not be sad. This is a time to rejoice. We are here to welcome you to womanhood." Kaya squeezed her fingers and gave her a smile. "There is much to learn in the desert. Collect some saguaro wood and let us study the stars to see who is looking down at us."

Hours later, the black sky sparkled with lights as Powaqa threw wood on the fire and stood. The smell of the fire was comforting. Something familiar among all the newness Kaya had introduced. This was her last night in the desert, and she felt changed. She'd been an innocent child when this journey began. Now, with the knowledge of what was to come, nothing would ever be the same.

From the medicine bowl she withdrew a handful of sage and threw it into the flames. Her gaze followed the sparks as they rose into the darkness. The fragrance of the sacred herb wafted to her nostrils, and her mind calmed. Arms raised to the sky, she spoke to the stars. "Oh, Great Spirit Sotuknang. Thank you for giving me life. Guide me as I learn about your gifts. Empower me with understanding and courage to do the things I must."

Raising her own hands to the heavens, Kaya stood beside her. "Spirits of the Kahoti, I present to you Powaqa, no longer a child but a woman. Look upon her with kindness and provide her with protection so she can fulfill her destiny."

The chilling cry of a wolf sounded on the night breeze.

Powaqa stilled. The sound resonated with her body as if played by a master musician's fingers, plucking a finely tuned instrument. "I recognize his voice." She gasped. Her mind filled with warmth, and her senses tingled.

"I feel him in my mind." Excitement burst through her body. Every cell of her being aligned itself with the animal's call. Quickly, she turned to the one person she trusted to explain this unexpected occurrence. "I've heard this voice before, haven't I?"

She knew the answer without asking. All through her childhood, she'd been aware of a presence. Even when she'd felt alienated by her differences, the being had been there. Not until she heard the chilling call from the hilltop did she realize—they were the same.

"Yes." Kaya picked up the bowl and threw a handful of herbs onto the fire. "Brother Wolf called to me the night you were born. He kept you safe until I came for you."

Emotion welled within her breast. She'd never been alone, not even now. She turned toward the darkened hill where the howl had sounded and raised her voice. "Thank you, Brother Wolf, for keeping me safe."

She then cupped her hands around her mouth and released an eerily realistic howl of her own. When her howl was returned, girlish laughter spilled from her lips. "Well, at least someone likes me."

Kaya's eyes widened and her face held a look of puzzlement.

"Is everything all right, Kaya? I was just playing, please don't be upset."

"I am not upset, just surprised. I did not know I had

raised a child who could howl at the moon. Are you sure I will be safe to sleep in the same tipi?"

The two laughed together, then entered the shelter to sleep.

Chapter Two

Kahoti Indian Reservation, 2232 A.D.

The early morning sun cast a pink glow on the flattened Mesa. Powaqa knelt before a small ritual fire, burning within a circle of round, white stones. The ceremonial cloth that once covered her at birth draped her shoulders. With tentative fingers, she touched the faded blood stains on the sacred wrap, symbolic of her impending sacrifice to the Great Spirit. A flash of heat invaded her mind followed by the image of a cold, dark night and a giant wolf. She grasped at the image, but it rushed beneath the darker edges of consciousness. She opened her eyes, gazed into the flames, and blinked back tears.

Today she turned twenty and would be blessed and renamed. A time for rejoicing and change. She should be overjoyed on such a momentous occasion, but her heart did not sing. Memories clouded her consciousness. Her very name, Powaqa, brought pain.

"Powaqa is a white devil," a cruel boy once taunted as the others on the playground laughed and jeered.

Most times she endured the taunts, but on that day she'd had enough. Her albino eyes, weakened from lack of protective pigment, made her even more of an oddity. To protect them she wore thick, green-tinted glasses. Modern technology could have fixed them, but that wasn't the traditional Kahoti way.

The voices of children from her past echoed in her mind. *"What has two pink eyes, two green eyes, and is white all over?"*

She touched the tiny streak of black at her temple, the only bit of color in her white hair. Slathered in sunscreen and protective clothing, her lack of pigment was a jarring reminder of how different she was from her peers. In these times of enlightenment, skin color shouldn't be an issue. Hadn't the Kahoti people been persecuted because of color themselves? Shouldn't they be more accepting?

Though the Kahoti had isolated themselves and returned to the old ways after *The Great Transition*, Kaya insisted she leave the reservation to attend university. "The world contains more than Kahoti, and to remain ignorant of it makes one vulnerable."

She had hoped to find acceptance at university, but she found the outside world a cruel place for someone so different.

"You must not question what the Great Spirit has deemed, child." Kaya stood across from Powaqa, staring as if she read her thoughts. "You must let go of the past and focus on what must be done. Your psi power strengthens, and the time for your transformation is near."

"I'm sorry. I still find it difficult to believe the Great Spirit has a special job for me. Why doesn't he call upon a more traditional Kahoti?"

"Traditional? Tell me, who is more in sync with Kahoti tradition than you? You have been trained from the time you could walk to embrace everything Kahoti."

"But I don't look Kahoti."

"As if the Great Spirit cares about your appearance. It is what you have inside which counts."

"But—"

"Stop it. You are the chosen one. I was there when Brother Wolf warmed your skin to keep you alive. I saw you in my visions, years before your birth. Child, you have been out into the world. Have you not seen what the Kahoti have become? We are among the few peoples who still honor the Old Ways."

"The people have lost faith before, and the world survived. Why is now so different?" She looked up as the sharp call of an eagle sounded high up in the sky, as the bird drifted on the warm currents. It wasn't that she *didn't* believe; part of her didn't *want* to believe. "The Mayans predicted the world would end in twenty twelve."

Powaqa added to her argument. "People world-wide panicked and made all kinds of preparations. Fifty years passed before *The Great Transition* occurred. Now, here we sit, and the world still spins." She tried not to think of the disasters which had occurred recently. As if to remind her, the ground trembled in another quake, the second since midnight.

Undaunted by the trembling earth, Kaya stood her ground, continuing the conversation without interruption. "Those were the confused ones, the unenlightened. Yes, the Mayan people knew a change would occur, but it wasn't about ending; it was about a new beginning, a rebirth where man and the universe once again become harmonious. Remember how many people came back to the simple ways and the world improved?"

She didn't answer. Head down, she struggled with her emotions.

"If you do not believe, all will be lost."

She heard defeat in Kaya's voice yet remained silent.

"Are you afraid, child? Is that why you hesitate?"

Tears burned her cheeks as she looked into the eyes of the only person who had shown her love. "No, I accept what I must do, but...I do not wish to leave you. My heart is heavy with grief."

"You will always be with me in my heart, so let your heart sing with gladness. I have received the message in a vision from Grandfather. The world is on the brink of destruction, and it is time for you to do what you were born to do. We must prepare and be ready."

The earth shook violently, the quiet broken only by the cries of birds scattering in flight. Their instincts forcing them to flee in fear. She felt kinship with them as she swayed with the Earth's movement. Kaya dropped to her knees and grabbed her, holding tight until the shaking stopped. Once the world finally settled, she leaned back into the strong arms holding her. "Forgive me for being selfish. I won't let you down."

Kaya placed a gentle kiss upon her brow and let her go.

Regretting her obstinacy, she stiffened her shoulders and took a deep breath. She exhaled, blowing out all uncertainty. Her thoughts turned inward as she felt for the power flowing through her veins.

Kaya's voice echoed in her mind. *"That's it, feel the power of the Earth around you."*

She closed her eyes. Reaching outward with her mind, she focused on subtle vibrations of energy. The variations in chemical compounds sang to her like music. From their song she absorbed energy and then concentrated it with her mind. An electric sizzle arced into her body from the ground. Her body attracted life force energy given off by the plants, rocks, and all natural things. The tangy scent of burning sage and other sacred herbs drifted through her senses, filling her with calm.

"You will no longer be called by the name spoken at your birth. You shall be called Tiponi, a child of hope for our people."

The Kahoti often took new names to commemorate important events in their lives. Tiponi opened her eyes and nodded her acceptance of the gifted new name.

Kaya stood and reached inside her buffalo hide bag. She removed a fan of twelve spotted eagle feathers secured with tanned hide. Hanging from the sacred feathers, circles of four colors representing the four corners of the universe dangled in the sun. She dipped the feathers in the gourd filled with blessed water and sprinkled droplets over Tiponi's head.

"Grandfather sky," she prayed, "touch this woman and make her waken."

Heat poured into Tiponi's body as each drop of holy water touched her skin and hair. Hot energy shot into her veins from the air around her.

****

As Kaya's words faded, the rising sun crested the mesa, bathing Tiponi in a brilliant glow. Her hair appeared to flame, giving off sparks where the light beams touched. The shadow cast by her kneeling figure took the form of a buffalo, and then changed back into a woman.

"It is done."

Kaya dropped her arms and began to put away her ceremonial items. She looked down into the upturned face of the young woman she had raised. Her love for the girl must be put aside for the greater needs of the clan. Tiponi belonged not to her, but to the universe. Uncertainty appeared in the pale eyes staring back at her, but no fear. Good. Grandfather had chosen wisely. Tiponi might not understand what she faced, but she was not afraid. Indeed, her courage was inspiring.

"Your journey has begun. Tonight, when all the clans come together you will be purified. You must follow the teachings of Grandfather and complete his quests. Only then will the universe return to balance and our people and those of the other clans will be safe. Your journey will be dangerous, but you will not be alone. Grandfather has provided a protector. Trust him with your life, Tiponi, for he is a great warrior."

"Who is this warrior? When will I meet him?"

"Patience, child. All will be revealed in time. Now, we must get you out of the sun and prepare for the festivities."

Tiponi nodded respectfully, then picked up a handful of red sand and moved around the circle in the way of the sun. Stopping at each of the four directions, she bowed. When this was done, she poured the sand over the sacred flames. As smoke rose from the dying fire, she moved her hands through it, wafting it over her body. Only when the last smolders had disappeared did she rise and accompany Kaya down the slope.

High above the mesa, in the sacred mountains, a

large mushroom-shaped cloud formed, nearly obliterating the mountain peaks. Kaya stopped, pointing to the clouds.

"See, child? Those clouds are not natural to these mountains. They are created by those who come to visit. Our people have long believed they were brought to this place, taught the ways by those who knew, and left to live in harmony with the world. Sometimes there are visits when special things happen. Magical things, like your birth. You entered the human world through the Slipstream twenty years ago. Tonight, because those clouds look down upon us, exciting things will happen."

****

Hania, in his man form, stood at the window. Peering down through the cloud, he watched the ceremony on the mesa. Tiponi had grown into a beautiful woman since he'd last seen her on the night of her birth. He'd spoken to her in the desert on the night of her coming of age but hadn't dared look at her. Her unusual coloring caused many of her kind to think her ugly, but he saw only her beauty. Beauty he could never touch.

He turned at a soft sound behind him.

"Hania," Grandfather said. "My son, your task will be difficult. Tiponi is unaware of her special powers and her destiny. You are her spirit warrior, her protector."

"I understand my job, but you've placed temptation in my path. She has grown into a delightful woman. I am attracted but can't touch her."

"You are wise, my son, to see what many cannot. Your time will come, but first we must put the universe back into harmony. I have felt evil in the currents of the Slipstream. There are some who wish this world to be destroyed."

"I've felt it also and will be diligent." As he spoke to Grandfather, his eyes remained on the woman below. "Is it fair to ask this of her? Must she be the one?"

"No, it is not fair. But it is the only way. I have need of her special powers."

Hania felt Grandfather's gaze studying him. He couldn't turn away from the window, nor could he hide what he felt. Tiponi was born to be his mate, and he wanted to protect her from this.

"I think it would be wise if you show only your animal self to Tiponi. She may feel more comfortable with you in that form."

Hania raised a brow at his elder, but when he spoke it was to acquiesce. "It will be as you wish." He bowed to the old man. A puff of gray smoke rose up around his body and then disappeared.

He stood before Grandfather in his gray wolf form.

Chapter Three

The Clans Gather

Evening drew near as Tiponi entered the ceremonial encampment. Excitement fluttered in her belly as she took in the sounds and sights of the crowd. She'd been a child the last time the clans had met and barely remembered what it had been about. Tonight would be different. It would be her last night with her Clan and Kaya. Pain tugged at her heartstrings, and the view lost some of its appeal.

"Enough," she chided herself. She glanced down at her sleeveless white blouse, embroidered with butterflies and flowers. She had chosen it for the celebration, deliberately flaunting her white arms. It wasn't as if anyone would ask her to dance anyway. She could at least pretend she was pretty and listen to the music. The village took on an excited, festive air as members of their seven clans gathered. The pounding drums and chant-song brought a smile to her face. She moved closer to the chief's tent to gaze upon the leaders dressed in their beautiful traditional clothing.

Chief Honaw took his place of honor among the six other clan chiefs. As chief of the Bear Clan, he was the most powerful.

"It is good to hear the old songs and see the young people dress in the old ways," Chief Honaw said to the clan chief to his left.

The chiefs were adorned in feathered head dresses and beaded waist belts. Several of the younger men wore elaborate breast plates made from bone, shell, or quills, each reverently handed down through generations. Buckskin breeches showed off the powerful legs of the ceremonial dancers, many of whom were dressed as Katsinas or spirits. Masks hid the features of the dancers, and paint adorned the faces of the chiefs and the people crowded near the ceremonial fire.

A willowy woman walked between the visitors, offering harvest treasures spiced with herbs from the surrounding desert. The mouth-watering smells of roasted goat, corn, and squash permeated the air. The dancers flashed a myriad of color with rhythmic moves to the drumbeats—a delight for all the senses.

"Good evening, Kai," Chief Honaw said.

"Good evening, chief," Kai responded, then leaned in and whispered something only he could hear.

All eyes followed his as he turned and gazed upon several maidens. They wore their hair in squash blossom forms on the sides of their heads. The girls sat to the side of the crowd, encouraging hopeful suitors to admire their beauty.

"Is she ready to marry already?" Honaw asked.

Kai spoke softly in her response. "She is eighteen—well past the time for a girl to wed." Kai bowed and moved away.

Tiponi stepped back, pain slicing through her heart. She would never wear her hair in a squash blossom, and there would never be a hopeful suitor. She swiped an angry hand at her tears and moved closer to the dancers.

The crowd chanted with the rhythmic pounding of drums. Dancers mimicked the steps of age-old legends, victories in battles, and successful hunts. Turtle-shell rattles kept time to the beat, as the singing and music rose to a deafening crescendo, and then suddenly stopped.

The crowd became silent.

From the direction of the setting sun, Kaya stood straight and walked proudly to the center of the gathered circle of people, wearing a dress, hand-made from the softest white deer-hide. Around her neck she wore a breastplate beaded with porcupine quills and colored beads in sacred patterns. Her silver-streaked, black hair hung loose except for a lock on the left side which was tied with white buffalo hide. Her feet were adorned with white moccasins that rode high up her legs, nearly meeting the hem of her dress. The peoples' four colors: red, yellow, black, and white, adorned the edges, and tufts of buffalo-hide fringed the tops. In her arms she held a bundle wrapped in white buffalo skin.

With respectful anticipation, the eyes of the crowd followed her. Stopping before the chief, she bowed, then circled the fire four times. Each time she moved around the circle, the drums pounded an extra beat. Kaya stilled and the drumbeats died. She opened the bundle and motioned to a small girl, to whom she handed the buffalo skin. In her hands the woman held the *chanunpa*, the sacred pipe, given to the people in early times.

Using the language of the tribe, Kaya told the legend of the White Mesa Woman in a strong voice so all could hear.

"Long ago after our people came out of the ground

and lived in the light. They were ignorant and knew nothing. The clans gathered together and made camp. Food was scarce, and two scouts were sent out to search. For days they looked and found no food. A large bird appeared and perched on a rock above them. Uneasy, one man brandished his knife and tried to kill the bird.

"Fool. You cannot destroy a sacred spirit," cried the bird.

Seconds later the bird disappeared in a cloud of smoke and a beautiful woman sat where the bird had been. The man who had held the knife reached for the woman with lust. A bolt of lightning struck him and turned him into dry bones. His bones crumbled and turned to ash. To the man who had treated her as waken, she said, "Go back to your people and tell them, a holy woman is coming with news for the buffalo people. The people should make things ready for my arrival."

The young man hurried back to his clan and told everyone what the waken woman had commanded. Respectfully, the clan erected the medicine tipi and purified it. Four days later the woman arrived dressed in her sacred clothing and carrying a bundle. The chief invited her into the lodge and spoke to her respectfully.

"Sister, we are glad you have come to teach us."

Upon entering the tipi, she commanded they build a sacred altar in the center with a buffalo skull and a three-stick holder on it for something holy. From the bundle she removed a sacred pipe and held it up for the people to see.

She put Red-willow-bark tobacco in the bowl, then threw a dried buffalo chip on the fire. She lit the pipe *and spoke. "The smoke is the living breath of the Great Grandfather." She showed them the correct way to pray, both words and gestures. She taught them the pipe filling song and how to hold the pipe up to the sky, Grandfather, and the earth, Grandmother.*

"The red bowl represents the buffalo and the red man; the wooden stem represents all living things which are connected. The twelve feathers and the skull are from the spotted eagle, Grandfather's sacred messenger. The seven circles on the bowl represent the seven sacred ceremonies in which you are to use the pipe.

"The pipe is a living thing. As long as you keep it, you will walk as a living prayer. Take care of the pipe, and it will take you to the end. I represent the four ages, and I will visit you in each age." She walked back the way she had come. Before she was out of sight, she stopped and rolled over four times. The first time she stood up as a black buffalo, the second time she stood as a brown buffalo, the third time she stood as a red buffalo. On the last turn, she stood as a white female buffalo. A white buffalo is sacred. After White Mesa woman disappeared, the buffalo arrived in great herds and allowed themselves to be killed, providing everything the people needed.

Kaya completed her story and reverently handed the pipe to the chief.

"Thank you for your story, sister, it is good for the young ones to hear and learn."

Chief Honaw grasped the pipe in the correct manner, then with the aid of a friendly hand he made his way into the buffalo hide tent, which had been set up for the celebration of clans.

Tiponi quietly followed the chiefs. She couldn't enter, but she could watch through a small crack in the side of the tent.

Chief Honaw sat on the rugs before the altar and, using the sacred fire, he lit the pipe. Placing the end of the pipe in his mouth, he drew in the living breath of grandfather. He puffed several times, blowing the smoke out slowly toward the next person of importance. With a few words of prayer, he passed the pipe to the chief to his left. After each had breathed the smoke from the pipe the chief stood. "Kaya," he said. "Waken medicine woman, you have told me of a vision about one of our own. Bring this person before me and make known the vision."

Stepping outside the tent, Kaya looked at Tiponi. "It is time, child. Be strong and remember my teachings."

Tiponi placed her cold hand in Kaya's and lifted her chin. She wouldn't let Kaya or her people down.

The group gasped in surprise as Kaya led her to the center of the tent.

She looked around at the group of elders. "This child was named Powaqa by her mother who died giving her life. Brother Wolf called to me on the night she was born, and I brought her to our village to rear. In my vision, Grandfather said White Mesa Woman would visit us again in human form. He said this child was to be renamed and purified. This morning, I spoke her new name, Tiponi, a child of hope. She is White Mesa Woman. After she is purified, she will make a vision quest. Grandfather has need of her. She has been sent to save us from terrible disasters that are to come."

Silence reigned after Kaya's words. The group

respectfully waiting as Chief Honaw made his decision. Slowly, the chief circled Tiponi, then looked at the medicine woman. "Kaya, your visions have always been true to our traditions, and you have done much good for our people. Times are indeed uncertain; events are happening which we cannot control. If this girl is the one you say, we cannot disobey the will of Grandfather. I will have the sweat lodge set up as you need. Who would you like to help with this?"

She responded, "I would welcome the medicine man or woman from each of the clans to be present."

Chief Honaw looked at the others, who all nodded. "It shall be as you say."

He then turned to Tiponi. "Speak your wishes."

Tiponi swallowed nervously. Her gaze darted over the assembled group and Chief Honaw. This was her one chance to back out. She had a choice but knew she couldn't say no. All her life, she'd known she had been placed on Earth for a special purpose. This was the moment of truth, and she gathered her courage. Her people needed her, and she wouldn't let them down. Her voice rang out strong and without hesitation. "My will is that of Grandfather. Let it be done as he wishes."

Honaw returned to the circle. "It shall be so."

Kaya took her hand as they walked from the tent. "There is much to be done, and time is running out."

With a pat for Tiponi's hand, she led her from the celebration.

Chapter Four

A Vision of Grandfather

Hands damp with nervous sweat, Tiponi wiped
them down her skirt before entering the sweat lodge.
Met by semidarkness and a blast of steamy heat, she
paused in the doorway, excitement and fear churning in
her stomach.

Kaya beckoned her to take her seat in the circle.
"Quickly. We must not release the steam."

Tiponi dropped the flap and edged toward the
empty seat. She nodded respectfully to each of the
waken elders, one from each of the seven clans. All her
life, her appearance had garnered stares, but this was
different. Here, she sat among the most waken people
of her tribe. The fate of her people–indeed all people on
Earth–rested with her and Kaya's vision. She
swallowed painfully and caught her Earth mother's
gaze with her own.

Be at ease, child.

Tiponi grasped the calming words in her mind and
relaxed, glad that Kaya understood her nervousness. A
young man brought in hot stones and placed them in the
small pit, never making eye contact with the
participants inside. Kaya spoke the words of a prayer,
opened her medicine pouch, and withdrew a handful of
dried plants. She tossed the sacred herbs onto the stones

where they smoldered. Pungent aromas saturated the air, as the hiss of steam rose from the water she doused on the stones. Heat and moisture thickened the air as each of the seven spoke an ancient prayer.

Hiss—more water hit the rocks.

Kaya poured a dark acrid, smelly, potion from her medicinal gourd and handed it to Tiponi. "Drink this, child, and seek the vision of our ancestors."

She grasped the ancient bowl with both hands, its fragile thinness a reminder of the sacred journey she would soon take and raised it toward the sky, "Grandfather Sky, show me the way." She then lowered the bowl to face level. "Grandmother Earth, guide my steps."

Placing her dry lips against the pottery bowl, she quickly swallowed the bitter concoction. She knew it contained herbs to relax her body and open her mind. Fire burned in her belly as the potent liquid entered her bloodstream. Beads of sweat oozed from her pores. Energy flashed through her body, pulsed in her mind, and her head began to swim.

The spinning universe with all its stars slid past at cosmic speed. Her body became weightless as she moved with those heavenly bodies. Gentle hands lowered her body to the floor of the sweat lodge, but her mind was no longer there, it was part of the cosmos.

Voices and beings passed around and through her as her consciousness sped through the universe like a stick floating upon a swift stream. Beings young and old, familiar and unknown touched her mind. Her body slowed, and a great cloud appeared before her, seemingly white, but with brilliant colors shining from its center.

****

"Welcome, my child." The deep voice anchored her in space.

She floated into a room where sacred gold symbols adorned the white walls. Tiponi gazed around trying to focus. She lay on a buffalo hide, her skin now cool where it had been hot before. Her weak eyes blurred but were able to distinguish the form of an old man sitting before her. His ancient face held such beauty it was difficult to look upon. "Are you Grandfather?"

"That is one of my names, but I have others. I am many things to many peoples, but you may call me Grandfather."

"Why am I here? I mean, why was I chosen from my people?"

"You were not chosen, Tiponi. You were sent. Your birth on the chosen day was planned so you could help your people."

"I don't understand."

Grandfather paused. "The universe flows like a stream with no past, present, or future. In the spirit world, this is called the Slipstream. Those who understand how it works move freely through the worlds both in spirit and in form. I brought your spirit here, but your body is still on Turtle Island with your people."

She smiled at the ancient name her people called America. She had read of it in her studies but had never heard it spoken. "So, am I doing this or are you controlling my spirit?" The idea of no past or future was hard to imagine, much less having her spirit in one place and her body in another.

"You spoke the words allowing me to bring you

here. Later, as you learn more, you will be able to move freely through the stream as others do."

My will is that of Grandfather. The words came back to her. Chief Honaw had insisted she state her wishes so she had given Grandfather permission to bring her here.

Accept.

The single word appeared in her confused mind, bringing with it comfort and warmth. She had to know more. "Are there others like me—I mean do humans come here?"

"Many beings come here, and yes, some are human," the old man answered without elaborating.

Urgency tingled at the back of her neck. "Why am I needed?"

"There is a disturbance in the Slipstream and unrest in the universe. Balance is gone, and the people have moved away from the old ways. Without balance, great catastrophes will occur, and many will die."

Tiponi sat up, bringing her face closer to the old man. "I am but one woman. I know nothing of disasters or how to stop them. How can I help?"

"You have great power within you, Tiponi, but you must work to bring it out. I will guide you as you go through each of the steps, but beware. Powerful entities exist in the universe. Some are evil and thrive upon chaos and destruction. They will try to stop you."

She found it hard to imagine someone or something stronger than Grandfather. "Are these beings as powerful as you?"

"Maybe more powerful. This is why I need your help."

Overwhelmed by what he described, she didn't

want to offend but needed to know. "I thank you, Grandfather, for this honor, but where do I start?"

"First, I have a gift for you, one that will help you to see things in a different light. Lie back and close your eyes."

Trusting though still unsure, she lay back on the rug and closed her eyes. Taught from birth that Grandfather was all powerful, she put away any doubts about beings more powerful and lay quietly. The click-clack sound of a turtle rattle moved over her body, then a warm, sticky ointment, smelling of jasmine and citrus, flowed across her eyes. Braced to keep from flinching, she lay still and listened to Grandfather's melodious voice as he chanted a prayer in the sing-song voice. As his voice stopped, he covered her eyes with his hands. Reverence filled her. Energy flowed from his hands to her face, jolting her momentarily, and then gentle fingers wiped her eyes with a soft cloth and continued through her hair.

"Open your eyes, Tiponi, and see the world differently."

She opened her eyes, dazzled by the sharpness of her vision. For the first time in her life, she saw without blurring. Emotion welled, making her unable to speak. Excitement shot through her, and she couldn't wait to see butterflies and flowers. They'd always been her favorite things. She could never quite see the intricate patterns with her blurred vision and now eagerly looked forward to seeing them.

"Come, see your gift."

"But I do see, Grandfather. I can see you clearly."

"I said you would see things differently; come and see the difference."

She followed Grandfather to a pool at the back of the room. As she knelt and looked into the water, she saw her eyes were no longer colorless. The face staring up at her had vivid turquoise blue eyes and light golden-brown hair.

"Remember: White Mesa Woman changed four times, representing the four corners of the universe and the four ages of man. So shall you. When you have completed your journey and changed four times, your powers will be strong enough to save your people."

She listened attentively to the solemn words, then gasped. Hundreds of butterflies, glowing like jewels, flew up through the water and hovered around the newly formed flowers. Both the flowers and the butterflies were in every possible color, and each finely etched detail was there for her to see. How had he known? Her mind questioned as she stared with wonder at the beautiful display of fluttering color?

Her vision now clear, Tiponi saw they were not alone in the room. Standing to the side was an enormous gray wolf. His sinewy muscles were still but conspicuous, as were the powerfully built jaws that could easily crush bones. Silver-gray fur covered his form, accented by a small tuft of black hairs on his massive head, a head so large it should strike fear into her heart. Having never seen such a powerful animal up close, she should feel terror; instead, she was overcome by a feeling of recognition and familiarity. Why should this animal seem familiar?

"Your wolf is beautiful."

The wolf uttered a low guttural growl, and Grandfather laughed. "Don't be offended, Hania, she also thinks my old face is beautiful."

She gasped as she realized he had read her thoughts.

Grandfather motioned for the wolf to come closer. "Hania takes offense at being called beautiful and my wolf. He is a free spirit and not mine. Your journey will be dangerous, and Hania has been chosen as your spirit warrior. He will die for you if he must."

Her heart skittered as the wolf padded slowly toward her. His giant paws made no sound on the floor. *How can such a large animal be so silent?* Muscles rippled with each step the wolf took. He stopped before her, sniffed her hand, then licked it. He sat back on his haunches and howled. Goosebumps raised on her skin as the sound skittered down her spine.

Grandfather laughed. "I agree, Hania, she will do."

Tiponi smiled down at the wolf and rubbed the spot on her hand where the animal's tongue had touched. The damp area of her skin tingled. He *was* beautiful, regardless if they thought her idea of beauty strange.

Grandfather motioned for her to return to the rug, and then sat cross legged beside the spot where she had entered. "For your first quest, you must find the peoples' first *Kiva*. There you will find a sign that will lead you further. You will know you have succeeded when you undergo another change. Now close your eyes and think of the Slipstream. Your body is in danger, and your mind must return."

There was no time to question his statement or feel fear because she immediately felt the stars moving past her consciousness and heat flowing across her body. Other minds touched hers, old and ancient, and then she felt her body wet with sweat and the earth moving beneath her.

****

"Wake up, we must get out of here. The earthquake caused a rockslide." Kaya's words brought Tiponi back to the moment. She became aware of her surroundings once more. "Hurry or we will be crushed."

The earth was indeed moving, and she grasped Kaya's hand as they stumbled from the sweat lodge. Still groggy from the herbs, she tripped and fell.

Kaya jerked her arm as she ran on wobbly legs. "Quickly, Tiponi."

Rocks crashed from the hillside, smashing everything in their path. Shouts sounded from the encampment. Spurred by the command in Kaya's voice, she focused her thoughts with clarity and urged her legs forward. A terrible crash sounded behind them, and they turned to see a pile of rocks where the sweat lodge had been. Screams filled the night air as the ground continued to shake. Abruptly, the earth stilled. Shouts sounded amid the chaos as they made their way to the buffalo hide tent.

Kaya entered the tent; the oil lamp in her hand lit a horrible scene. A mere wisp of smoke remained of the sacred fire beside the overturned altar. The seven chiefs, including Honaw, lay on the ground. Some of the men were unconscious while others were bloodied.

Chief Honaw struggled to sit up. "Waken sister, he has come and danced before us."

"Please be still, Brother, so I might tend to your wounds." Kaya dabbed at the nasty gash across the chief's forehead. A blue feather fluttered to the ground.

A collective gasp came from those gathered. According to legend, the Blue Katsina would return, dance for the people, then remove his mask. This would signal the beginning of the end.

"It is true. The Blue Katsina came and danced. We fought him, trying to keep his mask from coming off. He removed his mask, and a glowing light shone instead of his face.

Kaya helped the chief to sit up. "Honaw, who hurt you?"

"We tried to put the mask back on the Blue Katsina, and he threw us high in the air. When we hit the ground, he was gone."

"Honored father," Tiponi said from her place near the altar. "Where is the sacred pipe?"

Honaw pushed Kaya's hands away and whirled to face the altar. In a voice laden with sorrow he said, "The sacred chanunpa is gone. Our people will suffer and much of the world will be destroyed."

Tiponi fell to her knees at his feet. "No, honored father. Grandfather has said I can save the people and has given me a quest."

Kaya grasped her arm and shushed her. "Do not speak the words, for the air has ears and the wind can share what should be kept silent. Come, you must leave before others know of this. I have prepared a pack for your journey. I can keep you here no longer. The universe is calling, and your people need your help."

Remembering what Grandfather had said about those who wanted destruction, Tiponi hushed as together they climbed the ladder to their home. Though damaged, the door was unblocked. Dodging the rubble and tossed kitchen items, Kaya reached the peg on the back of the door. She grabbed the large sack made from buffalo hide and draped the strap across Tiponi's head and shoulder. "Know this, child, my love for you knows no boundaries." She looked closely at Tiponi's face and gasped. "Your eyes and hair have changed."

"They were a gift from Grandfather. Will I see you again, waken mother?"

Kaya wrapped a large buffalo blanket around the girl's shoulders. "I will always be with you, Tiponi, and one day, perhaps we shall be together again. All these things I give you for your journey. Walk with our ancestors, child, and help us put the universe right."

"How do I know where to start?"

"From whence you came, you shall return. It calls to you, Tiponi. Go find it." A wolf howled in the desert. Kaya smiled. "Remember another time a lone wolf called so boldly. You will not be alone. Grandfather promised."

Tiponi kissed Kaya on the cheek, straightened the sack, and walked toward the north.

Chapter Five

A Journey Through the Desert

All Kahoti knew the legend of where their ancestors had emerged from the Earth. According to their creation story, her people lived below ground when the world was still dark. A mockingbird stood at the hole where they emerged and named each tribe and gave them a language to speak. She had to find this place, go down into the earth, and figure out what she must do.

Moonlight guided her footsteps into the stark desert. Like a fledgling bird, she'd been pushed from the nest to face the unknown. Twenty years ago, on a cool night such as this, she had been birthed in this very desert. Now, she was back. Would her journey end here as well? No—she mustn't think such thoughts. Her people needed her. Warmth and awareness seeped into her. She gazed at her surroundings, searching—her gaze drawn to a shadow in the moonlight. A lone wolf stood silhouetted against the moon on the hill before her. His cry echoed off the plateaus sending a chill down her spine, but she no longer felt alone. Hania, her spirit warrior, was with her.

The sweat-lodge had drained her strength. Overwhelmed by what she had seen and done, her footsteps slowed. It was time to rest. She found a large outcrop of rock where she dropped her sack and gathered saguaro wood for a fire. Kaya had provided flint for her in the sack. The dry wood caught quickly, and she inhaled the scent of smoke as she dug through the bag.

Rewarded in her search, she pulled out a bag of jerky and a water bladder. Drinking deeply, she quenched her thirst, then crunched on the dried meat. The fire offered warmth against the cold desert air but only a small measure of emotional comfort. The desert could be frightening at night. Strange animal calls, tiny footsteps, and the flap of wings brought a feel of unease.

Grabbing the carry bag, she rolled it into a pillow as she wrapped snugly in the buffalo blanket. Kaya had provided well for all her needs. She had known what was ahead. Her gaze fixed on the fire, her one source of comfort. The hair rose on her neck. She looked up from the flames. Three sets of yellow eyes stared back at her from across the fire. Fear shot through her body as she returned their gaze.

She had no weapon to use against three hungry coyotes. Thinking back on all the lessons Kaya had drilled into her, she remembered the touching of minds. The same energy which created visions allowed her to use psi energy to touch other minds. She'd never really practiced this because it was an intimate act. To touch another's mind would be an insult in her culture. It was only done in special circumstances and then rarely. Kaya had touched her mind, but she was family.

She drew a deep breath and bravely returned the predatory stares. Energy from the rocks and plants entered her body as she reached out and touched the largest coyote's mind. *Malevolence, fear, hunger.* The negative energy of the animal slammed back at her. He resisted her mind's influence. Another wave of energy came back at her. They would come for her when the fire went out.

Tiny pebbles rained on her from above. Ice chilled her blood. Were there more of them? Had they surrounded her? She fought panic, quickly looked up— and relaxed. Hania stood just above her on the ledge. He raised his head and howled his fearful alpha cry.

The three sets of yellow eyes slunk away without sound or fuss.

As if satisfied with what he'd done, the large wolf moved down the hill toward her.

She tensed at his approach. He was huge and as he moved out of the darkness, his eyes blazed eerily red. The wolf had felt familiar at Grandfather's, but alone in the desert, with glowing red eyes, she was jumpy. As if sensing her thoughts, his eyes faded to yellow, and he stopped several feet from her.

"Hello, Hania. Thank you for scaring the coyotes away." Her trembling voice betrayed her fear. "I don't know if you understand me, but you frighten me a little."

The giant wolf bowed his head, then looked back up at her.

Surprise jerked her head up. *Had he understood her?* Sitting up, she put her hand out toward him.

The wolf leaned forward and licked the back of her hand. Immediately, her hand tingled and warmth filled her mind. She touched the top of his head, all the while feeling the warmth. The wolf stepped into her embrace, and she drew comfort from him. Pulling back, she looked into his eyes. Why did he seem so familiar?

Weariness overtook her, and she lay back on the buffalo blanket. So much had happened tonight. Images flooded her mind as she turned her gaze to the fire. Her first vision quest, meeting Grandfather, getting new eyes. She could see clearly! Now she faced a momentous journey, a journey fraught with danger and so important to the lives of her people. Moments later she felt the warmth of Hani's large form behind her. Relaxing against him, she slept.

****

Wisps of cool air teased her skin as warm fingers of sunlight rippled across her face. She woke—alone. Hania was gone. She tried not to miss him as she rolled up the blanket. Her breath fogged in the cool morning temperatures, and hunger burned her belly.

With fingers stiff from cold she rekindled the fire and boiled herbs for tea. She picked prickly pear cactus, removing the spines with the sacred knife from her bag. It felt strange to use the waken weapon for such a mundane task, but survival was paramount. After breakfast, she knelt before the fire and sprinkled sacred herbs on the flames and prayed.

"Honorable Grandfather, you have set before me a challenge, requiring strength and fortitude. For my people, I ask you to help me complete these tasks. Use me to accomplish what must be done." She poured sand on the fire, moving her hands through the smoke until the last breath of Grandfather was gone.

Unsure how long her journey would take, she took stock of her supplies. On foot over the desert and mountains, it would take almost a week. Water would be the most crucial element, and she'd need to make some sort of weapon. The knife Kaya had placed in the pack was an heirloom, a piece of Kahoti heritage, handed down through generations. It would work up close, but she would prefer something she could use at a distance.

If she walked in the cool of morning and rested in the heat of the day, she would save energy and water. Her skin would burn without protection, so she cut off a triangle from the blanket and fashioned a cover for her head. A thought flashed through her mind as she was about to put the knife away. She recalled the story of a boy named David from one of her ancient literature classes. The image of facing a giant in the desert in modern times made her smile. Regardless, she cut a strap and fashioned a sling. She picked up a handful of rounded stones and filled her pockets. She wrapped the sling around her waist, added the knife, and was on her way.

You much change four times before you gain your powers and are able to save your people. Self-doubt wasn't normally part of her makeup, but the task she faced now was daunting. Doubt filled her, weighing her down.

The screech of an eagle call high above the desert brought her gaze upward. She marveled at the deep blue of the sky with only a few puffy white clouds. It felt strange to be able to see clearly, with no need to protect her eyes behind the dark lenses she'd worn all her life. Quiet surrounded her with only the eagle for company. No airbuses or flying personal transports were allowed over Kahoti land. The clans had fought long and hard to preserve the sanctity of their small piece of homeland. Once she crossed into the Hotek lands things would be different. They maintained some of their traditions but freely used modern technology and economics.

By late afternoon, ominous dark clouds formed, blocking the sun as thunder echoed off the mesas and bounced back loudly around her. Her people did not allow climate control either. Their crops and lives were at the mercy of what the Great Spirit sent or didn't send. Sometimes he was more generous than others. The way the sky looked today she expected a gully washer. Fearing a flash flood, she climbed a nearby rocky slope. Rainstorms in the desert could be deadly. The sandstone eroded easily, and mud was also a worry.

Lightning struck around her as the heightened energy sought her out. She crawled beneath an overhang of boulders at the top of the rock formation. Large, heavy drops of rain splattered off the rocks, hitting the sand below with a dull plop. The drops joined and soon blood-like trickles turned into rushing red channels as the water mixed with iron oxide pigments in the sand. Damp earthy smells filled her nostrils as a chilling breeze came with the rain. Sharp forks of lightning blossomed across the horizon, quickly followed by the heavy rumble of thunder.

Head thrown back, eyes wide, she reveled in the raw, primal scene exploding around her. Hair rose on her arms and neck as power flowed from the elements, entering her body as if drawn by some unknown supernatural attraction.

"*Tiponi.*"

She gasped, startled at the sound of her name being spoken. At once, her attention was drawn away from the storm. Where had the voice come from? Rain splattered her face as she looked out from the overhang, searching the area.

The voice sounded near. "*I am here.*"

Again, she cast a look around the area and saw no one. The voice was not familiar, and she was starting to doubt her hearing.

"*Don't look with your eyes, look with your mind.*"

"Who are you? You have no right to my mind." She deliberately spoke the words aloud, emphasizing the lack of respect the entity had shown her.

"*I am a friend. I can help you on your journey.*"

"I don't have any friends, and why should I trust you? Are you with Grandfather? If you are, show yourself. Don't insult me with your lack of manners."

"*We will meet soon. I will walk in your dreams.*"

Lightning flashed nearby, struck a shrub, and caused rocks to dislodge and fall. The storm exploded into a furious downpour while the sky illuminated constantly with zigzag fingers of lightning followed quickly by crashing thunder. The wind whipped into a frenzied tantrum, blowing the rain into watery darts that stung her skin. The metallic smell of ozone from the lightning strikes caused a frisson of unease to crawl across her skin.

The sound of the voice in her mind unsettled her. Kaya had done it before, but only on special occasions or when it was urgent. Entering a person's mind was a very intimate thing. The Kahoti people were very private and guarded their personal contact with others. Who would do such a thing and why?

It wasn't like the experience with Grandfather, who had read her mind, but not entered or intruded. He'd spoken to the beautiful wolf, Hania, but to her knowledge the animal had not spoken in return, though truth be known, they had conversed somehow. Confused and unsettled she drank deeply from the water bag, then refilled it with rain running off the overhang. Rolling out her blanket, she settled to rest until the storm abated.

Desert storms might be furious, but they were short-lived. The sun appeared, drying up the water as quickly as it had appeared. Refreshed from her rest and cool from the rain, she traveled quickly for many miles before noticing the different landscape ahead. She had reached the Kahoti-Hotek border. She continued across the boundary though there was no visible line.

Modern technology immediately assaulted her. An airbus floated across the sky leaving no trail, but the sound of it abraded her sensitive ears after the quiet sanctity of Kahoti land. The bright lights of the Hotek Spaceship Casino gleamed against the desert horizon. Gambling survived regardless of what century or planet you were on. While at the university, she'd seen holograms of one of the new Moonshine Casinos on the lunar surface, along with all the exotic resorts to accompany it.

While gawking at her surroundings she was unaware of her close proximity to the cruiser lane and was startled by the sound of a child's voice.

"Hey, Mom, look—it's an Indian." The words had been spoken by a young boy in the backseat of an open personal cruiser.

"Raja, don't be impolite, they like to be called Native Americans." The boy's mother corrected his crass remark, then said, "Maybe she'll pose with us. The people back at the sky-base won't believe we saw a real live Native American."

The man turned his camera away from the mountains he'd been holo-graphing and instructed, "Madeira, get on one side and Raja stand on the other."

Tiponi stood in unbelieving silence as the two bumped up against her and grinned at the holo-cam. She blinked at the flash and moved her hand upward to shield her eyes in an old habit no longer necessary.

Mistaking her movement, the woman said, "Don't worry, dear, George will give you some credits."

The man quickly reached into his pocket and dropped some platinum credits into her palm, then turning, the three got back into the cruiser.

"I don't think she was full-blood. Did you see her eyes? We'll have to photo-rez the image." The woman spoke as crassly as her son.

The words floated back to her as she stood in amazement, while the trio sped off in the cruiser. She felt like she was in one of the old trickster tales Kaya had often read to her. She looked down at the credits in her hand and then back up at the skyline, deciding to stay in one of the sleep cubicles at the casino across the lane. She might be on a quest for Grandfather, but she didn't have to sleep on the ground as long as she had a handful of credits.

Chapter Six

A Room with A View

Laser lights created holo-bursts in the sky above the hotel. It was about as different from her simple adobe home as a palace to a hut. Dressed in her hand-loomed cotton skirt and simple white top, Tiponi caused quite a stir as she approached the brightly lit doors of the dome shaped building.

A young man in a shiny silver uniform stood before her, blocking the door. "I'm sorry, Miss, you can't enter wearing that."

Admission could not be based on appearance. There were laws against it. "What do you mean?"

"Weapons of any kind are forbidden in the building." He tried to make his voice authoritative, but Tiponi heard an underlying unease.

"You mean my knife?" Her palm touched the antler-handled knife at her waist. "I'd forgotten."

"Yes, Miss. You can leave it in a lock box here and pick it up when you leave."

She was hesitant about giving it up, but slowly handed it to the young man who immediately admired the craftsmanship. "Wow, this is a fantastic piece. Is it a replica or real?"

"It is real and has been handed down for generations." She watched the attendant run his fingers along the carved antler handle and touched the ancient symbols. "Are you sure it will be safe in the lock box? I would hate to lose such a sacred piece of Kahoti history."

The young man straightened from his exploration of the knife. "I'll keep it in the box closest to me and guard it carefully. I'll personally hand it back to you in the morning."

She had little choice. If she intended to enter the building she had to comply. "Okay."

The attendant indicated the box. "Place your hand here, Miss."

She placed her palm on the outside of the box and it beeped, then locked. "Thank you."

"Enjoy your stay, Miss."

She removed the buffalo hide from her head and ran her fingers through the silky strands of her hair. She didn't want to scare anyone. As she wove her way through the throngs of laughing and drinking people, they parted and left a path for her to walk. Once again, she looked down at her simple clothes and then at the other guests who were arrayed in shiny bejeweled fabrics, sleek dresses and perfectly cut suits. Her chin jutted upward, and she continued through the crowd. Finally, she made it to the desk and was glad to see a somewhat familiar face.

The middle aged Hotek man eyed her clothes. "May I help you?"

Her voice quivered a little but she cleared her throat. "I would like to rent a sleep cubicle, please."

"I'm sorry, Miss. We have a convention of college students in for the weekend and all of our sleep cubicles are booked. May I get you a room instead?"

Tiponi looked at the small handful of credits, knowing it wouldn't be enough. Smiling, she shook her head. "I guess I'll sleep elsewhere." She'd had her heart set on a bed. She'd just have to suck it up and head out to the desert.

She felt his presence before she saw him reflected in the mirror behind the counter, and their glances caught. He was the most handsome man she had ever seen. Her breath sucked inward, and her pulse quickened as he moved to stand directly behind her. She felt the heat from his body; his gaze held hers in the mirror. Dark sparkling orbs took in each detail of her appearance before he moved beside her and spoke to the clerk.

"Redhawk, I have been called out of town unexpectedly. My suite will be available for the lady's use." He turned those obsidian eyes on her, watching her every move.

As his masculine smell drifted toward her, she was barely able to string the words together. "That isn't necessary, sir, I'll be fine."

Butterflies took off in excitement in her stomach. He filled the space between them with energy. His jeans clung to his long legs and curved around his tight butt. She felt the heat of a blush at her thoughts. She looked up and knew he'd caught her staring. Something flared in his eyes—made him look dark and dangerous.

"My name is Sam Greywolf, and it is no problem at all. Another storm is scheduled shortly, and I'd hate for you to go back out into it."

He turned to look at Redhawk, who immediately spoke up. "Shall I have your bags brought down, sir?

"No need, I'll get what I need when I take Miss…"

"Tiponi." She supplied the name at his questioning look.

"I'll take Tiponi up and show her around, and then bring my bag down. I'll only be gone for the night. Have my hover brought around, please."

"Yes, sir." The clerk touched an invisible spot on the counter, instantly bringing up a 3D-holo-communicator.

"Mr. Greywolf, I thank you for your generosity," she said. "It's *really* not necessary."

"Call me Sam. Do you really want to sleep on the ground when you can have a nice bed?"

She looked at him warily as he put his hand on her elbow and led her toward the antigrav lift. "How did you know?"

"Does it matter? You need a room and I have one. I promise, you'll be quite safe." He turned as they entered the lift, his black hair swinging in the ponytail that hung in a slim line down his back.

How could anyone wear jeans, a simple white shirt, and dress jacket and look as good as this? She thought it had more to do with how he carried himself rather than the clothes he wore. He had presence, an old-fashioned word, but apt. He might have stepped from the pages of a four-hundred-year-old history book.

As the lift doors closed, a mechanical voice asked, "What level, please?"

Tiponi startled out of her musings, embarrassed to be caught daydreaming.

"Penthouse." Sam's voice filled the car. His lips curved upward at her look of shock.

"You didn't say you lived in the penthouse," she accused.

"You didn't ask. Besides I don't live there. I just sleep there when I'm in town."

If his words had been meant to reassure her, they failed miserably. There was no time to ponder them, however, as the lift hissed open to a luxurious entry hall, decorated with earthy tones and a desert feel.

"Have a good evening." The mechanical female voice spoke as the doors closed.

They were alone, and she was desperately aware she was at a disadvantage should this man have miscreant plans.

After he looked into the retinal scanner, the door slid open, smooth and silent as still water. "Make yourself at home. I'll just be a minute getting my things." He walked toward a door at the end of the hall.

While he was gone, she took the opportunity to study the apartment. The main room was decorated in understated elegance with a slightly masculine flair. Each piece of art seemed carefully chosen and was displayed for maximum effect. Her fingers itched to touch some of the pieces, but she dared not. The Sikyatki Period pottery belonged in a museum. She recognized one or two Nampeyo polychrome pieces which had to be several hundred years old. She wasn't an expert by any means, but one clay pot looked to be Second Age. That would make it at least a thousand years old.

She sucked in a quick breath as she caught sight of the painting above the mantle. The painting captured a magnificent Native American Warrior—tall, broad shouldered, with chiseled features. His long blue-black hair flowed over his shoulders freely. A beautifully beaded headband wrapped his brow and flowing locks.

The markings on the band were unique, and sacred. Attached to the left side, spotted eagle feathers and rings of colors adorned the band. His fiercely black eyes sparkled with power in a face tanned golden by the sun. Taken one by one, his features were harsh and cold, but together, they were striking, creating a face of savage beauty.

"Sam," she whispered. Without thinking her fingers reached to trace the firm lips.

"Do you enjoy art?" His voice came from just behind her, giving her a start.

Tiponi pulled her hand back with a guilty start as heat rose in her cheeks.

"You have quite a collection, Mr. Greywolf. How can you bear to only see it when you sleep here? Maybe you should keep it in your permanent home."

"I will, when I finally decide where that is. Look, I have to run, so please enjoy your stay and make use of anything you need."

"Thanks, Sam, have a safe journey."

With a wave he left, and she was alone in the vast room, which suddenly felt very empty without his vital presence.

****

Tiponi stared at the closed door. How had she gone from hiding from storms in the desert to sleeping in the penthouse suite at one of Arizona's top casinos? And who was Sam Greywolf? Why had he happened to be there at the exact moment she asked for a room? It was too much to think about. She was tired and hungry. Kicking off her moccasins, she flexed her toes. She was on her way to the kitchen when the door chimed.

"This is room service. Mr. Greywolf ordered your

dinner and asked for it to be delivered." The voice came though the speaker beside the door.

Tiponi smiled. She'd only known Mr. Greywolf less than an hour, but she'd bet he hadn't *asked* anything. "Just a minute." She pushed the button on the speaker, and a mini-cam picture appeared on the screen. Wearing a crisp shiny uniform, the young man stood by an antigrav cart laden with covered dishes.

She felt silly asking the question, but it didn't have a handle and she didn't see a button. "How do I open this door?"

"It is voice activated, Miss. Just say 'door open'."

"But I don't live here. Why would it listen to me?" She bet Sam hadn't thought about that little detail.

"Mr. Greywolf took care of it before he left. It'll respond to your voice."

"Door open," she said hesitantly and stepped back.

As the door slid silently open, the young man immediately made his way to the dining room and set the table with silver, crystal, and candles. She watched wordlessly as he completed his task and started to the door.

"Enjoy your meal, Miss. Just call downstairs if you need anything."

Smiling, he left before she could offer her meager credits for a tip. No doubt that had been taken care of too.

The tempting aromas from the table were irresistible and answered her rumbling stomach's call. She sat and ate. It took several minutes before her hunger abated enough to allow her to actually enjoy the savory dishes. Sam had good taste in food as well as art. She finished the delicately seasoned chops with sautéed vegetables and sat back.

Mineral water in hand, she wandered over to the balcony and looked out over the desert. From this height she could see twinkling lights in the distance, and if she used her imagination a little, she could almost see her homeland. Overwhelming fatigue crept into her body, and she made her way to the opposite room Sam had entered. She was curious, but not brave enough to invade his sanctum.

Delicate, sandy shades adorned the walls and floor of the room she entered. Minimal touches of greens and browns gave a feeling of being embedded in nature. The large bed was layered with several shades of green covers. Brown pillows in every shape possible rested against the headboard. She was tempted to fall on top of the covers and give in to her tiredness but decided to clean up first. The adjoining en suite was breathtaking and included a natural pool surrounded by rocks fed by a small waterfall. She resisted the urge to play in the water and took a quick sonic shower, donned the fluffy robe from the hook, and jumped into bed.

****

Blistering heat seared her skin as she walked over the sand toward the red hills. She needed to go somewhere and do something, but what? A tall saguaro cactus, spiny arms upraised, appeared before her—again. She was lost, and it was dangerous to wander in the desert in the heat of the day. Why was she here anyway? As if answering her question, the sharp cry of an eagle drew her eyes upward, halting her steps. The bird was huge, casting a shadow which completely covered her and brought relief from the sizzling sun.

Her attention shifted downward at the first ominous

rattle just a foot ahead. One more step and she would have stepped on the rattler.

As a child, she and the other Kahoti children had tended the snakes, gathered by the clansmen, weeks before the sacred Snake Dance. The priests would dance with the poisonous snakes in their mouths, and then release them back into the desert to carry the prayers of the people to the Great Spirit.

This snake didn't look friendly and was actually growing larger. Muscles stretched, elongating the coiled body upright until the head was almost even with hers. She stared back at the snake, frozen in place, not from fear, but because she couldn't help herself.

Tiponi. The snake called to her. She could feel the familiar and hypnotic voice in her mind. This was the same voice she'd heard during the storm. A fierce shriek from the sky was her only warning as the snake's head reared back, fangs dripping, and struck.

A rush of wind pushed her backward. The eagle swooped down and grabbed the snake with enormous steel talons. She lay in the sand, watching as the snake fought to coil around the majestic bird. The eagle shrieked loudly, tightened its claws into the writhing snake, and flapped its wings as they rose from the desert floor. Sand swirled in a small twister as both bird and snake became smaller the higher they climbed. Finally, they disappeared.

Tiponi, wake up, you are in danger.

The urgency in Kaya's discorporate voice pierced her sleep. Unease rippled along her bare skin as she searched the dark penthouse room for danger. Her slight shift halted abruptly as she heard an all too familiar rattling sound.

This was no longer a vision; this was reality.

Like Kaya, she didn't dream. What she saw in visions came true. She swallowed with a mouth dry from sleep, as her mind raced with ideas for escape.

The malicious voice forced its way into her thoughts. *"Lie still and your death will be painless."*

Tiponi wrestled to free her mind from the evil hypnotic words emanating from the reptile. She revved up her psi power, drawing as much energy as possible from the rocks and water in the next room, but this wasn't enough to block the menacing thoughts. Helpless, she watched the snake grow larger at the foot of her bed.

Grandfather? Hania?

A low, ominous growl sounded from the door seconds before the enormous wolf leapt forward and grabbed the snake in his massive jaws. An evil hiss shook the room as the wolf shook the snake, slamming the writhing reptile against the floor. As in her vision, the snake grew larger, nearly filling the small space. Untangling her body from the covers, she stood, backing as far from the battle as possible. A high-pitched yelp in the darkness struck a chord of fear in her heart.

"Hania?" The startled cry tore from her lips. Had her protector been hurt? Unthinking, she took a step forward.

The wolf dropped the snake and jumped onto the bed, placing his body between Tiponi and the reptile.

The snake seized the opportunity and slithered quickly from the room. Hania lurched forward and gave chase. The walls shook as the two animals fought with unearthly strength. The glow from eerie red eyes lit the battle scene as the two rolled across the once pristine hallway carpet. The fight moved to the living room, destroying priceless art and furnishings. Once again, the lupine's powerful jaws grabbed the snake as it grew larger, attempting to immobilize the wolf in its coils. The serpent's body grew so large, the embattled pair pressed against the wall of glass doors. Stricken by horror, Tiponi screamed when the two broke through the windows and careened off the balcony, still gripped in their struggle.

"Hania!" She sprang forward, her view below shrouded by darkness. Silence—no yelps—nothing.

Sobbing, she leaned over the rail, desperately searching, listening, and hoping. Pain squeezed her chest as she waited. She stood for long minutes before the cool desert night chilled her. Her heart heavy with grief, she turned back into the room.

Could Spirit Warriors die?

Grandfather had said there were forces stronger than he. Was this serpent one of them? It had been after her, and Hania had sacrificed himself for her. Empty and alone, she moved to the corner of the living space and sank to the floor. Chilled in spirit and body, she hugged her arms around herself for comfort.

"Fire on." Most of the devices in Sam's home were voice operated.

Sam! How could she explain what happened to his beautiful home? He'd think her crazy when she babbled about talking snakes and wolves that were really spirit warriors. She'd have to find some way to make him understand. Right now, she needed to do something— anything to help Hania.

From her bag, she removed the buffalo skin and

placed it before the fire. She settled, removed sacred herbs, and sprinkled them on the fire. Inhaling their essence calmed her. She reached for her knife, at once remembering it was locked away downstairs. Her eyes were drawn to the display of ancient Kahoti artifacts on Sam's wall. From the case she removed a deer horn knife and gently grasped the old clay bowl she'd admired earlier. Explanations and apologies would come in the morning. Hopefully, Sam would forgive her.

With the words of an age-old prayer on her lips she slid the blade across her palm. Blood gave life and was required for a sacrifice like this. Shakily, she squeezed her fist, and her blood dripped onto the flames.

"Honorable Grandfather. My blood and that of my mother stained the sacred blanket the night of my birth, a sign of sacrifice for you. Tonight, another may have died as a sacrifice for me. Take my blood as an offering of my pledge to my quest. Please, let him live."

She ran her fingers through the blood and drew two vertical lines under each eye and down her face. With water from her bag, she rinsed her palms over the flames. She removed a small mother of pearl box from her provisions. The bitter scent of mind-opening herbs teased her nostrils when she lifted the lid. Before she lost courage, she shook half of the herbs into the bowl. She added water, then swirled the contents. As she had done in the sweat lodge, she raised the bowl up and down accompanied by a chant. Finally, she drank the contents and gently set the bowl aside. Dizziness was immediate and filled her head as heat from the herbs burned her insides. She fell on the buffalo blanket and closed her eyes. The world spun.

Sentient beings passed her spirit as she moved on the psi current of the Slipstream. Her body stilled, and she opened her eyes. She was alone in the room where she'd first met Grandfather.

She sat up and made a visual search of the room. "Hello? Grandfather?"

She stood and moved to the pool. Her image, reflected back on the water's surface, was still strange to her. She placed one hand on the rocky ledge and the other in the water. Psi energy resonated and flowed into her body.

"Grandfather?" She called him with her mind, channeling her thoughts.

"I am here, Tiponi. Why are you so troubled?"

"Grandfather, there was a snake—but he wasn't a snake—and he entered my mind and was going to kill me." She paused for breath. "I'm sorry, I'm not being very clear."

Grandfather said nothing as she stumbled through her story, then came to an abrupt stop. "Is Hania dead? I saw him fall over the balcony with the evil serpent, and I just have to know. Can spirits die, Grandfather?"

"Would you like some tea?" The question was so mundane, she was stunned into silence.

"Tea?"

He walked over to a small table with two chairs which hadn't been there moments before. "Yes, I find it very calming." He indicated the chair opposite him and poured aromatic tea from a pot beautiful in its simplicity. "Please, sit and let us talk as we drink."

"Death in the spirit world is different from your world, Tiponi. Humans think of their bodies as 'alive' and their spirits; if they believe in spirits, as something separate. Here there are only spirits, and though they can be destroyed it is very difficult."

She asked the most important question. "Does that mean Hania has been destroyed?"

"He was chosen for your spirit warrior *because* he is difficult to destroy. He is very powerful, but he would sacrifice his soul, for lack of a better word, to prevent your death."

She didn't want anyone dying for her, even a spirit wolf. "But why am I so special?"

Watching her face, he answered her question with one of his own. "Why is Hania's fate so important to you?"

Tiponi felt the heat in her cheeks. "I can't explain, exactly. Even as a child, I felt him. When I first saw him, he was familiar. And when he touched me, my skin burned. I know it sounds crazy, but it's like we're connected." Her voice dropped lower as she said the last few words.

Grandfather sipped his tea while she waited for his answers. Finishing, he set the cup aside and looked into her upturned face. "Your world will end if you do not complete the quests and your transformation. I am powerful, but I will need your special gifts to be successful. I cannot explain further. It could alter your world's timeline. You must discover your own unique powers for yourself. Think outside the Reservation, Tiponi. You are more than Kahoti, and the world is made up of many kinds of people."

"I gave my oath in blood, Grandfather. I might not understand, but I will accomplish what you ask."

"Good. Kaya has done well with your education."

"And Hania?"

Suddenly, warmth began to spread through her mind; the spot on her hand burned. She turned, and he stood behind her. With tentative fingers, she reached out and touched his muzzle. When she looked into his eyes, she knew it was her spirit warrior. She didn't understand how he'd survived, but she was satisfied with the reality.

Hania was alive.

The pull of the Slipstream caught, then tugged her through the swirling cosmos.

Chapter Seven

The Morning After

Tiponi's nose twitched at the enticing smell of scrambled eggs and toast. Her taste buds danced with the aroma of herbal tea. As the warmth of the fire radiated across her body, she stretched—then was jolted into awareness of her surroundings. She was lying on the same rug where she'd been last night. The apartment appeared in perfect order. The windows were intact; artifacts lined the lighted shelves as before.

Had the events of last night really happened?

"Good morning." Sam entered, carrying a tray loaded with breakfast items. "I'd hoped you would enjoy a good rest in the bed. I'm glad you at least got some sleep by the fire. You can start with this while I bring the fruit."

He placed the tray on the low table beside her. He brushed her hand aside and poured tea into her cup.

"You didn't need to fix my breakfast," she said in a voice husky with sleep. "Your hospitality has been more than generous. Did you just get in?"

"I didn't need to be away as long as I'd thought. I returned home several hours ago, and I always cook breakfast for my guests. Cooking relaxes me."

"Does your job entail a lot of stress?"

Sam paused on his way back to the kitchen. "It has

its moments. Now eat your breakfast."

The eggs smelled wonderful, and she took a bite before speaking. "Did you notice anything unusual when you..." She hesitated before continuing. "I mean...was the apartment okay when you arrived?"

His eyes looked intently into hers. "Certainly, was there some reason it shouldn't be?"

Breaking eye contact, she lowered her head to take another bite of food, chewed for a few moments, washing down the savory bite with tea. She knew he waited for an answer, but she decided to ask a few more questions of her own.

"Who are you? Why did we meet at this particular time? You know who I am and what I must do, don't you?" Her tone was accusing though not angry.

At first, she thought he wouldn't answer and jumped as he folded his tall frame on the couch beside her. "You're right, I do know who you are. I've known Kaya for many years, but until last night, I had only seen you twice."

His words held an underlying note of seriousness, grabbing her attention immediately. "But she never mentioned you. Why did we never meet?" Her fork was forgotten as she stared into his handsome features.

The sofa crinkled as he leaned back and pressed into the soft leather. She breathed his masculine scent mingled with the essence of fine leather, and her pulse quickened.

"Do adults tell children everything?" He raised an eyebrow. "I'm not saying Kaya would keep secrets from you, but some things are best discussed at the appropriate time."

"Are you kidding? She waited until I was twelve

before telling me I wasn't human." Immediately, her hand flew to her mouth as if she could force the words back in. It was obvious, *she* couldn't keep a secret. "I can't believe I blurted that out."

He merely studied her face, which warmed with her discomfort.

"Aren't you going to question my sanity or move farther away from the crazy woman?"

"You're not crazy, and I'm not afraid of you."

"I just told you I'm not human and you're *okay* with that? Like, you *happened* to appear with a room, when none were available? What if I told you strange things happened here last night and your apartment was destroyed?"

"I would believe you." His eyes never left her face during her questions, and his reply came without hesitation. A smile spread across his face as he gazed around at the apartment. "I must say, you've done a hell of a job cleaning up, if that's the case."

She recognized his attempt to bring some humor to the situation but found his calm attitude difficult to understand. The things she'd told him were strange by anyone's standards. She reached over and pinched his arm. When he laughed and pinched her back, she jumped.

One brow rose in question, and he laughed with a deep-throated chuckle. "May I assume we've just proved we're both real?"

His laughter made her itch to touch him again. Growing up, she hadn't heard much laughter, at least not the sharing kind. She'd heard plenty of the mean, taunting kind, the kind that hurt instead of made you feel alive and carefree as Sam's laughter had.

Tired of dancing around the questions she needed to ask, she placed her cup down decisively and turned toward him. "If I ask you a direct question, will you give me an honest answer and not prevaricate or distract me?"

"I will never lie to you. If I'm unable to give you an answer, I will tell you. But be careful. Sometimes we discover things we'd rather not know."

He took the pot, pouring himself a cup of tea as she studied him.

"Were the two of us meant to cross paths at this this time and place?" She studied his face, searching for signs of a lie.

"Yes," he said after a sip of tea and placed the cup gently on the saucer.

Excitement filled her as she gained this bit of information from him. Maybe she wasn't crazy after all and was getting closer to her goal. She digested the little scrap of information she'd managed to extract from him and took her time before asking her next question. Unconsciously, she ran the tip of her tongue along the edges of her lip. "Do you know Grandfather?" She didn't elaborate. He would understand her question if he indeed knew him.

"Yes, we're acquainted."

He hadn't expounded on either of the answers, but then he hadn't said he would. If he knew Grandfather, then of course he would understand her not being human. Nor would he be surprised by strange things happening. Did that mean he wasn't human? Her eyes roamed over his face, and she quelled the urge to ask— he'd said to be careful. She wasn't ready for that question yet. Grandfather's final words prompted her to ask one more question.

"Are you outside the box, Sam?"

"Yes, I believe I can truthfully say that for certain."

"Good. I've always colored inside the lines. I might need a little help with stepping out of bounds." The cup rattled against the tray when she nervously set it down and stood. "I think it's time for me to get started. It's a long way to the Grand Canyon."

"There you go, staying in the lines again. You don't have to walk the entire way. I have a Hover Explorer Craft downstairs, and she loves to cover rough terrain."

"Your hover is a she?" she quipped smartly.

"Aren't they all?"

"I wouldn't know, I've never had one."

He pointed to the counter. "I picked up a few things for you on my trip. Change and we'll get started."

He left the room before she had a chance to respond.

She took a quick look at the robe and then at the bag. Before she could question his motives, she grabbed the bag and headed for the bedroom.

The denim jeans, knit shirt, and hiking boots were a far cry from her normal clothes, but they were much more practical for climbing around the canyon. Denim, like gambling, was something which never got old or went out of style. Cotton was so scarce now, only the rich could afford its extravagance in everyday wear like jeans. A grin flashed back at her in the mirror.

Not bad for a Rez-girl.

Grandfather had said to think outside the reservation, and he was right. Except for her years in academy study, she'd been isolated on the reservation and knew little of the outside world. It was time to broaden more than her horizons. It was time to start thinking of all people, not just the Kahoti.

Sam was dressed in similar fashion, except for the boots. His were old fashioned cowboy boots. She smiled at the choice, remembering the history of the cowboys and Indians.

She placed the large bag onto the counter and removed the water skin. "Do you mind if I restock my water and food?"

"Please do. I have some nutrition bars in the storage bin."

Neither spoke as they entered the lift and rode down to the casino floor. The sunlight hurt after the low lighting inside, and she paused to let her eyes adjust to the brightness.

"Miss." The voice came from the behind her. "Don't forget your item in storage."

Tiponi whirled around, angry at herself for forgetting something so important. "Thank you for reminding me. I would hate to lose it." Her smile was gracious as she placed her palm on the cool metal plate. The locker buzzed, then popped open.

The young man reached in and handed her the knife.

Sam discreetly handed the young man a tip, then stood with his hand on her back. An ultra-modern, racy looking personal hover glided to a stop in front of them. Silver and black, the machine purred as Sam helped her in, then took the controls from the valet.

Her hand slid over the seat cover in a caress. "One day, remind me to ask how you became so rich."

The hover took off in a smooth motion as Sam steered it toward the desert. "You like it? Once we clear town, I'll show you what she can do."

"It's beautiful. How long will it take to get to the canyon?"

"That depends on how fast you want to go. We could be there in three hours or…" He flashed a rakish smile at her. "We could be there in two. The choice is yours."

"I have a feeling you want to soar, so let's see what she can do." Tiponi felt lighthearted, then thrilled as the hover gained speed and the scenery became a blur. The movement reminded her of the Slipstream, but she didn't voice her thoughts. That topic would need to wait until another time.

Two hours later, Sam slowed the craft beside a sign which read, *Park Hovers Only from This Point*. He turned a somber face to her. "This is as far as I can go."

"I can't tell you how grateful I am for all your help."

She reached over and placed her palm against his cheek. A jolt of electricity streaked through her hand. She hastily jerked her hand back, surprised by the itchy tingle on her skin.

Sam sat facing straight ahead, the muscles in his jaw clenched and his lips tight.

"Good luck, Tiponi. Remember, you are not alone."

"Goodbye, Sam." Her voice wobbled a little as she slung her bag over her shoulder and walked down the red dirt trail. When she turned moments later, he was gone.

****

"All right, Tiponi, time to get started." She gave herself a pep talk as she continued down the track.

She waited until the park rangers and tourists crowded near the geological cut-out wall left, then slipped behind the ticket building. To preserve the pristine environment, the Rangers kept groups small and restricted permits for exploration of any ruins. Her destination was an area strictly off limits, with no permits allowed.

Her journey would take her down into the earth in search of the third world. The point of emergence was where she'd find the first kiva of her people. Held secret by the sacred elders, she had no knowledge of the exact location. Not surprising, as women had rarely been allowed in the kivas except to clean or serve food. Legend described it as a place of great cosmic energy. To discover the opening, she'd need to use her ability to detect and manipulate psi energy.

Her people revered the canyon as sacred. They believed spirits returned here after death and re-entered the underworld from where they had emerged. Scouts made trips into the edges of the canyon for salt but kept to specific sites. Besides priests who made sacred pilgrimages, few Kahoti would dare explore farther than the salt deposits. The last pilgrimage had been over a hundred years ago, and the priest had not returned.

Tiponi firmly believed the legends. Prickles of unease ran down her skin as she took her first tentative steps into the jagged scar scouring the mesas. A burgeoning wave of psi energy slammed against her psyche, nearly short-circuiting her consciousness. She opened her mind, absorbed it as best she could, and bravely entered the canyon. The calm vastness drew her in, filling her with healing strength.

Treacherous and steep, the goat path down to the river required her full attention. She clung to the cliff wall, stepped over loose stones, and eased around rock protrusions. The distance to the bottom doubled when taking the twists and loops into account. She was in good shape, but it had been a while since her last long hike. By the time she reached the bottom of the canyon, she was winded, overheated, and her legs shook like feathers in the wind.

At the edge of the Colorado River, cool water splashed over rocks sending droplets up to bathe her. She reveled in the coolness. The Chaco Caves loomed a thousand feet off the canyon floor. Her heart quickened at the ancient site. These caves belonged to the Anasazi, ancestors of the Kahoti, but they were not her destination. Scientists had studied the caves repeatedly through the centuries, chasing clues as to the disappearance of these mysterious people. They, like many, forgot to look with their eyes instead of their instruments. Anasazi blood ran in the Kahoti along with the blood of the Aztec.

Briefly she rested, pulling deeply on the water bladder to rehydrate. Overwhelmed by the task ahead of her, she began to seriously doubt her qualifications. She didn't lack courage, but...*You are the chosen one.* Kaya's words flashed in her mind. Grandfather had said she'd been sent. That was that. If Kaya and Grandfather believed in her, she couldn't be the wrong person for the job.

Tiponi took a deep breath and slowly released it. Why hadn't she picked up a map in town? Three dimensional vertical rocks made navigation difficult, especially when the coordinates were unknown in the first place. Oh, and she could have gotten a kayak. Sam had been right. She hadn't needed to walk the entire way, but it would have been hard to sneak into the canyon with a kayak and camping gear. Though the trip would have been quicker floating on the river, she might have missed the signs if she'd been passing quickly on the water.

As she followed the river eastward, her eyes scanned the towering red walls for symbols or other indications of Native American habitation. Hours passed, and still she walked with no clues. Her journey *had* to begin in the park. There was no other way to reach her destination. It was totally inaccessible from any other direction, and off limits to even Park Rangers. The Kahoti and Hotek were the only people allowed into the three mile stretch of canyon. Of those allowed, only a few had made the pilgrimage over the ages.

Bands of red and brown rock painted a colorful history of the area's geology. The bands matched on both sides of the canyon, only darker where the sun cast long shadows across the canyon floor and the rushing river. Darkness would come abruptly because of the steep walls. She would soon need to stop and make camp for the night. Her eyes scanned the walls around her in one last effort before nightfall. Psi energy hummed along her skin, and she stilled. She moved closer to the wall of rock and touched it with both hands. Energy hummed through her hands and aligned with her psi signature. There was something here. She stepped back and craned her neck to gain a better view.

There, high above her on the cliff wall was a sign.

She carefully studied the small symbol. Had

someone been reading her mind again? If she hadn't been looking so carefully, she'd have missed it. A hundred feet above her on a small outcrop was a pictograph of an ant person.

Eyeing the narrow ledge, she wished for one of the pueblo ladders as she checked for handholds on the rock surface. She'd never done any serious rock climbing but was strong in both flesh and will. The pictograph alone told her nothing; there must be something else nearby to guide her. Preparing her mind, she touched the rock surface. Psi energy pulsed into her hands. The wall was like a living, breathing entity, emitting an energy signature unique to this spot. If she'd had doubts before, she was now reassured. This was the place.

Before she lost her nerve, she began to haul her body up the canyon wall. It took all her concentration to place her hands and feet securely in the shallow niches. About twenty feet up, she paused and leaned back to look at the symbol. Impossible, she couldn't see it from this angle, and if she leaned back too far...Gravity pulled down on her straining muscles, and her hands began to shake. One moment she rested securely on the wall and the next she was free-falling backward.

As she gazed up, her eyes fastened on the dark shape of a crevice against the lighter bands of rock.

Chapter Eight

Powering Up

As Tiponi plummeted toward the canyon floor, she had only a glimpse of the orange sky of sunset before her body slammed into the hard rock of Mother Earth. Stars flashed, and her vision blurred. She squeezed her eyes shut, trying to blot out the pain in her head and back. Robbed of air, her chest burned, craving oxygen. Her hands clawed the rocky soil, trying to pull her body upright. Panic made her efforts frenzied. Fear seized her mind as she fought spasms of pain. Would she die without saving her people?

Be at ease.

The words filled her mind with warmth and a sense of calm. Her thoughts cleared, and she understood what she had to do. Opening her mind to her surroundings, she channeled psi energy from the Canyon into her lungs.

Whoosh. Air rushed in, and she savored a deep, shuddering breath.

With her lungs filled, she took stock of the rest of her body, moving her arms and legs. She lifted her head and immediately regretted the movement. Her skull throbbed, and blood trickled from her nose. Okay, she'd lie here a few minutes, *then* figure out how to reach the crevice.

Quietly, she listened to the sound of her breathing. She focused on the pain, centering her mind on her body. Her thoughts followed the path of her blood as it pulsed through her veins, passed through her lungs and into her heart. The rapid beating slowed as she concentrated on healing her body. Her breathing evened as she moved deeper into her mind and entered a meditative state. The pain eased as her muscles relaxed. Free of pain, she slowly sat up. When no dizziness ensued, she turned her attention to the wall in front of her.

Amid the smooth rocks and brush, there were tiny handholds. She'd almost reached the ledge. Why had she fallen all of a sudden? Was her body too weak? Or had she been deliberately kept away? She had found the sign easily—too easily. Was there a protective force around the place? It would make sense. Not every curious person could wander by and invade the holy place of her ancestors. How had the priests gotten in when they made their pilgrimages?

Tiponi pulled the buffalo bag from her shoulder and grabbed the water bladder. She drank thirstily from the sack before capping it. The Colorado River splashed briskly yards away, and she was drawn to the water's edge. Taking her time, she refilled the bladder with the cool clear water. A century ago, she couldn't have done so. Too many cities had dumped wastes and other impurities into the water. At least the Great Awakening had made the world's population more protective of the environment. Now, humanity was threatened by the very Earth itself. It somehow seemed like poetic, if delayed, justice.

She turned to look at the cliff once more. Her

heartrate took off as her stomach dropped to the pit of her stomach. The crevice and the ant symbol were gone. Had she missed her opportunity and failed in her quest already? The symbol and the crevice had been there. Frustration ate at her nerves. The earth rumbled beneath her as if mocking her feeble attempt.

She stood, faced the canyon wall and raised her voice. "Kaya raised no weakling, and Grandfather does not choose unwisely. I am Tiponi of Kahoti, and I will succeed."

The earth stopped rumbling, and she turned back to the water—the clean, *pure* water. Could that be the answer? All those who came before were priests, holy ones. Maybe she should cleanse her spirit before making another attempt. She'd been cleansed before her visit to Grandfather, but the entity last night…She shuddered at the memory. That vile creature had been in her mind, been privy to her thoughts. Her skin crawled at the image. Without another thought she stripped bare of her clothes, momentarily reveling in the warmth of the late afternoon sun.

With care she entered the water, securing her footing against the swift current. Her skin pebbled with gooseflesh as she allowed the water to flood her skin. Emptying her mind, she lay back in the water. All thought washed away as she bent her knees and sank, allowing the flood of water to cleanse her mind.

Beneath the surface she heard only bubbles and the beating of her heart. She counted each beat and felt her heartrate slow. The molecules of water began to change around her. They spoke to her in a way only a person tuned to psi could understand. She became one with the water; it followed the tiniest movement of her hands.

When her lungs burned, she pushed down with her hands and surged upward with a mighty leap. Energy buzzed around her body, and when she opened her eyes, she was suspended ten feet in the air, cushioned by a waterspout. Shock kept her balanced delicately on the plume of water, but a moment of doubt broke the surface tension, and she plopped back in the river with a splash. Sputtering, she resurfaced and heard male laughter. Indignation warred with self-consciousness.

"I don't recall ever seeing a waterspout on the Colorado," Sam Greywolf said with a wicked smile as he lazed on a rock beside the shore. "How exactly did you do that little trick? It could come in handy."

Tiponi quickly ducked her breasts beneath the water and sent him a glare. "You have me at a disadvantage. This water is cold." She totally ignored his question, the discovery too fresh in her mind.

Teeth chattering, she struggled to keep irritation from her voice. "Sam, would you turn around, please?"

He didn't move. "Where are my manners?"

As she continued to wait, he stood and with exaggerated reluctance turned his back.

Tiponi rushed ashore, grabbed her clothes, and struggled to pull them over her wet body. She'd lost time while she'd played with the water molecules, and now shadows moved down the canyon wall creeping ever closer to the water. She still couldn't wrap her head around what had happened. *She could move water.* Not control water. It felt like the water had a mind of its own and allowed her to manipulate it. Like the keys of a piano reacted to—

"You're shivering," Sam admonished as he dropped the buffalo blanket around her shoulders.

Starting at his voice, she murmured a quick, "Thanks," before moving away to sit on a large chunk of driftwood. She drew the blanket up and over her wet hair as the wind picked up.

"I'll collect some wood."

She gave herself a shake and began selecting stones for a fire ring. She had the ring complete and the log pulled closer when he returned. Using the handful of dried grass he'd found, she lit a fire and carefully coaxed a good blaze.

"Why are you here, Sam? I thought I had to do this alone."

"Never alone, Tiponi." His voice deepened as if in promise.

"I know, I have my spirit warrior, Hania, but are you a part of this, too?"

His dark eyes gazed into hers, and she saw shadows of things she didn't understand. "I can't answer that question."

She waited, but he didn't elaborate. Just as he hadn't last night. Well, he'd said he wouldn't lie.

Sam threw a stick into the fire, sending a cascade of sparks upward on the breeze. "But I can answer the first. I didn't like the way we left things this morning. I wanted you to know that I would come with you if only it were possible. There are those far wiser than you or I who hold our fates in their hands. I must bow to their judgement."

Tiponi watched the sparks rise skyward only to blink out of existence before reaching the heavens. Were her people doomed to the same fate? No, not as long as she breathed and Grandfather kept his promises.

"Is this goodbye forever?"

"Forever is a long time. Let's just take one day and then another."

In the distance a wolf howled. She turned toward the sound but knew it wasn't Hania. There was no warmth in her mind. With a sigh she pulled the buffalo bag over and rummaged through the contents. "May I offer you some tea?" She raised an eyebrow when he burst into laughter.

"What's so funny?"

"Not funny. You sounded like a friend of mine." He moved to sit on the log as she shifted to the sand near the fire. "Are you afraid?"

Tiponi paused in her preparations for tea and looked back at him. She took her time and searched her soul carefully before she answered. "I'm unsure of my way but unfearful of my destiny."

"Uncertainty is easily cleared up. One only has to explore the different options. Fear, on the other hand, can lead to failure. I think you will be fine."

"Thank you, Sam. You've been so kind."

His face changed, hardened.

"What is it? Did I offend you? I'm sorry." She yelped as her fingers burned on the hot pot. Dumping tea leaves in the pot, she gave thanks to the plants for their sacrifice. The silence grew thick around them, but she didn't know how to dissolve it.

Sam's voice broke the tension. "Be at ease. I get surly sometimes."

She laughed as she poured tea into the metal cup and handed it to him. "I can't imagine a face as well formed as yours turning surly."

He raised the cup in a silent toast and drank. "You say the kindest things."

Tiponi stared at his bronzed profile, mesmerized. When he tipped his head back, her gaze followed the motion of his throat as he swallowed. An ache welled in the pit of her stomach as an unfamiliar yearning constricted her chest. She quickly looked down as he turned to return the cup. Why now? The safety of her world depended upon her gaining the rest of her powers. Sam might be handsome and intriguing, but she couldn't be distracted by personal cravings.

"I must leave you now. Take care on your journey." He stood and walked away from the circle of light—into the darkness and gone.

As he disappeared into the night, she whispered, "Goodbye, Sam."

Chapter Nine

Friend or Foe

Morning brought a chill wind and sand in her face. Sputtering, she sat up and gazed upon the cloud filled sky. High cirrus clouds promised snow before nightfall. She stood and shook the sand from her buffalo blanket before quickly rewrapping it around her body and sashing it with her belt. The sudden cold and promise of snow quickened her preparations. No time for hot tea this morning. She had to find her way to the first kiva. A quick drink of water and jerky fueled her movements.

The winds heightened, becoming frenzied.

She loved storms. The fury of their psi power called to her, entering her body more readily than any other time. She spread her arms skyward. Sparks from the ionized sand grains collided with one another, forming larger arcs. Eyes closed against the grit, she cleared her mind and concentrated on the buzz of electrons. Mere minutes passed before the electric arcs became large ropes which reached for her. Like a lover's caress the ropes draped around her arms. Using her senses, she looked inward and saw the ant man and the ledge.

The ropes thinned, melding into an electric glow around her body. "Holy Grandfather, guide my steps."

Keeping her eyes shut, she ran toward the canyon

wall. The harmonic frequency changed. She clapped her hands together and jumped. An explosion of energy jettisoned her up, slamming her into the wall. Quickly she reached out, and one hand caught the edge of the ledge. The pulse of energy depleted, leaving her hanging by one hand as the wind buffeted her like a doll drying on a clothesline.

Wrenched by her landing, her left arm shook with pain. She had to hurry, or she would fall. Using her feet, she found a small protruding rock on which to rest her weight. The wind, which had helped before now turned against her. It spun and swirled all the while draining her strength. Waiting for it to shift, she used its forward thrust to throw her other arm on top of the ledge. Ever so slowly, she inched upward as her legs scrambled for footholds. The ledge was barely a foot deep. She had to get at least one leg up and lie flat against the rock. With her energy waning, she pulled one leg and then the other onto the narrow ledge.

Using her free arm, she reached inside the crevice and leveraged into an upright position. She waited for the dizziness to fade, then used the last fading rays of sunlight to peer into the void. A cavity opened up behind the rock fissure. Elated, she wiggled her body through the slit opening, dragging her pack behind her.

Blackness engulfed her.

Her breathing was labored, amplified in the otherwise quiet cave as she rested on the rocky floor. The wind reached with clawing fingers to lash at her through the opening. No light penetrated the slit opening, and she was afraid to move. As with all caves, this one could turn suddenly up or down or drop into nothingness. Without light, she couldn't determine her path. She reached for her flint, and her hand encountered something strange in the buffalo bag. Where had it come from? Her mind recognized the shape as a chem-glow. Used by campers as a portable form of light, it was perfect for the cave. Sam must have put it in. Her heart lightened at his kind gesture.

A quick twist and artificial light illuminated the cave, leaving only the edges in shadow. The cave was quite large and showed evidence of previous pilgrimages. An altar made from cedar driftwood stood to one side. Cedar was one of the Kahoti's most sacred plants for ceremonies. Kahoti and Hotek spiritual symbols were burned into the wood. A buffalo skull and hand-made pottery bowls sat among offerings left by those before her. In the center of the cave a large fire pit had been scraped in the hard floor and was prepared with logs.

"Thank you, ancestors, for providing for me." She bent to light the fire. Once it blazed with warmth and light, she sprinkled herbs on the flames and knelt to pray. "Oh, Great Spirit, I thank you for leading me safely to this place. I ask your continued guidance on my quest as I journey into the unknown. Help me to act wisely so that not just the Kahoti, but all people might be safe."

Tiponi sat in quiet meditation, her gaze focused on the flames. The fire popped. She blinked and turned her thoughts from spiritual to survival. She drank water, chewed on a nutrition bar, and thought about her next move. Using the chem-glow she moved into the shadows to check out the rest of the cave.

The back wall stood nearly twenty feet tall and contained several ledges where others had left offerings. Beads strung in decorative patterns, hatchets with embellishments, and pottery lay scattered on the shelves. Some of the pieces were ancient, and she could feel the spirits of her ancestors in the cave. Tiponi removed her turquoise earrings, her own offering, and placed them on the nearest ledge, then continued to investigate.

To her left, she found a passageway. Hewn by hand, the rough passage ended after a few feet. A heavy wooden door blocked the way. No lock or handle broke the smooth façade. How was she supposed to enter? Raising the light, she studied the symbols chiseled into the rock surrounding the arch. Another Ant person was depicted on the left side of the door. It stood on a reed raft with the symbol for water beside it. In the center of the arch was a drawing of an ant mound with a door on top. A door that opened! That must represent the sipapu, the opening to the next world. Excitement coursed through her at discovering her first clue. This passage must lead to the kiva!

Delight was quickly tempered by common sense and the realization that something wasn't right. The sacred first kiva of her people couldn't be this easy to find. Anyone with a little knowledge of hieroglyphs, a bit of luck, and determination, could have found this place eons ago. She studied the wall closely. On the right side of the doorway was another symbol, a rounded maze—the symbol for rebirth or new life. She paused to think about how to interpret all of the symbols. They told a story.

The world flooded, and the people used rafts to get to the safety of the kiva. They came through the sipapu into the new world and a new life. This was the story of the great flood. Christians had a similar story in their Bible which told of an ark that saved Noah and the chosen animals. Tiponi carefully studied the archway, then reached out and touched the symbol of new life. Her body nearly buckled from the psi power that jolted through her, but she held on, listening to the voices of the ancients as they spoke to her.

Death!

She broke contact with the archway and knelt on the floor. The sign for death, Maasaw, was always placed low and usually under a rock or in a crevice. With her fingers, she brushed away debris near the outer wall of the archway; she saw a small arrow pointing down. She gently scooped out some of the earth, and there it was. The skull-like head with large vacant eyes and sharp teeth. Maasaw, the death Katsina. The face which scared children when the men danced the Katsina dances.

She moved away from the doorway and returned to the fire. She needed time to think about the symbols and what they meant. If this was truly the passage she needed to take, she'd have to reconcile herself to the idea that she could die. Maybe the symbol was there to warn her that this wasn't the way. Maasaw did everything backward, because that was the way it was in the underworld. The arrow pointed down. Did it mean she needed to look up? Grandfather, Kaya, and even Sam had told her she would not be alone on this journey. Where was everyone now? She needed guidance or at least some feeling of support.

Outside, the wind picked up. As it blew through the narrow crevice, it created a strange melodic whistle. The breeze moved the flames, and dancing shadows appeared on the wall as the fire danced. *Yes*! The fire *was* dancing, and the sound was like a flute. She had Kokopelli for company tonight. Watching the shadows on the wall and listing to the sound of his flute, she relaxed. Kokopelli represented spring and was a fertility spirit. Not very helpful at the moment, but at least his music was calming. She spread the blanket from her bag, reclined on her side, and watched the flickering shadows on the ceiling of the cave.

Psi energy seeped into to her from all directions pouring more power into her mind and body. The cave felt sentient, like an entity, with a life-force of its own. Had the other visitors felt this same aura—or pull? No, something would have been passed down in the oral history if they had. This place was unique, but she was aware of things others had not seen or felt.

The flute sound resonated at a different pitch, causing her skin to tingle and her mind to sharpen. The roof of the cave no longer looked the same; it appeared as the night sky with twinkling stars in constellations she knew only too well. The outstretched arms of the Galaxy spun in the darkness of space. Feeling the pull of the energy at the top of the cave, she opened her mind to it. A movement at the back of the cave caught her eye and broke her concentration.

"Hania, I've missed you. I thought earlier how nice it would be to have some company or support." She smiled at the gray wolf, who stared back at her. "Come and keep me company while I tell you about the things I saw and did today."

The wolf stayed where he was and continued to stare at her.

A tingle of unease crawled up her spine as she

noted his aggressive stance and lack of welcome. "Is everything okay?"

She sat up and moved closer to the fire. Her head swiveled around to check for danger in the cave. She saw nothing out of the ordinary, but her hand cautiously slid down to her waist and pulled out the ancient knife. As her hand touched the handle, the wolf lowered his head in a challenging move. Understanding flashed through her with a jolt.

Hania had a shock of black hair at his temple, this wolf did not. This wasn't her friend, her warrior spirit; this was an enemy. She should have known it wasn't Hania. When he was around, she always felt warmth in her mind. She felt nothing from this impostor. Wolves weren't that common, even with the reintroduction programs ecologists had enacted. This couldn't be any ordinary wolf. Piercing sound invaded her mind, pitched so high, it nearly burst her eardrums—definitely not an ordinary wolf.

Bent with pain, she reached down and grabbed a stone from the fire circle, ignoring the burns to her skin. Her aim wasn't great, but she managed to strike the animal, bringing a moment's respite from the ultrasonic blast. Before she could mount a counterattack, the animal leaped toward her, mouth snarling and hideous growls coming from its throat.

She wasn't a trained fighter, nor was she overly strong. In a fight her only hope was her psi energy. Opening her mind to the sacred surroundings, she pulled in energy from the walls and psi remnants from her ancestors. The cave began to buzz with the sound of ionic charges, and flicks of electricity sparked in the air as her body absorbed the psi power. Just as the beast was in midair above her, she pointed the knife outward in a protective stance. Lightning bolted from the cave walls, passed through her body, into the knife, and then arced into the wolf. Snarls were replaced by screams when the hot energy struck his body, flinging him upward. The smell of burning flesh assaulted her nostrils. The beast writhed in mid-air.

Stunned, Tiponi stood and gaped at the falling animal. Unable to move, she gasped in pain as razor sharp claws swiped her arm in one last effort to kill her. The animal collapsed on top of her, gasped one last shuddering breath, and died. Air rushed from her lungs as she collapsed to the floor beneath the weight of the corpse. Struggling, she pushed with all her might and managed to roll the wolf off her chest.

Breath returned to her lungs.

Her stomach heaved as bile rose in the back of her throat. She swallowed, pushing the gastric fluid back down, then slowed her breathing. Shakily, she dragged her quaking body over to the fire. It still flickered cheerfully and cast shadows on the wall.

But Kokopelli no longer played his flute cheerily, and the shadows had lost their bouncy step. Her ragged breathing and pounding pulse had replaced his music with discordance.

What had just happened? How had she managed to do that?

Still reeling from the aftereffects of adrenalin and psi drain, she fell back on the blanket and closed her eyes. Her mind filled with warmth. She jerked when she felt the tickle of fur against her arm. Her muscles bunched in fear before recognition brought ease. It wasn't just the dark patch of fur she recognized. Her mind recognized him, Hania, her true warrior spirit.

The wolf bent his head to lick her arm, and she jerked back, afraid, not knowing what to expect. He paused, sat upright, and looked into her eyes. They continued to stare at each other as moments turned into minutes. Finally, her fear abated and she lowered her arm. The wolf gently licked her wounds. She felt intense pain at first, then burning warmth pulsed through her arm. The wounds faded and disappeared.

Stunned, she watched as Hania walked over to the dead animal and placed his paw on the grotesque body of the dead wolf. Glittering crystal-like particles appeared over the body. Both the crystals and the body floated upward and disappeared into the roof of the cave.

She looked at him with new respect. He was her guardian, a spirit, but she hadn't quite understood how different he would be. Grandfather and he had communicated—no—Grandfather had communicated with him. Obviously, he had powers other than brute strength. Her arm had been healed by his touch, and now he had made the wolf float away. Was he like Grandfather?

She heaved a sigh. Her mind was too small for such big thoughts just now. Exhaustion made her body ache. She threw more wood on the fire and lay down on the blanket, smiling when she felt the large wolf curl up behind her. She might not understand who or what he was, but she certainly felt comforted by his presence.

Chapter Ten

The Earth Continues to Shake

An eerie howl sounded the only warning before the
ground and walls began to shake. Rocks and debris
showered down upon her. Startled awake and slow to
react, she offered no complaint as Hania covered her
body, shielding her from the heavy altar as it careened
toward her. Crashing thunder sounded as boulders
ripped from the ceiling, smashed into the floor, landing
close enough to feel the wind of their passing. Seconds
later all was silent.

Tiponi sucked in a breath and gagged. Spitting out
dirt and grit, she coughed to clear her lungs. Hania
moved from her body, making it slightly easier to
breathe. The fire was gone and with it, all light. She
scrambled in the direction of where she thought the
opening should be. Impeded by rocks and the uneven
floor, she gave up trying to stand. On her hands and
knees, she continued toward the opening. Where was it?
She was hopelessly turned around.

"Hania?" Her voice croaked. "Which way?"

A wet nose bumped her arm. She grabbed a
handful of fur and pulled up. With the wolf's superior
vision and senses, they crept slowly to the opening.
After only a few feet she bumped into her pack and
bent to retrieve it. She snapped another chem-glow, and

the cave glowed a spooky green. She turned toward the outside—only now there was no outside. The entrance was completely blocked by a boulder. They were trapped.

Claustrophobia engulfed her as she imagined no way out. Panic wasn't her normal reaction, but it had been a harrowing night. Gathering her courage, she inched toward the tunnel. Icy fingers of fear slid down her back when she saw that the tunnel had disappeared. Not blocked—completely gone. Her options were limited…all right hopeless.

"Think, Tiponi." She spoke the words aloud seeking comfort from the sound of her own voice. She circled the cave but found no other tunnels or crevices. There *was* no way out. Frustrated, she shook out the buffalo blanket and sat down.

"I don't suppose you know how to get out of here?" she asked Hania as he lay beside her. "Never mind. Even if you could talk, you couldn't help me. I understand the rules. I had hoped to do better at this."

With a heavy sigh, she lay back and closed her eyes. There had to be a way, and she'd find it. Images of the ceiling spinning like the galaxy and the surge of sentience she'd felt had her opening her eyes. The ceiling had been high before, but now, it looked twice as high. Where the light from the chem-glow reached, it sparkled off the surface of something other than plain rock.

"How skilled are you at climbing walls?"

She laughed as the wolf stared back at her. She grabbed her pack and blanket, slung them across her body, and started to climb the wall. As she neared the top, she felt moisture on the rocks and slowed to keep from sliding. The entire ceiling, covered in large crystals, glowed with a greenish-yellow light. The huge crystals acted as a light source. This didn't look natural. A superior technology or intelligence had a hand in this. As she pulled her body up and over the last part of the wall, she shrieked when her hand touched something hairy and very much alive.

"I'm not even going to ask how you did that, though maybe one day you'll show me how." She spoke to her furry friend as if he understood every word. "This climbing stuff is so overrated." She hadn't given any thought to how the wolf would climb the wall, but then, he did a lot of things most wolves couldn't do. Hania just looked at her, his tongue hanging out, looking very much like he was smiling at her.

When she stood, the crystalline ceiling was at least six feet above her head. She moved down a corridor which had definitely been hewn by careful hands. Lighting was much improved in the corridor, so she shoved the chem-glow back into the pack. The corridor was lined with a mica-like mineral which reflected the light and seemed to intensify it.

As she moved farther into the tunnel, the floor became polished and the walls even shinier. This didn't look like the work of ancient Kahoti people, but then some of the legends had spoken of a time of great technology. With Hania walking beside her down the hallway, she felt reassured—until the corridor ended. Here again she encountered an archway. This time it contained a closed door.

Directly above the archway a single symbol of a handprint, painted white, impressed into the rock. A handprint could mean many things in the Kahoti language. This was the left hand, a spiritual sign, like a signature representing a person's existence and accomplishments. She felt no hesitation in touching it and gently placed her left palm against the symbol, matching it to fit exactly. A slow hum began where she touched, and the palm print lighted with a blue glow. The light pulsed back and forth against her palm. She held her palm still, quelling the urge to jerk it back. The ancients would have protected this sacred place. What would happen if she wasn't the right one? The buzzing stopped, and the light went out. Silence pulled at her nerves as she stood anxiously watching the door.

A strong voice filled the air around her. *"Choose."*

She looked, searched frantically for an idea of what to do next. "Choose what?"

Symbols, illuminated by white light, began to appear at random around the doorway. Tiponi knew it was vital she pick the correct one. There were so many, some she knew, others she didn't recognize. There was her clan sign, the bear, the snake, the buffalo, the wolf—how was she to know? She closed her eyes, and pondered the symbols and dismissed each one, with no reason, but knowing they weren't right. How could she pick with certainty or feel the rightness of the symbol?

Relying on Kaya's teachings and her own feelings, she stopped thinking and focused inward. She cleared her mind and immediately felt the psi energy from each of the symbols. Each emitted a different wavelength of energy. Her body was drawn to the one with the highest energy. She put her faith in her own power. Without opening her eyes, she placed her hand on the symbol. Pulsing energy poured into her body. Her eyes flew open. Anxious, she removed her hand. Had she chosen the correct symbol? She stared at the blinking symbol on the arch. She had chosen the white buffalo.

"*Welcome, we have long awaited your arrival.*" A woman's voice spoke to her, and the heavy door slid open.

Chapter Eleven

The First Kiva

Tiponi took a tentative step forward, and the door slid closed behind her. She whipped around, realizing she was alone. Hania had not entered with her. Dry mouthed, she swallowed and took a deep breath. She studied each of the smooth plaster walls which surrounded a hard-packed dirt floor. Wooden poles covered by clay tiles formed the ceiling. It looked exactly like the one in her home on the mesa.

Light fell from the ceiling like rays of sun, but she saw no opening. The air in the room smelled fresh, unlike a place which had been sealed for hundreds of years. Could there be others like she, on a quest for Grandfather, and this was some elaborate testing facility? No, that didn't feel right. Kaya believed so it had to be for real.

An old-fashioned weaving loom sat against one wall. Men were the weavers in Kahoti culture; the looms were in the kiva for this reason. Men wove the cloth their brides wore on their wedding day. Cloth and other Kahoti articles hung from the loom.

Her heartbeat accelerated. There was the sipapu a few feet from the fire pit. It was the opening to the underworld. Though every kiva had a sipapu, they were merely for tradition. This one was different. This was the real thing. As a child she'd listened to the stories of how the Kahoti had come to be on Turtle Island. Everything was in the correct place according to tradition.

Her heart lifted, and she wiped at the wetness on her cheeks.

She had found the first kiva.

She had been expecting a cave like the one below, not something so similar to the kiva still in use today. Placing her bag on the floor, she took several pieces of dried cottonwood from the wood box. Cottonwood trees were common along the river in the canyon. The dried wood was very lightweight and perfect for carving the Katsina dolls used by the tribe. It was also very easy to ignite. She arranged the wood in the shape of a tipi over tinder and struck her flint. With a little puff of air, flames engulfed the dry wood.

The room quickly took on a rosy hue with the glow from the pit. She sat before the fire and sprinkled it with sacred herbs. She must cleanse herself before performing the ceremony to help bring harmony back to the universe. A smudging ceremony would remove ill spirits from her body.

Removing a wrapped bundle from her sack, she gently opened it to reveal a small, shallow pottery bowl used in her smudging rituals. She placed the bowl before the fire, then removed a smudging stick made from a bundle of white sage wrapped with string. Sage was a sacred herb known for its power to drive out negative spirit energy and also purify a person. The sacred plants must be shown respect as she asked assistance for their healing power.

Tiponi sat cross-legged, grasped the smudge stick,

and lit it from the flames. As she placed it in the bowl, a pungent aroma drifted upward from the smoldering stick as the flame went out. Lifting the bowl, she pointed it in each of the four directions. She took the spotted eagle feathers from her pouch and gently fanned the smoke toward her. Reverently, she began her prayer to the spirits.

"Oh, Great Spirit, you placed all life on this land

Each being, including the plants were given life-force or chi

As in all things there is good and evil within each of us

Allow this sacred herb to cleanse me of any evil spirit or energy."

She fanned the smoke toward her left foot, the entering side of the body, then moved upward over her heart, pausing for several moments before going over her head and back down and out through the right foot. This was a simple yet essential ritual, and she felt her psi energy resonate with the cleansing. She stood and took the bowl to each corner of the room. In the shadows, beneath furniture and under the roof beams. She fanned the smoke into all the places where negative spirits could abide.

Having driven all the negative spirits from herself and the room, she stubbed out the sage stick and picked up the most sacred of smudging herbs, sweetgrass. Braided, like hair, and precious because of its scarcity, she lit it as she had done with the sage and moved through the room again, this time using the powerful herb to bring positive energy into the space. The sweet scent of musky vanilla filled the room and her senses. The air became charged with energy which she felt as vibrations across her skin.

After smudging the room, Tiponi began preparations for the four directions of harmony ceremony. This was a sacred ceremony, one usually done by the Katsinas during the festival dances. Doing it alone would be difficult and would require agility and stamina.

Normally the sipapu would be open during the rite, but since this was the actual opening to the third world and not the symbolic hole in the kivas at home, it would remain closed. She doubted it would open anyway until the ritual was complete. Everything had to be perfect for the ceremony to work, and a quick look at her clothes made her regret wearing the jeans Sam had purchased for her. She moved to the loom and wasn't surprised to find the finely woven garments a man would make for his bride.

She stripped completely, threw more sage on the fire, and wafted the smoke with the eagle feathers, cleansing her bare skin of the taint of modern clothes. Barefoot, she walked over and donned the white cloth, wrapping it around her form in the correct manner. Soft white moccasins and jewelry hung from the end of the loom and nearly completed her change.

Lastly, she placed the head band around her head, adjusting the eagle feather which hung from the left side. Sacred symbols were etched into turquois and attached to the band. She gently touched the bear, her clan sign and the symbol for courage, Kokopelli the sign for harmony and fertility, and the symbol for the four ages of man.

Now she was ready to begin.

From a small cotton bag, she removed a bag of

sacred cornmeal, ground from the first corn of the harvest. She outlined a large circle with the cornmeal, then used more cornmeal to draw an "X' over the circle. The lines reached out of the circle and toward the corners of the room then bent to the right. Now, she had marked the way the tribes had walked after emergence. Her people call this the wheel of life. To the uninformed, it looked like a swastika. The swastika symbol had been used by Pre-modern people worldwide, long before Hitler had raped the symbol of its meaning and used it as a symbol of evil.

Finally, she picked up her antique turtle rattle along with the eagle feathers and crouched in the center of the circle. Her head was hidden beneath the feathers. Her body was like a child in its mother's womb, and she must be born or emerge and go forth—just as her ancestors had emerged from the sipapu and spread out in the four directions.

WO—HA—LI

A piercing wail erupted from her body followed by a long shuddering motion as that of a child kicking in the womb. Using the turtle rattle to keep time, she sprang upward, arms lifted to the ceiling, and started a slow circular dance and a sing-song chant.

So—tuk—nag—Wa—ken Tan—ka
E—LO—HI—NO, E—LO—HI—NO
Oh, Great Spirit, giver of life to all things
You called to me and I was born
The Earth trembled with pain
And my people emerged from its depths
So—tuk—nag—Wa—ken Tan—ka
E—LO—HI—NO, E—LO—HI—NO
We knew nothing and you sent us Katsinas

Tiponi

They taught us how to grow crops and live
We were told to live in harmony with other creatures
And honor your spirit and creations
So—tuk—nag—Wa—ken Tan—ka
E—LO—HI—NO, E—LO—HI—NO
You gave us different colors and directions
Wisely you sent us on a journey to find our way
Some followed your teachings
Many others have turned away
So—tuk—nag—Wa—ken Tan—ka
E—LO—HI—NO, E—LO—HI—NO
We seek a return to your harmonious ways
As I repeat those journeys for my people
Help us to bring balance to the universe
And return the cycles of the Earth
So—tuk—nag—Wa—ken Tan—ka
E—LO—HI—NO, E—LO—HI—NO
North, the way our White Brothers walked, they are
qöötsa — Guardians of Fire
South, the way our Red Brothers walked, they are
paalangpu — Guardians of the Earth
East, the way our Yellow Brothers walked, they are
Sikyangpu —Guardians of the Wind
West, the way our Black Brothers walked, they are
qömvi — Guardians of Water
So—tuk—nag—Wa—ken Tan—ka
E—LO—HI—NO, E—LO—HI—NO

Tiponi left the circle following the way north along the line and danced to the corner of the room. She removed the white circle from her eagle feathers and attached it in the north corner of the kiva. Then, dancing back to the center of the circle, she spun as she continued her chant. She repeated her dance, followed the way south, placing the red circle in the corner, then danced back to the center. Repeating the same ritual, she placed the yellow and then the black circle. Exhausted from her dance and chant, she stilled in the center of the circle and one last time lifted her arms.

"I am Tiponi, and I am forfeit for the lives of my people and all the peoples of Turtle Island."

Her voice rang out loudly, echoing back to her. A loud buzzing sound came from the ceiling and as she watched in astonishment, a bolt of lightning flashed down and struck her in the chest. The powerful electrical surge lifted her body from the floor, then dropped her like a broken Katsina doll.

****

An image of Tiponi completing her harmony ritual filled the large screen along the white wall of the room. Hania, in his man form, watched the beauty of her movements as she completed the steps with perfect balance and grace. Melodious words of prayer slid from her finely formed lips in sync to the shaking of the turtle rattle. The traditional white, woven garments accentuated her beauty, giving her the ethereal appearance of a Kahoti goddess. He had sat at that very loom and woven them in the age-old tradition of Kahoti men. With each pass his hand had made with the shuttle, he'd thought of the woman she would become. He could have made them magically but had wanted to touch the fabric as he weaved his spirit into the fibers. His quiet admiration was extinguished as a bolt of lightning struck her in the chest, lifting her from the floor.

Emotions cascaded though his body along with tremendous power, blotting out all thought but her safety. Bright light flashed around his form as…

"Hania, no! You must not interfere!" The sharp words of Grandfather halted him when he would have transported down to be with her.

"She could die!" His voice was sharper than he'd meant, but so was the pain of watching this.

"We knew it could happen before she started the quests. She must do this and find her power."

"We promised her she wouldn't be alone in this," Hania insisted stubbornly.

"And she is not, I see everything," Grandfather gently reminded him. His face took on the benevolent look of a father to a child. "Look with your head, not your heart."

They stood staring at each other, both strong willed and unflinching. Finally, the younger man nodded.

"Forgive me, I overstepped."

"There is nothing to forgive, my son, now look inside your mind and find peace."

Hania took a deep breath, closed his eyes, and reached out for Tiponi with his mind. *Pain!!*

"She's in terrible pain." His breath came quickly as the feeling of her pain flooded his body.

"Well see," Grandfather's words held a humorous note, "Dead people don't hurt." He cackled with laughter.

Hania felt his face stiffen with anger. "I do not find this amusing." He gave the old man a harsh look and without speaking another word, vanished in a puff of smoke and light.

Chapter Twelve

The Third World

Excruciating pain radiated from her chest, moving through her limbs, bringing her to one conclusion: she was alive. Realization was quickly followed by a vivid image of what had happened.

She'd been hit by lightning and survived.

Darkness, black as ink, surrounded her. Blinking her eyes changed nothing. Had the lightning bolt taken her vision and not her life? The smell of sweet-grass and sage permeated the room and her senses. A feeling of ease came with the smell. It was familiar. The odor was clean and untainted, with no nauseating smell of burned flesh.

That was a good sign, but still…she reached up and touched her chest. No gaping wound as she might expect, no blood, and her clothing was still intact. She'd survived the ceremony, but had she been successful? Had she undergone a change as Grandfather said?

Tiponi attempted to sit up but failed. Her thoughts turned inward. Effortlessly, she channeled psi energy to her limbs, amazed by the power of the energy surge. Within moments she felt wonderful. Her power had grown much stronger. She was amazed at the ease she directed the psi energy. This must be what Grandfather meant.

A blood curdling howl shattered the darkness. Her heart leaped into her throat. She willed her psi energy to 'see' the doorway.

"Hania?" she called hesitantly. Hopefully he was the only wolf in the area. "I'm okay."

She infused her voice with calm. Had the wolf known what had happened in the room? If so, he was probably quite worried about her welfare. The door burst open, and green light from the crystals penetrated the inky blackness. The wolf bounded to her, nudged her chest with his nose, then licked her face. His fur tickled her cheek as she snuggled against his strong neck.

"I'm so glad to see you, Hania. Things got a little hectic in here, but I'm fine." She pulled back and raised her hand to pet the dark patch of hair on his forehead. Her hand stopped in mid stroke. In the filtered light her hand was clearly visible. She was no longer white; her skin had changed to a warm reddish brown.

"Hania, my skin has changed color. I look normal."

Her words were greeted with a low growl and a bump on her hand from the tip of his nose. "What's that you say? You liked me the way I was? Well thank…"

Yes, your white skin was beautiful.

Astounded, Tiponi dropped her hand and used it to propel herself away from the wolf. Had she just heard that or was her mind playing tricks? "Hania?"

Yes, you heard me.

The wolf's thoughts projected to her mind in a warm masculine voice.

"I can't believe I'm hearing your thoughts."

Don't worry, Tiponi, it's really me.

"Well, the last time I heard a voice in my head, the

experience which followed was quite unpleasant. You can't read my thoughts, can you?" She gave him another anxious look.

A growl came from the animal, but in her head, she heard rich laughter.

Do you want me to read your thoughts, Tiponi?

"I do not. Thank you very much. You can't, can you?" For the life of her, she couldn't stop her thoughts from chasing round, wondering what she'd thought about when she was last with him.

I could—but only if you wanted it. To do otherwise would be quite rude.

"Heavens, we can't have that, now can we?"

Are you trying to infuse humor into an awkward situation?

Laughter spilled from her lips. "Yes, I am. And by the way…all those times you looked at me with your tongue hanging out, were you smiling at me?"

Another growl.

I was either thirsty or hungry. I can't quite remember at the moment.

"Who's being funny now, fur ball?" She reached out and playfully ruffled his fur before standing.

Fur ball?

Indignation heated her mind. She smiled at such a human reaction.

Just stick to Hania, please. The wolf bumped her shoulder.

"All right, what's next?" She began to circle the room as she talked. "I found the first kiva, performed the ceremony, and changed color. Step one complete, so what do we do…oomph."

She tripped over something on the floor, barely

managing to remain standing.

Hopping around on one foot, she saw the cover stone to the sipapu. The cover had been completely locked earlier and now lay partially open. Excitement rippled through her. Legend said this tiny opening led to the third world. Scrunched on the floor, she peered over the edge, hoping to see her people's past. Useless. The cover wasn't off far enough, and the darkness below the small crack concealed any secrets.

"We've got to move the stone to get a better look down there." She found herself casually conversing with the animal. "It's quite nice having someone to talk to, even if your paws aren't very helpful with moving rocks." The growl she heard was just that—a growl this time. "Come on. Where's your sense of humor?"

I'm not sure I have one.

"Sure, you do. You need a little practice, that's all." She grunted with effort to move the heavy cover-stone but managed to drag it completely off the sipapu. The hole was quite large, easily big enough for an adult to go through. Darkness still hid what lay beneath the surface. Hania nudged her arm, and she turned to find him beside her, another chem-glow delicately held in his huge jaws.

Laughter burst from her lips. "Well, I see you can be useful after all." She took the chem-glow and held it over the hole in the floor. A sudden rush of light radiated from the hole. She opened her mouth, but no words came. Awestruck, she stared down—down into another world.

"I don't think we're in Kahoti-land anymore."

Her oblique literary reference was meant to calm her nerves as much as to have something—anything—

to say. A sturdy metal ladder disappeared into a churning swirl of red, yellow, and turquoise spirals that were eventually swallowed by a deep indigo. The colors spiraled up then sank into the blackness only to be reborn again and again. The pulsing movements were hypnotic, pulling both at her psyche and her body.

"Is this the third world?" She dragged her gaze away and looked at her friend who remained silent, picking up on the nuances of his stance. "What's wrong?"

I can't answer your question. It's forbidden. I can only protect you from evil—not help on your quests.

His words flooded her mind with warmth. This was how she'd always known him. "It's all right. I don't need your help to figure this one out. This is the most beautiful thing I've ever seen, and the only way to find out more—" She paused to rub his muzzle before stepping into the unknown.

The whirling colors turned into a blustery wind, dragged at her clothes, and tugged her down. She placed her head through the strap of her pack and tightened her grip on the ladder.

Then, she stepped into nothing.

A strong gravitational force like that of a moon to a planet sucked her down. Muscles in her shoulders screamed in complaint, and she tightened her grip on the ladder. The colors changed from lines into sparkles. Fear, sharp and acrid, tightened her throat and filled her mind.

Helplessly, she clung to the last rung of the ladder—her only tie to her world.

Let go.

Hania's words warmed her mind but chilled her

blood. He wanted her to release her hold on the one piece of reality she could feel? Her psi senses reached out and she felt him—not just in her mind, but all around her.

"Are you sure about this?"

Trust me.

The two simple words evoked calm in her mind and body. Microseconds passed. She responded with warmth and thoughts of trust. Reassured, she pushed one last nervous twinge out of her thoughts.

One of her hands let go and she fell into the swirling sparkles.

Chapter Thirteen

Out of This World

In free fall, her body spiraled downward. The sparkling lights flashed faster and brighter, blurring at the edge of her vision. Time became nonexistent. Images of her childhood and adulthood mixed in a myriad of flashes though her mind. In the Slipstream, she had felt similar sensations but had experienced the consciousness of others. Here there was only her and nothing—no sound, just light.

Sweetgrass. The smell came just before her body touched a cool surface and stopped. The light dimmed until she was again in total darkness. Pressure filled her ears, and the space around her filled with a thick atmosphere. Unease tickled at her subconscious, alerting her survival instincts. She hurled her body upward and shakily stood. Instantly, the room illuminated with the familiar green glow. Shiny metal and clear crystal made up the walls while the ceiling had the familiar green crystals.

"Hello?" Her voice echoed back to her. What if she'd transported into a crystalline version of a jail? No doors or windows, her mind registered. The opening was gone. Cut off from her world and alone, fear oozed from her pores. "No!" She couldn't afford to panic. The sound of her own voice comforted her.

"I am Tiponi. Grandfather has sent me on a quest. Where do I go from here?"

Her words met with silence. Curious, she walked the perimeter of the circular room. Mesmerized by the crystal and metal wall, she tentatively touched it. Her hand sank into the crystal. She had no time to react as psi energy surrounded her. Consciousness flowed through her arm into her body. *Life*—she felt life in the wall. This wasn't just a room, this was a living being, and she was inside it. Pulling, she tried to remove her hand from the wall but couldn't. Prickles of sensation moved up her arm bringing with it the realization that the wall was transforming her body into crystal as it moved upward.

"Wait—Don't do this. Please stop." Her voice shook, as icy tendrils of fear stiffened her spine. The crystal stopped moving but stayed in her arm. "Please tell me what's happening. I won't be afraid if I know what's going on." Fearful that any movement would shatter the crystal and damage her arm, she stood rock still.

A multitude of colors sparkled in the crystalline structure on her arm while the wall remained clear.

I am Leah, and I mean you no harm. Your body is fragile and must be protected for the journey. No harm will come to you.

Tiponi heard the words in her mind followed by warmth filling her entire being. "Will I stay like this?" She felt strange talking to a wall, but no stranger than conversing with a wolf.

Your body will return to its natural form when you arrive. Until then you will be aware, but unable to move.

The voice broke off as if waiting for her to make her decision.

Shall I continue?

"All right, but can you tell me where we're going?"

We are going to the beginning.

"Thanks for being so vague." Tiponi mumbled under her breath then, "Okay, get on with it." Her patience was rapidly changing to annoyance. She was a willing participant in all this but when would she find out her next quest?

Sit down.

Her gaze swerved behind her. An egg-shaped chair made of crystal was growing from the floor just behind her. "That's handy." She tried humor to calm her nerves, then tentatively sat on the edge of the chair. She had expected the chair to be cold and hard like crystal, but as she leaned back, the chair softly molded to her contours and emitted warmth and psi energy, just like the wall. She hoped the rest of the process was as comforting.

Don't be frightened.

Tiponi watched the crystal structure move up her arm and over the rest of her body. As it reached her face, her heartrate accelerated, and claustrophobia crept into her mind. The crystal continued, covering her eyes and entering her mouth and nose.

Be at ease, Tiponi. I will breathe for you.

Calmness filled her and she felt her lungs move, bringing oxygen and a slight sweetgrass smell into her body. She tried to open her eyes and couldn't.

Do you wish to see?

"How did you know?" Tiponi added as much sarcasm as she could under the circumstances.

We are together now.

"Then tell us, what the hell's going on?" She wondered how Leah would react to that.

We have a sense of humor, yes?

"Please tell me what's going on."

The crystal shifted around her, and she tensed as her body moved upward and tilted.

We are about to take off.

"What?"

Then, there was no more time to think. The entire room moved. She was glad she was immobile; otherwise, she'd be running in the other direction. Absently, she wondered where they were headed. Without warning, a picture formed in her mind—space with stars moving past so fast that they looked like streaks against the blackness. She was in space—which meant—she was on a spaceship.

We are going home.

"Where is home?" She had to ask, though she doubted she'd get a straight answer.

I believe you call it, The Eye of God.

"Holy crap, we're going to the Helix nebula?"

Chapter Fourteen

Another World

A fit of coughing roused her from a sound sleep. Her eyes cracked open to bright sunlight. Wincing, she squinted to filter the intense rays. Clouds of red dust billowed in the air, made breathing difficult and clear sight nearly impossible. Thunder sent jagged shards of pain straight through her eyes, striking sensitive nerves, then pinged around her brain before dulling to a horrific throbbing pulse.

The large open area where she lay smelled of dried grass and animal musk. Roaring thunder moved ever closer, increasing the pounding inside her head. Funny—the air didn't smell of rain and felt too dry for an approaching storm. Groggy, she tried to make sense of her surroundings. But as the ground began to tremble, a nervous twinge ran up her spine. Instinctively, she jerked upward to get a better look at her surroundings.

Holy Grandfather! Were those buffalo?

She'd never seen one outside a rehabilitation facility. Now, from the look of it, there must be thousands of them spread across the plain, frantically churning up dust as they ran. Awe at their magnificent presence paralyzed her, and she was slow to realize her very real danger. She was lying in the dirt directly in their path. Seconds separated her from trampling hooves.

Behind her, above the roar of the pounding bovine hooves, she heard the labored breathing of a running animal. *Run, Tiponi!* Her brain finally kicked into gear, and she shot upright and stumbled to her right on wobbly limbs. Her next step was a giant leap as rough hands hooked beneath her arms, jerked her up and over the sweaty body of a horse.

Awkwardly, she clung to the mane of the horse and the buckskin-clad leg of the person riding the beast. Dangling across the horse, pain jabbed her stomach and chest with each forward lunge of the animal. Upside down and dizzy, the world flew past in a blur of color and sound.

Foam from the animal's mouth and skin flew into her face. Its sides heaved, straining to bring air to bursting lungs. Finally, the horse slid to an abrupt stop, snorted loudly, and released a cry of fear as thousands of hooves stampeded the area where they had just been.

"Whoa, boy," a man's voice soothed the horse.

She felt a muscled arm pull hard to hold the frightened animal. That same arm pressed down into her back as the buckskin leg disappeared and the man quickly dismounted. Strong arms lifted her and pushed her to the ground behind a large rock edged with shrubs. Head down, she tried to breathe without sucking in mouthfuls of dust coming from the stampeding animals.

Bellows and grunts of fear joined the pounding, adding to the assault on her ears as she crouched close to the rock. Long minutes passed, while the strong arm held her firmly in place. Soon the herd thinned, leaving only a few stragglers who followed the exodus across the plain. The silence now broken only by the faraway hooves and the raspy breathing of the horse.

"Are you okay?" The words were spoken in her native Kahoti language, something she hadn't heard in quite a while.

"I think so." Her words came out shaky and a little hoarse from her dusty, fear-dried throat. She sat back as the hand released her and lifted her face with a thank you on her lips. The polite response turned into a raspy gasp instead as she got her first glimpse of her rescuer.

From the ground she gazed up at him as he towered above her. He stood out vividly against the bright sunlit horizon. Raven black hair flowed loosely around his shoulders held at the temples by a headband decorated with feathers and colored medicine circles. Obsidian eyes returned her stare from a face chiseled finely by what could only be a genetic artisan. Firm, unsmiling lips above a strong chin completed the finely crafted face. He said nothing, as if allowing her time to absorb everything and become acclimated to the new situation.

"Sam?" She voiced the unbelieving question as her heart pounded with something quite different from fear.

He reached down and pulled her to her feet. Her eyes were level with his chest. He stood nearly a foot taller, forcing her to tilt her head back to appraise him. Muscles rippled along his bare shoulders as he removed a small water skin from the belt at his waist. He uncapped it and offered her some.

"Drink. Your body will be weak for a few hours after your long journey." He lifted her chin with his fingers and tipped the water into her gaping mouth.

"Stop," she choked out as she bent over to cough

and catch her breath. "Can't breathe," she managed between spasms of coughing. "I don't understand; how are you here? Where are we?"

She followed him as he walked over and poured water into his cupped hand for the horse.

"Slow down and let your brain and body catch up," he cautioned as he stood with his back to her, carefully wiping the sweaty horse down with dried grass.

"Thank you." She touched his arm as he worked at cooling his mount. "You saved my life." She was unprepared for the jolting shock from the contact. Quickly, she jerked her hand away and took a wary step back. Tension filled her body when he turned to look at her with his eyes molten and muscles taut across his cheeks.

"Sam?" Her question carried so much more than his name. Infused in the single word were hundreds of questions. What was happening—why did his touch affect her the way it did—why did he look so stern? The world around her was forgotten along with her reasons for being here—it was as if she was in a bubble, suspended from the normal time space continuum.

"Let's walk while *Cheveyo* cools down." His words discharged the electricity between them and broke the tension.

"That's funny," she laughed. "Your horse and my…I mean—someone else I know…have names with similar meanings." She looked down at her feet as they walked, self-conscious and not sure what to say.

"Does your friend's name mean Spirit Warrior?"

"Yes, but his name is Hania. That's kind of strange—but then everything about this is strange."

"I agree, and it will probably get stranger still."

"Is that a warning?"

"No, just a gentle reminder."

"I'm definitely outside of the box this time, aren't I?" Her gaze fixed on his eyes, watching every nuance as she waited.

"Actually, you're completely out of the solar system." He paused as if to gauge her reaction.

"I gathered that when *Leah* said we were going to the Helix Nebula. This isn't exactly what I expected to see. I thought all nebulae were made of gases and debris. This looks like a planet. Which is it?

"Things are not always what they seem. A planet, a place, the Slipstream—they're just ideas we create in our minds to describe things—to help us understand."

Tiponi glanced uneasily over her shoulder. Her psi senses were telling her they weren't alone. All she could see, however, was the large rock they had used for protection during the stampede. She could have sworn they had walked much farther, yet the rock was only a few yards away. Her sense of time and space must have been altered by the trip. How long had it taken? Days? No, nothing could travel that fast; it must have taken at least weeks or months.

He continued to study her face as they walked. "Don't fight it; just accept."

"But I don't understand how any of this works. I'm—" Her words broke off, and once again she stopped and looked at the rock.

"Understanding takes time, which is irrelevant in this case. The sun moves across the sky from sunrise to sunset and you accept this. It is the Earth which moves, but do you truly understand the physics of it? Is it not enough to just know that it is?"

"Now you sound like Grandfather." She laughed, then stopped and pointed. "I don't understand it, but that rock is staying close to us. Is that the sort of thing you're talking about?

Sam's face broke into an enormous grin. "Exactly!"

She paused, waiting expectantly. "Aren't you going to tell me how it can be?"

"That's an easy one; it's not a rock." He leaned his head back and blew between his lips, producing a high pitched, ear ringing whistle. *The rock* stood up on thick stubby legs as a long, flat tail unfurled from beneath it and poked out from the back. At the other end, a boxy head with shrubby frills turned in her direction and blinked enormous, bulbous, brown eyes at her. As Sam clapped his hands and whistled again, the thing screeched indignantly and waddled off in the other direction.

Tiponi stood gaping at the thing. Sam must think her a nitwit, the way she stood gawking with her mouth open. She managed to close her mouth and force sound across her vocal cords.

"What..." No more words formed.

"It's a Rock Dragon. Mostly, they're harmless, especially ones that small. He's just a baby."

"I don't think I want to stick around to meet his mother, if that's all right with you."

Laughing together, they continued to walk from whence the buffaloes had come and finally arrived at the edge of a valley where the land sloped away to a small muddy stream, now nearly dry after servicing the herd. From the stream the land rose steeply, forming a high sandstone cliff which towered above the surrounding area. Earthy red in color, the formation showed dark hollows which had been modified into crude dwellings.

Tiny forms which looked ant-like from this distance crawled up the sides carrying large chunks of bloody meat as they deftly climbed to the dwellings. These were pueblo people, just like the Kahoti and the Zuni tribes on Earth. Where was this place which was so similar and yet so strange? She could have been back home, albeit hundreds of years earlier. Carried on the breeze, the pungent smell of buffalo dung teased her nose as it burned hotly on the fires.

Tiponi strained to get a better look at what was happening in the community. "Are they making pottery?" She knew true Kahoti artisans still used dung to fire their pottery, swearing by the age-old method which produced such fine results.

"Why don't we find out?" Sam indicated they should walk onward.

"We're just going to walk in unannounced? Are you sure?"

"Oh, we were announced a long while ago. You just didn't see the scouts, nor hear the messengers." He laughed at her puzzlement. "These people may look peaceful and harmless, Tiponi, but like all people they have enemies. They will have scouts and ways to send their messages. Are you ready to be the center of attention?"

"Wait—Sam." She ran after him as he walked on. "I don't know anything about this place—who these people are—what will I say to them? Are they part of my quest?"

"Are you shy?" He smiled at her blush. "I would

have never guessed. Be yourself, and you'll get along fine."

****

Curious stares never meeting her eyes bored into her skin as they entered the camp at the base of the cliff. Fires burned hotly as women tended the meals and men wandered to and fro, attending various jobs. Children with wide, rounded eyes peeked from behind their mothers' skirts, eyeing the strangers with excitement and not an ounce of fear. Voices called back and forth and up and down the cliff as groups parted, allowing the strangers through.

At the base of the cliff sat an adobe structure, which looked ceremonial in nature. Circular and large, it would hold most of the people present. Off to the sides were smaller rooms, probably used for storage. Over her shoulder, Tiponi noted the crowd had formed a half circle behind them—not threating, just following. Finally, they stopped in front of the central structure where an older man stood waiting.

"Welcome, Katsinas from the mountains." The old man spoke to Sam but included Tiponi in his gesture of greeting. "We are honored by your visit. Come let us refresh ourselves."

They followed as he led them into the dwelling where they took low seats around an already blazing fire. Those who entered behind them sat on the ground. From the back of the room two young women entered and indicated Tiponi should follow them. Uncertain about protocol, she looked to Sam who nodded slightly.

Exiting through a narrow opening in the back, the three women immediately climbed a set of ladders leading to the adobe houses above. Here, the two women prepared a water basin with fragrant flower petals and without another word began to undress her.

She was indeed being honored—so much water gathered at such great labor would only be utilized for bathing in the rarest of circumstances. That they went further and scented it and were about to bathe her was extraordinary indeed. Unused to such attention, she was slightly embarrassed by the ritual bathing. She couldn't risk insulting them, however, and passively stood for their ministrations.

Sam seemed familiar with the planet and the people, yet—they had called them *Katsinas.* Did they think she and Sam were Spirits? Kaya had said she was from the spirit world, was Sam? It was far too confusing. She'd have to wait for answers or until her role in all of this became clear.

After drying her skin, the women rubbed oils over her body and dressed her in a simple white dress made from finely tanned hide. Around her neck they hung an ornate necklace of the finest turquoise—the exact color of her eyes. Each piece of the gem had been hand-fashioned into an arrowhead complete with notched sides and wrapped with silver wire. The tip of each stone had been dipped in melted silver, drawing attention to the lethal points. The piece was exquisite. Nervously, she fingered the arrowheads as the women continued to work their magic on her appearance.

A tortoise comb untangled her hair, which was then topped with a headband decorated with eagle feathers and medicine wheels. It was exactly like Sam's. Soft moccasins completed the outfit. The two women stood, gave her shy smiles, and picked up her Kahoti dress to take it away.

"No! Please—"

She hadn't meant for the word to sound so harsh, but she couldn't bear to part with the wedding outfit someone had so lovingly made on the old loom. She chastised herself when she saw the fear in the eyes of the two women. Of course, they were afraid of offending her—they thought she was a spirit.

"Please, it's okay. I would like to keep the dress with me."

She then took the garment, gently folded it, and placed it in her ever-present bag. She wasn't sure they'd understood her words which she'd spoken in Kahoti. She had no idea what language they spoke, nor who they were. If only Sam had explained more. For some reason he was holding back. Maybe it was because of her quest. Her thoughts were interrupted by the sounds of chanting and drums below them in the gathering place.

The smell of some sort of tantalizing stew greeted them as they re-entered the adobe structure and sat near the fire. She was seated on the left side of the old man, obviously the chief of the tribe. To his right, Sam sat watching the group of men dressed in buffalo leggings, woven fiber kilts, and painted faces. The top and bottom of their faces were painted black while a swath across the middle a vivid red. A headpiece with a buffalo horn on one side and six eagle feathers on the other covered their heads. Several women adorned in feather headdresses and carrying rattles and plants joined the men. Their dresses of woven cotton bore beautiful markings with bright colors and intricate beading.

Tiponi had watched the buffalo dances before at

home, but this felt totally different. This was much more primal, stirring the blood with all the sights and smells which could only be experienced fully in primitive rituals. Back in Ondrone and Horetec, the dances had become almost a theatrical performance rather than an expression of thanks for the sacrifice made by the animals.

This was real. Life versus death—man and nature—spirit and mortal. Her blood sang with the experience, raising gooseflesh as the dancers left and re-entered from a ladder in the floor. The drums kept time as the dancers moved around the room, chanting the age-old story of the buffalo hunt. Excitement filled the air, yet not a word was spoken in the crowd as the buffalo dancers were chased by the hunter and slain. These people were not acting a part; they were the hunter and the buffalo.

A woman placed a bowl of stew in her hands, breaking her enthrallment of the scene. After tasting the delicate flavor of the stew, she ate quickly. Her thoughts turned to what she'd learned about her hosts so far. The people with whom she dined were a curious blending of plains and pueblo people. They were at a transition point between a nomadic life chasing the herds and an agrarian life on the mesa. What had spurred the change? They obviously still hunted the buffalo, yet she sensed a sort of pathos in their dance— as if they were thanking the buffalo but...she couldn't quite wrap her head around what was bugging her.

As the meal and dancing progressed, Tiponi sensed an air of expectancy—as if those gathered were waiting for something special. A glance at Sam didn't help, his face was as stony as the Rock Dragon they had hidden behind. He knew something was up and he couldn't tell her. He wasn't pleased about it either. His eyes were flinty and the muscles in his cheeks were taut. He wasn't just displeased, he was angry. Surely, *she* hadn't done something wrong or offended someone, had she? The answer came rather suddenly as the drums increased in tempo and then abruptly stopped. The chief stood beside her and made his way to the center of the floor.

Heavy with silence, the air filled with anticipation as each man woman and child stilled to respectfully listen to their leader.

"Today we have been honored and blessed by the Great Spirit. The Lahapi people have suffered much loss and endured many hardships. Our sacred Keresan Tiponi was taken from us by those who have much power but no conscience. Since then, the buffalo have not come, and we went hungry. Our enemies have pushed us up against this tall rock that we now call home. That time is now over, and the tears of pain have turned into tears of joy. According to prophesy, the sky rock formed from these tears now adorns the savior promised, the one who will help us become strong again."

All eyes swerved to look at her, as she sat listening.

"According to legend, a visitor with eyes the color of sky stone would come to us in our time of need. She would arrive in a cloud of red dust accompanied by a great warrior. Sakwa Posi will bring the buffalo back to us so that we do not go hungry again. She will climb the rocky pyres of Mount Andro and defeat the terrible dragon which holds us hostage. Then having defeated the Evil one, she will fly over our rock home in victory, and we will again be strong." At the conclusion of his words, the crowd cheered and pounded the drums in celebration.

A terrible sinking feeling in the pit of her stomach made Tiponi wish she'd eaten considerably less of the fragrant stew. Sakwa Posi meant blue eyes in her language. Grandfather gave her blue eyes as a gift. Some gift.

Her name, Tiponi, had several meanings in the Kahoti language. One meaning was a sacred item like a talisman or fetish which represented the faith of the people. The four parts of the sacred rock given to the leaders of the four races in the beginning of the fourth world were the most sacred Kahoti Tiponi.

If the Keresan or Buffalo Tiponi, *had* been stolen from the Lahapi people, then they would indeed suffer until it was returned. It was truly uncanny how closely the Lahapi paralleled her own people. Many of the words were the same or similar, and the beliefs were almost identical. Though leery of the dragon mentioned by the chief, she was anxious to start her quest and hopefully find out more about the missing Chanunpa from her tribe. There must be a connection, or she wouldn't be here.

Chapter Fifteen

Dragon Slayer

Before the sun had peeked over the horizon, Tiponi became aware of him in the room.

Their eyes met, hers sleepy, his bright and alert.

"It's time." His words were but a whisper. "I'll meet you at the base of the mesa."

Tiponi listened hard, trying to detect any nuances in his voice to indicate his mood. Last night his face had been almost frightening with anger, hiding the face of the man she knew. He was obviously unhappy about her quest, but unable to change it. This morning his voice was neutral, telling her nothing. Maybe he'd tell her what was wrong as they made their journey.

All hope of a quiet chat evaporated, however, as Tiponi met Sam and three others at the base of the mesa. It seemed that the chief had provided an escort for the two Katsinas to include an able looking warrior and the two young women whom she'd met last night. At least Sam's countenance was still unreadable and not angry.

She addressed the group in general. "Good morning,"

Sam stepped forward to help her mount a beautiful white and black Appaloosa which sported only a rope harness and a woven blanket for the ride.

One of the women handed her a water pouch and the other bowed before looking up at Tiponi with serious eyes. "Sakwa Posi, it is the wish of Chief Yuma that you take these gifts with the appreciation of our people." The young woman spoke the words as if reciting from a script, carefully enunciating the Kahoti words to make sure she had spoken them correctly.

"Thank you." Tiponi paused, not knowing what to call the woman.

"I am called Yamka, and that is Meda," she said, nodding at the other woman. Pointing to the imposing warrior, she lowered her eyes before saying, "And this is the son of Chief Yuma. He is called Qaletaqa, the guardian of our people."

Tiponi hid a smile. It was obvious Yamka was smitten by the man. Her eyes had difficulty avoiding a look in his direction.

She accepted the gifts, admired the lethal looking bow and quiver of arrows before adding them to the pouch and her bag which draped over her shoulder. "I am honored by your gifts and the confidence your people have in me."

She included the three Lahapi people in her thanks. Before she could say more, Qaletaqa gave heel to his sturdy black mount and started the procession. Each of the women mounted smaller brown horses and with one in front and one behind Tiponi they took off.

Sam fell in behind the group, riding Cheveyo and wearing a very grim expression as the red dust billowed up from beneath the horses' hooves.

The mesa terrain quickly gave way to desert. The desert stretched endlessly before them as the group moved silently across the sandy path. The riders sat listlessly on their mounts. Oppressive heat bore down on them as the horses plodded onward. Jostling with each movement of the animals, the travelers limited conversation, saving both energy and water.

Tiponi was excited at first, noting the different plant life that was almost familiar, but still alien in appearance. The spiny cactus plants were strangely shaped, and remembering the rock dragon, she wondered if these too were disguised. Just when she thought she'd go crazy with the quiet, the horses in front of her stopped and the riders dismounted.

Sam slid from Cheveyo's back and halted her horse before helping her to slide down. Stumbling against him, she was glad for his support when her legs, unused to such exercise, wobbled. "Take it easy," he cautioned. "The atmosphere is a little heavier here and can weigh you down."

She tried to ignore the sizzle of feeling where his hands touched as she accepted his help standing. "I thought I was just feeling the effects of too much stew." She tried making light of the situation.

Tittering laughter from the women let her know they'd heard and understood her joke.

"When do I find out what's going on, Sam? I've been picking up an oppressive feeling with my psi power. I…"

At one shake of his head, she ceased speaking. Either they couldn't trust their escorts or he didn't want them privy to the conversation. The women motioned to her, and she followed them on what she supposed was a nature call. She just hoped that any rock they hid behind was actually a rock.

Returning, they found only Sam with the horses.

"Qaletaqa has ridden ahead to scout out a place to camp," he answered her unspoken question as they approached. "We'll camp early tonight and discuss our plans. Tomorrow the topography will change and the going will be hard. We'll need to be well rested before entering the realm of the dragon."

At the mention of the dragon, Tiponi felt oppressiveness quite strongly and wondered if the dragon was as evil as the feeling suggested.

The women's faces wore a look of extreme seriousness, unusual in ones so young. She needed to do a prayer tonight and a smudging. She must be prepared for almost anything when they reached the dragon's realm. After drinking deeply from the water bags, they gave the horses a little before remounting and following the red dust cloud before them.

Unease kept intruding into her thoughts as they plodded toward their destination. Her mind grasped at tendrils of feeling, trying to make sense of what she felt sure was a warning. She wasn't having a vision but was receiving some sort of psi message which she struggled to understand.

If only she could discuss it with someone. She missed Hania and his ever-present feeling of warmth in her mind. Even when she hadn't been able to hear his thoughts, she'd felt his presence and been comforted.

The surrounding landscape changed, became rockier and sloped upwards. Cactus plants gave way to even stranger looking shrubs and stunted trees. The horses slowed, ears pushed back, eyes rolling as they sidestepped with unease.

"We'll stop here," Sam called as the women struggled to control their horses.

"Why are they so spooked?" Tiponi asked nervously.

"It's Chua Nukpana," Yamka answered. "They can smell it."

"Chua Nukpana," Tiponi repeated.

The name evoked memories of a childhood terror for Kahoti children. "The Evil Snake or Dragon," she translated the words softly. She thought back to whispered conversations which had stopped abruptly around children. Old men would sit around the fire and speak of the evil which could be present in flying serpents. No one had ever actually seen one on Earth, had they? They were just the stuff of myths and legends, right?

"Get a grip, Tiponi—you're daydreaming," she murmured beneath her breath. "How far away are we?" She held the rope tightly and slid from the horse's back.

Sam came up behind her and she felt a little safer with him at her back. "We're far enough away to be safe for tonight."

All eyes turned to the hill as Qaletaqa rode toward them. No one spoke as he dismounted. All eyes searched his face for answers to questions no one wished to voice.

"There's a small watering hole over the hill, but it might be best if we stay here for the night. All kinds of creatures will seek out the water after dark." His words caused a chill to descend over the group, sparking images of monsters in the minds of all.

"Did you see anything else?" Sam asked.

Tiponi looked at Sam. His expression told her that it wasn't the watering hole which had put such a look on Qaletaqa's face. He wore the look of one who had seen evil or death.

"Shall we start making camp?" Yamka asked of Meda and Tiponi.

The other woman must have read his face as well. Her question was an obvious ploy to leave the men alone to talk. Tiponi was having none of it. She'd seen the look which had passed between the two men.

"That's a good idea," Tiponi said, then surprised the women when she turned and walked toward the men. "You ladies start while the three of us talk."

Clearly, they were unaccustomed to women participating in men's conservation; she sought to reassure them. "I am Sakwa Posi.I can't hide from the evil I must face. I need to know all the facts so I can prepare."

Sam picked up the reins of the women's horses and walked toward the hill and the watering hole. "We'll talk while we water the horses."

Tiponi and Qaletaqa followed closely behind, leaving the two women to set up camp. From the crest of the hill, they looked down upon the small watering hole. The pool of water was dark—almost black, taking its color no doubt from the blackened rocks which surrounded it. Lava rocks? A few weeds grew at the edges, but the entire pool area was rather stark, almost forbidding in appearance. The horses shied away as their hooves stepped on the rocks near the water, but thirst overcame their fear. Soon they were drinking deeply as the men and Tiponi stood watch.

"Tell me what you saw," Tiponi asked Qaletaqa.

"Buffalo, slaughtered by the hundreds, left to the scavengers and maggots to feast upon. There was no honor in their death, only carnage. Their bodies were headless, their insides strewn about with none of the meat eaten or used. They were killed just for the sake of the killing." Rage filled his eyes, and he looked fiercer than Sam at the moment. One look at his stony visage made her glad he was on her side.

"Thank you for not sparing me the details. I need to know everything if we are to be successful. Would you take the horses back while I speak with Sam?" Her question had been a request, but he obeyed as if it were an order. She remained silent until the warrior crested the hill.

Without a word she went to Sam and placed her head against his broad chest. She calmed as his strong arms surrounded her, and she drew strength and solace from his being. Grandfather, Kaya, the Lahapi— everyone depended on her. A few weeks ago, she'd been carefree and unencumbered. Now, there were so many expectations.

"What have I gotten in to? Monsters—dragons and who knows what else is out there? Is it truly possible for me to kill this evil and bring back the sacred buffalo?"

She startled when the chest beneath her face rumbled with an answer. "You know I can't help you with the quest, but I am here along with the others to protect you. Grandfather has faith in you because he knows you can do this. He doesn't do anything without a purpose and believe me, he's extremely wise. You won't be alone in this; you can count on me to be at your back."

"After such a sweet statement, would it be mean to say I miss my Spirit Warrior?"

"If my horse will give you courage, you are

welcome to him."

"Your horse? Right—I forgot he's also called Spirit Warrior. You can make any situation more bearable. Thank you for that and the loan of your horse, but I was talking about Hania. I miss him."

"Are my horse and I not enough? What's he got that I don't?"

Tiponi couldn't help herself. "Fur."

"Sorry, I can't accommodate you on that one. What's so special about fur anyhow?"

Drawing strength from their banter, she said, "Actually, I enjoy running my fingers through his fur. It's comforting; and he always fills my mind with warmth." She was being deliberately provocative and loving it. She'd forgotten how much she enjoyed talking and being with Sam.

Both brows slanted upwards. "Should I be jealous of this Hania?"

"Oh, I don't think so. You're both charming in your own way. Are there any wolves on this planet? She walked over to a flat rock and kicked it. Assured it wasn't alive, she sat.

"There are animals called lupees that are very similar to wolves. They are larger and much more dangerous. Not only do they have fangs, they also have poison. I wouldn't suggest you run your fingers through *their* fur."

"There are so many things about this place and the situation I don't understand. Like, why didn't you want to speak in front of the others?" She watched idly as he sat on the dirt near her feet. "Can't we trust the people we're trying to help?"

"First, they think of us as Katsinas, and as such we

must remain separate from them. They look to us for help, and in return they do us honor. Second, I will trust no one but myself or Hania with your safety. The others are worthy of trust if not influenced by outside forces. We both know how easy it is for powerful beings to influence the mind."

Tiponi didn't need to be reminded of the voice in the desert and the serpent at Sam's home. If she, who had strong psi powers, could be influenced, then what chance did the others have against such forces? There was also the matter of the oppressive feeling which kept invading her mind. Was it trying to influence her or was her own psyche trying to warn her?

Would it be possible for her to influence minds? She had become much more powerful since the first change. She wanted to ask but knew he wouldn't answer. For now, she needed to concentrate on getting as many facts as possible.

"All right, what's the whole story of the dragon and the buffalo? Are you going to tell me, or should I ask the others?"

"I think it best if they gave you the details. Though some of the details may be distorted by fear or superstition, I think you'll get a better idea of what you're facing by talking to them."

"Are there any other unusual animals which I should be aware of before going farther?" She thought he would laugh and say no and was surprised when he answered.

"I've never been to the Dragon's Lair, but I've encountered some of the denizens on previous visits here. There are bat-like creatures called Chiropts which feed on blood and Lavarats who live in the lava tubes and eat anything. Shall I go on?" Sam asked as she stared back at him with disbelieving eyes.

"That's quite enough, thank you. Let's save some surprises for the journey, shall we? We had better go back now, but I need to be alone for a while later tonight."

"Are you going to talk to Grandfather?"

"There are things I need to ask him, and talking with him always seems to make me feel stronger."

"We'll sleep away from the others in camp; you can move away and talk to him then. I'll check out an area close by before it gets too dark."

"Thanks, Sam."

They rose and headed back over the hill.

Chapter Sixteen

The True Story

By the time they returned to camp, the fire was burning and something fragrant simmered in a cleverly rigged spit over the flames. The entire group had a very somber appearance.

The horses were tied on a line, stamping at flies with tails flicking back and forth while Qaletaqa sat nearby sharpening his blade. Meda and Yamka both were occupied with similar tasks.

"Something smells good." Tiponi tried to break the tension with her comment. Meda began filling wooden bowls with the stew and passing them around. "I hope you are hungry, Sakwa Posi, this stew will not keep another day."

Everyone ate quietly. Yamka broke the silence to ask, "How can we help you kill the evil one and get back our sacred Tiponi? So far, all those who have ventured there have not returned."

Tiponi chewed, trying to digest both the food and information. She placed the bowl aside and laced her fingers together in a calming pose. "Tell me the entire story; don't leave out any of the details, regardless how small. I need to know when this started and why."

Surprisingly it was Meda who spoke first. "I was about five when things started to happen. We lived on the plains then, not on the cliff. Something appeared, flying in the night sky. We were all afraid. Our parents would bring us close to the fire before dark, and guards surrounded us. At first that was all, then one night a terrible dragon descended from the sky and killed many of our people. Weapons were useless against it, and eventually everyone scattered. This happened for two nights.

"On the third night, smaller flying creatures came. The sky was thick with them, flying around us like flies, slashing with their sharp claws. When they were gone, the elders found Chief Yuma badly wounded and the Buffalo Tiponi gone. Soon afterward, the buffalo came in smaller numbers and then stopped coming altogether."

Yamka continued the story. "The first winter many died from starvation and cold, so when spring came the tribe moved to the cliff and made homes. We planted beans and squash and killed small animals for meat. We survived but did not prosper. The dragon has not come since we have been in the caves. Those who leave the area to hunt on the plains do not return. It's as if the dragon wants to keep us caged in this one small area."

Interested in hearing a warrior's point of view, Tiponi asked, "Qaletaqa, do you have anything to add?"

He paused in his task, then looked up at Tiponi and Sam. "They shouldn't have gone up the mountain and awakened it." His voice was harsh and condemning.

"Do you mean the dragon always been there? If so, why didn't it attack before?" Tiponi struggled with an uneasy thought. Maybe the Lahapi people had done something wrong.

"Yes, it has always been there, but has been

dormant for generations." Qaletaqa spoke the words without inflection. "Our legends tell of a time when the dragon roamed the skies freely. Those were times of peace and plenty—and the dragon was considered a sign of good luck."

"What happened to change all of that?" Tiponi prompted when he didn't continue.

"The land began to shake and tremble with quakes. The S*haman,* Lapu, made a vision quest to Htrae Mother to make peace and bring balance back to our people."

Htrae Mother, Tiponi thought to herself must be like Earth Mother to the Kahoti. "And what did the *Shaman* discover on his quest?" She asked.

"Htrae Mother said the dragon was lonely and needed a mate to make it happy. When it was happy, the dragon would sleep for a hundred years. During its sleep time the land would stop shaking." Qaletaqa paused, and Yamka continued the story.

"The tribe gathered to decide who would be sent to be the dragon's mate. The Chief's daughter was chosen as the best suited for the task. A beautiful ceremony was held, and the lovely maiden was taken up the mountain to the Dragon's Lair." Her voice softened before continuing. "The dragon became angry and ate the maiden. A mighty roar split the air causing the land to shake harder and smoke and fire to come out of the mountain. Two maidens were sent next, so the dragon could have a choice. Both suffered the same fate and the shaking continued.

"The shaman came up with a plan to help his people. He dressed as a woman and carrying his bag of magic he approached the dragon's lair. The dragon came out and seeing the woman swallowed her in one gulp before returning to the belly of the mountain. The *Shaman* had covered his body in a sleeping potion, and the dragon fell into a deep sleep. Protected by magic, the shaman crawled out through the chest of the dragon leaving a hole beside the dragon's heart."

"He used trickery instead of wisdom to solve the problem. Did the people not realize the dragon was female and wanted a warrior instead of a maiden?"

Tiponi couldn't keep the sound of her ire from her voice. So many deaths could have been prevented if someone had taken the time to get the facts. Noting the fearful look on Yamka's face, she took a moment to cool down. "I'm sorry, I didn't mean to sound angry. You were only telling me the story. Please continue." Her words were much softer than before.

"There's not much more to tell. The land stopped shaking, and the people lived peacefully." Qaletaqa spoke again.

"Something happened to wake the dragon, and it sounds like she was different when she woke," Tiponi interjected. "What happened?"

"Fifteen years ago, there was dissent among the people, and some decided to break away from the tribe and its ways. They moved to the mountain, and soon after the dragon awoke."

Tiponi sensed he wasn't telling her everything. "What are you not telling me?"

Qaletaqa exchanged looks with the two women before answering. "My father sent me to convince my brother to return to the tribe. He and his followers have broken many hearts with their departure. When I found them," here his voice became gravelly, "they were not the same."

"How were they different?" Tiponi questioned when he stopped talking.

"They had forgotten the ways of the Lahapi and worshiped the dragon. The dragon had become evil during its sleep and wanted revenge against our people for the trickery that had been used against it. Chua Nukpana took the form of a beautiful woman and seduced my brother. She gave him power, and together they inflicted pain on those around the mountain. When I arrived and tried to convince my brother to return, he became angry and we fought. Chua Nukpana actually laughed with enjoyment at seeing brother fight brother. She must have been controlling his mind—planting evil thoughts, because he accused me of coming to steal his wife. While we were fighting..." His voice broke and he could not finish.

"There was a child," Yamka interrupted. "When Qaletaqa fought with his brother, the child was accidentally thrown from the mountain and died. It was the child of his brother and Chua Nukpana."

Tiponi knew the story wasn't complete. "So, the dragon attacked your people and took the Buffalo Tiponi? I don't understand; why not just kill the one who had killed the child?"

"My brother said we had taken his heart and it was only right he should take ours. The Buffalo Tiponi is the heart of our people. By taking it the entire tribe suffered not just me." Qaletaqa bent again to sharpening his blade.

"So, we not only have to fight Chua Nukpana, but your brother as well." Tiponi summed it up with a cheerful voice. "What can you tell me about the dragon's powers?"

Sam interrupted before the others could speak "Why don't we take a little break? Don't you have something you need to do?

"I've prepared a place for us for the night. Rest may be the best way to get ready for tomorrow."

"I need to…" Tiponi looked at the group and noted the relieved expressions. Sam was right; they'd spoken enough for tonight. Time to make her preparations. "All right, sleep well my friends." She stood and nodded to each of the three before following Sam away from the others.

****

Peace seeped into her bones as the scent of sacred herbs on the flames enveloped her. She cleared her mind, letting in only the smell and the silence. Her body became light as her spirit rose above the desert floor. The Slipstream washed her into the cosmos on a giant wave. Thoughts touched hers as she passed along, and then hovering, she awoke.

"Welcome, my child. It is good to see you." The words were accompanied by a gentle smile.

"It's good to be with you, Grandfather. I've missed you." She hadn't meant for her voice to catch, but it did.

"What is it, child? I feel your unrest."

"Oh, Grandfather, I feel so—so inadequate. How am I suppose kill a dragon and return a sacred Tiponi?"

"Would you like some tea?" His voice was so calm and reassuring.

Tiponi smiled at him, remembering their last conversation over tea. "Is tea your cure for everything?" She laughed in spite of herself. "I would love some, by the way." She walked over and sat at the finely set table which had appeared as usual.

"Mm—this smells delightful, but it's different; what is it?" She relaxed in the chair and inhaled the hot mixture.

"It is a different time and a different situation, so yes, the tea is different. I call this my meditative blend. It helps me think." The old man joined her at the table and poured the hot brew into fragile, ancient patterned cups. "Do you like it?"

Tiponi was anxious to speak of other things but knew Grandfather did things on his schedule not hers. She sipped the tea and allowed the fragrant liquid to slide slowly down her throat. Her body began to relax almost immediately. "Are you sure this concoction is legal? It tastes and feels wonderful."

A chuckle came from across the table. "Whose rules are we going by?"

"I've always been a firm believer in—your house, your rules." Tiponi sipped more tea, enjoying the calming effect it had on her muscles and her mind.

"Ah yes, rules. I think that might be the problem, Tiponi."

"I don't understand; I follow the rules."

"You are boxing yourself in again. You are powerful, and yet you are reluctant to use that power."

"Dragons have power also, so what can I use to destroy it?"

"May I?"

At her nod, his hand reached over and picked up one of the turquoise beads on the pendant. "Exquisite workmanship."

Tiponi felt the beads warm beneath his touch. "The

Lahapi people called it sky stone and said it matched my eyes. What would have happened if you had given me brown?" She looked at him quizzically. "Everything you do has a purpose doesn't it?" She smiled at the crafty old man. "I suppose the necklace would then be topaz?"

His chuckle stopped, and she watched his face turn serious.

"You are very wise, Tiponi. I do like to plan ahead; it makes things so much simpler." He stared into her questioning face. "Trust in yourself. Use the gifts you were given."

"You have a strange way of saying nothing and everything, yet I always feel better after speaking with you."

"That is what I am here for, now I believe you have some planning to do. Think the unimaginable and do the unthinkable and you shall be fine."

"Wow, that's a tall order, but I won't let you down." As soon as the words left her mouth, she felt the tug of the Slipstream.

****

She became aware of the crackling fire and Sam sitting beside her.

"All is well?" Sam asked as she refocused her eyes in the real world.

"The tea was great, and I'm supposed to break the rules."

The perplexed look on Sam's face made her smile. "I'm okay. I just need to believe in myself and use the gifts I was given."

"Don't forget, I'm here for you. You might have to kill a dragon, but I'll make sure it doesn't kill you."

"Thanks. You can't know how much it means to me that you have my back." She reached over and placed her hand on his cheek. Pure electricity passed through her hand, jolting her back.

"Why does that happen when I touch you?" There—she'd finally asked the question which had been burning at the back of her mind.

"That is a conversation for another time. Tonight, we must concentrate on tomorrow, shall we?"

A little hurt by his rebuff, she wandered over to the bedrolls. Sam had gone to the trouble of removing the small rocks and softened the soil by digging. How could she be miffed at someone who had gone to that much trouble for *her*? He was a strange mixture of strength and gentleness. Maybe one day she'd figure him out.

After checking the bedroll for unwanted bedmates, she curled up and gazed at the sky. It was a slight shock to realize the stars above her weren't the same as those back home. It was just as beautiful though, and a feeling of homesickness overcame her. What was Kaya doing right now? Was she making piki bread to have with her supper? Maybe she was sitting beside the fire weaving herbs for drying. Such simple memories, yet so heartwarming. Even those memories of childhood taunts seemed trivial when put into perspective with what was happening now. Shaking her head to clear the nostalgia weaving webs in her mind, she sat up and looked across the fire.

She was restless and wanted company more than anything. "Sam, aren't you going to sleep?"

His voice rumbled from the shadows. "I don't usually sleep much. Are you having trouble?"

"I suppose I could blame it on Grandfather's tea, but actually I'm nervous about tomorrow. There are so many things to remember and so much at stake. I may never fall asleep."

"Shall I sing you to sleep like a little one?" His voice held humor, but he moved to sit closer to her on the other blanket.

"You'd do that for *me*? No one ever sang for me at bedtime."

"Then it is time to change that. Lie down and relax."

His voice was a beautiful baritone, and the melodic words rolled from his mouth with the ease of one having done this before. One more thing for her to ask about, when the time was right. Her list was mounting, she thought drowsily as warmth filled her heart and her mind.

****

Ho, ho, Watanay Sleep, sleep, my Little One
Ho, ho, Watanay Sleep, sleep, my Little One
Ho, ho, Watanay Sleep, sleep, my Little One
Ki-yo-ki-na Now go to sleep
Ki-yo-ki-na Now go to sleep

After Sam finished his song, he glanced down at Tiponi's sleeping form. There were so many things he wanted to say to her but couldn't. The role of Spirit Warrior was a difficult one. He had to tread a fine line between protecting her and allowing her leeway to come into her powers. His feelings for her mustn't interfere with her transformation. Her face looked childlike as she lay snuggled in the blanket.

He ached to touch her but couldn't risk it. She'd

already noticed the electricity between them as they touched. Instead, he took his own blanket and gently covered her. He gave her one last glance, and then with a puff of smoke he turned into his wolf form. Tonight, she would need the comfort only Hania could provide. Nuzzling her arm, he lay at her back all senses alert for danger.

Chapter Seventeen

Many Heads—One Solution

As Tiponi entered the cave, the stench of sulfur and rotting flesh overwhelmed her. Her heart pounded loud enough to be heard in the stillness. Searing heat and an eerie red glow in the distance indicated molten lava nearby. Surprisingly, the water which rose above her ankles was cool as she moved through the labyrinth beneath the mountain. Something scuttled along the walls and ceiling. She hoped it was only lava-rats in search of a meal.

The wealth of living material surrounding her sent her psi power into overdrive. The entire mountain was alive, and she could feel its pulse. Hot wind blew down the tunnel causing her torch to sputter and go dark. The wind was unnatural, smelly—*alive*. It came again in a rhythmic pulse—not wind, but breath.

Pausing in the darkness, she closed her eyes and reached outward with her mind—searching for the evil. Where was it hiding? Why couldn't she feel it?

Where are you?

No answer.

The floor rose sharply, ending at a set of rocky stairs. She grasped the slippery handrail and climbed slowly upward, her feet making wet squishing noises as she moved. When she could go no farther, she pushed at the heavy door blocking her entrance. There was no handle, and without a light she could see no markings.

The wind came again, hotter—*closer*. Behind her red light glowed, illuminating the stone walls and eerily casting her body in shadow against the door. She swallowed her fear, which threatened to show, and turned slowly.

Her breathing stopped altogether.

Not ten feet behind her filling the entire width of the tunnel was what she'd been looking for. It had found her instead. Two sets of glowing red eyes stared back at her—each from its own separate head. The heads weaved and bobbed, moving independently of each other but tied together by one body.

"Have you come to destroy us?" The left head asked. "Who are you to brave our domain alone and unarmed? You are different from the others."

"I am Tiponi of Kahoti, and I come from a different place on a quest for Grandfather. You hold something which belongs to the Lahapi people. I must return it to them as part of my quest."

"And what if we refuse to give this thing back to you? Will you kill us?" the dragon asked in a reasonable manner.

"I will do what I must to complete my quest. Killing you is not what I want, but if it must be, then I am prepared."

"Then prepare, Tiponi of Kahoti, to die with any others who try to help you." The dragon blew out a massive stream of fire at Tiponi. She focused her psi power and shaped the energy into a shield which pushed the flames back. Then, she formed the fire into a fine stream and severed the dragon's head. Turquoise blood poured from the wound, and the other head screeched in pain. Almost immediately the head regrew but now had the face of a Native American maiden. The second dragon head blew fire, and Tiponi severed its head. It regrew a male human head.

"Will you kill us too, Tiponi of Kahoti?" The male head asked. "And what of those who are hidden away?"

"What of my children, those innocents who have not had time to grow?" the female head asked.

"Who is hidden away? What children?" Was this some sort of trick or dragon sorcery? What would happen if she killed the dragon and the others died? Something had to be done to right the situation. She had to act. She pulled an arrow from the quiver and noticed the strange blue color of the tip. Air sucked into her lungs, then breathed out as she took aim and let the arrow fly. Just to the left of the dragon's heart, the arrow found its mark, penetrated the scaly skin, and exploded.

Terrified screams filled her ears, and something grabbed her. "Wake up."

Sam's voice finally penetrated her terror, and she stopped screaming. His hands pulled her up, enveloping her in secure warmth.

"Sorry." She slowly took in her surroundings and realized it hadn't been real. Footsteps sounded nearby announcing the rest of the group.

Qaletaqa stood with his weapon ready and a fierce look upon his face. "I am here, Sakwa Posi."

Sam moved to stand between Tiponi and the trio. "Be at ease. She had a vision which startled her. She'll be fine in a moment."

Tiponi stood to reassure the others of her safety

and moved to stand beside Sam. Shock darted through her system as she looked upon the face she had seen just moments ago. "Qaletaqa?" Her voice was hesitant as she broached the subject. "Do you look a lot like your brother?"

All eyes turned to look at him.

"We have the same face; we are twins. Is this important?"

"It's helpful, yes. I need you to do something for me before morning."

"Anything, Sakwa Posi."

"Good, the rest of you need to get some sleep. I will need your strength tomorrow."

She and Qaletaqa sat talking in whispers near her bedroll as Sam waited by the fire. After sending the young warrior back to the others, she approached Sam and sat.

"Do you want to talk about it?" he asked quietly as she stared into the fire.

"I'm afraid my task is going to be even more difficult than we supposed."

"I'm not sure how that could be possible, but I'm listening." Sam moved to sit beside her.

She saw the concern in his eyes, but he waited patiently for her to continue.

"I'm not sure, but I think the vision was trying to tell me not to kill the dragon."

"Could the powers of the dragon be influencing you and you saw it as a vision?"

"I felt…regret, and sorrow, but no evil or threat. How can I kill something that is not evil? Then—there were the faces. I believe the dragon is holding hostages in the mountain."

"The dissenters who left the Lahapi village years ago?"

"Yes and no. I think there are more beings there. A piece of the puzzle is missing. I've got to figure it out before doing the wrong thing. I need a promise from you, Sam."

"I can't promise what goes against my purpose. Your safety comes first."

"All right, I understand your duty. But promise me —you will kill nothing there unless I am in mortal danger. I can't explain more than that, but I need your promise."

His steely eyes stared back at her as if trying to read all the answers in her face. "I promise."

For minutes they continued to stare at each other across the flames, talking with their eyes and not words. "Thank you. And...?" She paused, looking for the right words.

"And?" he prompted softly.

"Could you...I mean...could Hania sleep next to me for the rest of the night?" Her eyes caught his look of surprise, then continued to watch every nuance of his features, hoping she was right.

Sam studied her intently then nodded. Moments later, Hania stood where Sam had been.

Pleasure washed through her as she watched her friend approach. Gently she touched the dark patch at his forehead before pulling him toward her and enveloping him in a big hug. "I'm so glad to see you. I've missed your company, my friend."

I've never left your side, Tiponi, nor will I.

The words came into her mind with the warmth she recognized. "I know, but tonight—tonight, I need my friend as well as my Spirit Warrior." She lay down on the blanket, feeling the warmth of his fur at her back.

Sleep. I am here.

****

Dawn was heralded by loud rumbling followed by an undulating wave of the desert floor. Frequent and strong aftershocks made gathering the supplies and horses difficult. Lightning flashed in a black sky—not from the night, but from smoke spewing out the top of the mountain.

"She knows," Tiponi said to no one in particular. "She knows, and she's angry."

Meda struggled to keep the animals from running away. "We can't take the horses any farther, Sakwa Posi. The rest of the journey must be made on foot."

Sam spoke up. "Let them go. There's no need for them to suffer such fear. They'll make their way home." His words brought a look of relief to the girl's face. He walked over to his own mount, speaking gentle words before slapping it on the rump. The horse leaped forward, running away from the smell of danger. With very little encouragement, the other horses followed.

Tiponi looked at each member of her small party, searching and listening for dissent. "There is no shame in leaving if any of you should choose to do so."

Qaletaqa spoke as the other two nodded. "Where you go—we go."

The trust she saw in each of the three faces gave her pause. These people believed in her totally. How could she doubt her own abilities when they had complete faith in what she could do? Emotion flooded through her veins, and her courage blossomed. She would not let these people down. Swallowing the lump in her throat, she straightened.

"Today you may see things that are unimaginable, but keep heart. I have been told by the highest authority—unimaginable and unthinkable are exactly what we must embrace. All right, Qaletaqa, since you're the only one who has been there, I'd like you to lead. Sam, as always, you've got my back." Tiponi picked up her bag, bow, and quiver and fell into step with the rest as they moved forward.

Beneath their feet, the land still trembled as ominous bursts of smoke billowed from the mountain above. Treacherous footing and falling rocks elicited no complaints from the group as they climbed higher. The air became hotter, and sulfur gases made it almost unbreathable. Reaching a flat area, the group halted, agreeing without words to stop for a moment's rest.

"It wasn't like this before," Qaletaqa murmured quietly.

"She didn't feel as threatened by you," Tiponi replied. "She knows things will change today."

"Will things be like they were before the dragon awoke?" Yamka's voice was hopeful.

"No, nothing can ever be the same as it was, but hopefully it will be better." In her heart of hearts Tiponi knew for some things would be much worse.

Shrieks from the sky had everyone racing for cover as ten large bird-like creatures dove down from the peaks. Similar to ancient Pterodactyls in size and shape, their bat-like wings were covered with iridescent scales instead of skin. Shimmering brilliant red as the light reflected from the scales, they were as beautiful as they were deadly. Snapping beaks, lined with razor sharp teeth glinted as they swooped at the group.

Sam and Qaletaqa threw rocks at them, more to deter the beasts rather than kill.

"These are her eyes." Tiponi spoke loud enough to be heard over the noise. "Throw ash and sand instead of rocks."

All hands scraped the ground, grabbing handfuls of dark ash and silt. As the flying red targets came closer, they threw a cloud of dust at them. Cries pierced the air from the first animal blinded by the cloud of debris. The rest of the flock responded by rushing the group in a marathon flapping of wings. Their efforts proved useless in the tight rocky crevices where the group had taken shelter. Then, as if responding to an unheard call, the entire group retreated, including the one blinded. Apparently, vision wasn't required for flight.

Tiponi fell to her knees, overwhelmed by an oppressive surge of evil, a punch to her psi senses. It was coming from the mountain, but from whom or *what*? She was almost certain the dragon the Lahapi people spoke of wasn't the source of the sinister feeling washing over her. They hadn't mentioned any other creature or being, but she felt it. There was another presence in or on the mountain, and she had to discover its motives quickly before blindly continuing the quest.

Lightning cracked the sky, arching jagged tendrils of pure energy above them. Tiponi closed her eyes and raised her arms to draw energy. Her body glowed a yellowish orange momentarily, giving her a ghostly appearance.

Yamka and Meda shrank against the rocks afraid, but Qaletaqa bravely reached for Tiponi.

"No, don't touch her." Sam stopped the warrior. "She is drawing energy into her body from the sky. It won't harm her but will kill you."

Blocking out the reactions of the others, Tiponi opened her senses to what was happening around her. The surge of power washed through her body like high tide pounding a rocky shore. Each and every cell of her body became energized, and her mind felt as if it was one with the cosmos. Grandfather had said she was powerful—now she felt that power as never before. She felt a curious sense of wonder and awe. No fear—only purpose. This is what she'd needed to bring her mind and body back into balance.

You are not welcome here. The malevolent voice interrupted as it sounded in her mind. *Go away or you will die.*

The words dropped coldly into her mind like cubes of ice in a drink. As if sensing her gaining strength, it needed to undermine her boost of rejuvenation. The words were meant to give her doubts—make her cower or second guess her actions. She heard the words and the evil behind them, but now there was no fear. Her mind and body were renewed and primed for duty. Laughter bubbled up into her throat and escaped her lips before she could stop it.

She opened her eyes, threw out her arms, and shouted to the cliffs around her. "I am Tiponi of Kahoti, and I have come for you." Wind gusted, blowing her hair riotously around her body as it buffeted the others against the rocks. Her voice echoed back over and over, bringing smiles to her companions. They grinned at each other as if she had just given a rousing, 'we're going to war' speech.

The mountain answered with a loud rumble, spurring the group to seek cover from falling rocks.

Tiponi picked herself up from the ground and dusted her hands on her clothes. "I think he got my message."

"He?" Sam and Qaletaqa asked in unison.

"I thought the dragon was a she," Meda chimed.

"She is." Tiponi confused them more with her reply. "But…the true evil one is a he."

"There's more than one dragon? Is it her mate?" Yamka wanted to know.

"No, there's only one dragon, but there are two entities. Our job will be tricky, but I think I now know what we are up against. Let's go find our dragon."

Chapter Eighteen

Hear No Evil

The climb to the top of the mountain was treacherous, and more than one in the group slipped dangerously close to the edge. Sam walked lightly with the grace of an animal familiar with steep paths and slippery slopes. Tiponi hadn't noticed before and did so now with only part of her attention. When this was over, providing of course they survived, she wanted to have a long talk with that man. There were so many things they needed to discuss.

They rounded a sharp turn and came to a flattened plateau which led to a cave. Puffs of foul, smelly smoke billowed from the opening. The bitter odor of sulfur stung their nostrils, nearly masking the scent of death. Scattered around the edges of the cave, buffalo and other unknown animal carcasses lay rotting in the heat. The stench combined with the heat thickened air, created an almost unbreathable potion.

At this height, the air should be cool, but the volcanic activity negated the advantage of altitude. Not a single plant grew in the area—not surprising with the high acidity from the sulfur gases. All in all, it was an unpleasant place to be.

Meda and Yamka pulled torches from the supplies and handed them to the men. They lit the torches and entered the dark maw of the mountain as a close-knit group. They followed the rough floor deeper into the mountain. Steam burst from cracks in the wall, spewing hot water on their unprotected heads. In the distance, Tiponi saw the red glow from her vision. The feeling of malevolence was tangible in the air. She heard rattling noises. In her vision she'd heard rats, this sounded more like chains.

"I feel many life forces nearby, not all are people." *We are walking among evil and only you and I are prepared for it.* She shared her thoughts with Sam.

The ground sloped downward, and water covered their feet, making the walk even more treacherous. Ahead, something splashed in the water, sending a small wave back at them.

Qaletaqa yelled back to the others as he pointed the torch at the water's surface. "Watch your feet."

"Here, let me." Yamka took the warrior's torch. "Keep your hands free for your weapon."

Sam passed his torch to Meda and likewise searched the water as they moved. Tension heightened. Everyone watched each ripple the water made as they continued forward. They'd gone only a few yards when Qaletaqa was pulled down into the water, his body surrounded by long, snake-like tentacles. The water churned as his body spun, then he disappeared into the depths. The pool was too dark to see anything—just splashing and tiny glimpses of a hand or tentacle.

"Qaletaqa! We've got to help him," Yamka cried.

Meda's hand tightly held her arm, holding her back. "No, you'll only get yourself killed. Qaletaqa is our strongest warrior. If the monster can be killed—he will do it." Her voice sounded confident, but her face showed as much fear as her friend's.

"Step back from the edge," Sam said with a frustrated look on his face.

Tiponi knew he wanted to jump in and help but wasn't allowed to do so. No—she was the only one who could save Qaletqa. She closed her eyes and looked at the water with her second sight. Using her psi energy, she found the creature and touched it with her mind.

No—let him go. She pushed the thought toward the primitive mind.

Fear, hunger, bounced back.

Infusing her thoughts with calming energy, she pushed against its mind once more. The animal's response was immediate. It hadn't understood her words but reacted to the calming energy by relaxing its grip on Qaletaqa.

Qaletaqa's arm popped up, and Sam pulled the sputtering warrior from the tentacles. Tiponi continued to hold the animal with her mind, sending thoughts of reassurance. Slowly she introduced the thought of *home* to the animal, hoping it would swim away and hide where it felt safe. She had to work hard to influence the creature, as it was driven by instinct rather than emotions. Finally, its tentacles flexed in a pulsing motion and it sped away.

Yamka checked Qaletaqa for wounds. "Are you okay?"

"I am fine," he reassured her, "but why did it let me go?" he asked as he dripped water and heaved in breaths of air. A few pounding whacks on the back and he coughed up a stream of water.

"I sent it home," Tiponi interjected. "It won't

bother us any longer. Let's take a different tunnel, in case there's more than one."

"Sounds like a wise idea to me." Sam indicated another tunnel to their left. "Were you able to get any information from it?"

"No, it was too primitive for thought and reacted on instinct alone. As far as it was concerned, we were merely dinner."

Qaletaqa stood to join the conversation. "Not a very cheerful thought."

Meda giggled nervously. "After smelling this place, I may never eat again."

Only Yamka remained silent. Her face was closed and tense.

Tiponi knew that nearly losing her warrior had shaken her, but she continued to follow at his back, ready to lend a hand if needed. She hoped there wouldn't be a need for it. She had no idea what awaited them and would have to rely on her vision and Grandfather's advice to save them.

A deafening roar echoed through the passage followed by scurrying feet and flapping wings. Dodging and ducking they managed to stay upright as the mass exodus of animals passed them. If the noise was an indicator of proximity, they were about to meet the dragon. Fearful cries came from other animals as they made their way down the tunnel.

Around a corner, they entered a gigantic cavern, complete with stalactites and dark pools of water. In the center of the floor, a large vat rested above a roaring fire. Located around the perimeter of the room were cells or stalls filled with many kinds of animals. Some she recognized, others were new to her. The lack of ventilation and the close confines created a rank odor. The metallic smell of blood and sweat added to the noxious smell.

Qaletaqa asked what was on everyone's mind. "What is this place? I do not recognize some of these animals."

"It looks like a zoo," Tiponi said without thinking.

"What is a zoo?" Yamka asked.

Tiponi couldn't keep the anger from her voice. "A place where people lock up wild animals so others can gawk at them."

Two hundred years ago, zoos were seen as an effort to save animals from extinction. Allowing the public to view the caged animals for a fee helped fund the places. Today no such facilities existed—only repopulating sites were allowed. These allowed the reintroduction of animals into the wild. The scene before her was barbaric.

"Don't they use them for food or riding or clothes?" Meda asked.

"No, they just cage them up." Tiponi's voice was even angrier.

"That's cruel. Even food animals in our world should have some freedom," Yamka said.

Sam approached the cages. "Let's take a look around and see what's here."

The four of them moved off as Tiponi lagged behind. Her heart ached at all the pain and fear she felt from these poor beasts. How could anyone be so vile as to harm these creatures? She heard all their cries, but one in particular spoke to her more than the others. She walked along a ribbon of rock behind the pools. The cages here were nearly in complete darkness. As her eyes adjusted to the dark, she was able to make out shapes.

She stood in front of a cage containing a full-grown white buffalo. Her heart raced as she stared at the beautiful sacred icon of her people. It was majestic. For a moment she forgot about the cage in her awe of the animal's beauty. Elation took a nosedive when she studied the animal more closely. There were small marks on the animal's neck—cuts. Tiponi struggled to bank her anger. Someone had deliberately bled the animal for some purpose. This wasn't good.

"Sam?" Her call came out weakly, but she felt his instant response.

His voice came from behind her. "What is it?"

"Someone is experimenting on these animals." She moved to the next stall, gasping at the animal she saw there. It looked like a white deer, but both its horns intertwined to make a central horn. *A unicorn?* Weren't they a myth? Disorientation washed over her. Where had these animals come from, and why were they here? In the next cage, she saw some sort of bird, large like an emu, and also white. They had the same markings as the buffalo. "What did you find in the other stalls?"

"Animals both indigenous and non-indigenous to this planet. There's even a small Rock Dragon. They all have one thing in common—they're albino," Sam said.

"Interesting—I'd say if genetics works the same throughout the universe, someone wants pure genetic strains for some reason. I found marks on their necks where they've been bled. How many dragons do you know who take blood from only pure white animals leaving small marks on the neck only?"

"None," said Sam.

"That's what I figured."

"What are we up against, Tiponi?"

"Evil; pure evil." She moved back to the cage with the buffalo. The animal snorted and jumped back from the cage opening, obviously afraid. How could something so big and strong be afraid of someone as small as she? Her gut clenched as she thought of the angst these beautiful creatures had suffered. "Shh, I won't hurt you, big guy." Her words purred from her lips as she moved closer to the gate. The animal's eyes widened, and it shrank even farther into the corner.

"It's hard for an abused animal to trust again." Sam's words softened to keep from scaring the animal further.

"Help the others calm the animals on the other side. This guy and I are going to have a little talk."

"All right. I seem to have better luck with horses anyway. What are we going to do with them while we track down the evil one?"

"Why, let them go of course. It should create enough of a diversion to help us get to where we need to be."

"And that is…?"

"The heart of the mountain. That's where we'll find them."

She turned to look at the buffalo. *I feel your pain;* she pushed the words into the mind of the buffalo. *I feel your fear.* Focused on calming the animal, she created images of grass, sunshine, and other buffalo in its mind. *Taste the air—smell the grass—feel the freedom.* She reached through the bars, holding her palm upward. *I need your help, friend. I need you to lead the others.*

The buffalo took a tentative step toward her hand.

She continued to send calming energy to it. Ever so slowly the animal inched forward, finally placing its nose in her palm. Gently she rubbed its face then slowly ran her hand down its cheek toward the marks. The animal jerked its head but didn't back away. "Shh, it's okay, boy. I'm only going to help you."

Tiponi placed her palm over the cuts and sent a pulse of healing energy through her fingers. Where her hands touched, the animal's skin glowed and healed. "Sam, have everyone find a safe place out of the way. I'm going to free them."

The words had barely left her mouth before another roar from the dragon created panic in the stalls. Fearful cries and agitated stamps magnified with each roar. The animals sensed danger and were reacting in the only way they knew how. She sent out a large pulse of calming energy, hoping it would be enough to prevent a stampede.

She unlocked the buffalo's pen and swung the door wide. "Take care, my friend." The buffalo edged out of the cage.

"You have wings." Her startled voice turned into a laugh at the beauty of it. A flying buffalo—what next? She concentrated on the cages and opened all the locks at once. The animals bolted out but slowed immediately when the buffalo stood solidly in their path. When all were out, the buffalo turned and led them from the cavern. She felt like Noah, sending the animals from the ark.

Tiponi made her way to the center of the cavern where the vat bubbled over the fire. Wafting the steam toward her, she cocked her head to one side, trying to decipher the concoction. Her nose wrinkled at the scent of magic. Someone was using medicinal herbs for magic potions. This wasn't any love potion or good luck charm either. The brew contained body parts and blood.

This was black magic and totally evil. She didn't delve into the black arts but had read enough to know that the Lahapi would need protection. Just as she could project thoughts and use psi energy in a good way, others could manipulate thoughts and energy for evil. She removed her buffalo blanket, cut three pieces of buffalo skin, and placed them flat on the floor. On each piece, she placed sage and cedar to keep their spirits clean. Next, she placed an eagle feather to keep them close to the creator and honor their bravery. From the gate of the stall, she removed some white hairs from the buffalo and added them to the squares. The white buffalo was the most sacred of symbols and would give them strength and keep their hearts pure.

At last, she reached up and snipped a lock of her own hair for each of the medicine bags. She wasn't completely spirit, but these people believed in her. Their belief, and carrying a part of her with them, would go a long way toward protecting them. No one knew what they might encounter when they entered the lair of the dragon. She murmured a prayer and words of blessing over the bags as she tied them with strips from the buffalo hide. All was set.

She placed the bags around the necks of her Lahapi companions. "These medicine bags should keep you safe from evil. I'm not sure how it will work on dragons." A violent quake shook the mountain. Immediately roars echoed off the walls.

"I think they know we're here," Sam said as they

started for the back of the cavern where the noise came from.

Several openings led to different tunnels, all leading down. They entered the closest one, which felt small and very hot. Sam passed the torch to Qaletaqa, who led the group swiftly through the passage. It was strange they'd encountered no one. Where were all the Lahapi people who had moved to the mountain when they'd split from the tribe? Could they all be dead? No, they were more likely being used by the same person who was experimenting on the animals.

Tiponi nearly bumped into the women as Qaletaqa abruptly stopped. He held the torch up high, illuminating a massive wooden door. It was the kind of door you'd expect to find in an old castle, with iron hinges and a huge lock. Light showed through the bars at the top, but it was far too tall to see anything.

"This is the place, Sakwa Posi," Qaletaqa said. "This is where the dragon lives."

"Why is there a lock on the outside if the dragon is in there? A dragon could easily break through this," Sam said.

"It wasn't locked when I was here before. Maybe it is to keep people out rather than dragons in," Qaletaqa added.

"Good thinking, gentlemen, but I'd say finding out what's on the other side might be prudent before barging in. Yamka, could you stand on Qaletaqa's shoulders and see what's on the other side?" Tiponi hated to ask, but of the two women, she seemed the best suited.

"Of course, Sakwa Posi." She climbed onto the warrior's shoulders and leaned against the bars. Her breath sucked inward audibly before she said anything. "It's like a room in a house, with chairs. The ceiling is very high and…" Her words cut off at the roar that sounded far too close. Sam caught her as she fell backwards.

"The—the drag—gon." She stuttered. "It's…" She took a deep breath, "…it's in the pool."

"Were there any people?" What about my brother?" Qaletaqa's voice was sharp, his concern for his alienated brother obvious.

"No, just the dragon." Yamka's voice dropped at the word dragon.

"Okay, I want you three go back the way we—"

"No, we cannot leave you, Sakwa Posi," Meda interrupted.

"You must," Tiponi insisted. "I have a job for you." She touched the woman on the shoulder to reassure her. "You three are going to find the people who are being held captive here. I don't know how many or where, but they're here. Take each of the corridors until you find them. Don't split up, and go directly to the surface when you release them. Sam and I will take care of the dragon and whatever else we find in that room. Does everyone understand what I need you to do?"

"Yes, Sakwa Posi," they all said, but looked far from happy.

Tiponi turned to the young man—brother to the dragon's mate. "Qaletaqa, I'm depending on you to carry out the plan." She stared directly into his eyes, seeing the strength she had known was there. "Now, go quickly."

As the three departed with the torch, she and Sam

were in the dark both metaphorically and physically.

Tiponi turned a calculating look at Sam next. His response was to quizzically raise an eyebrow. "Don't think you're getting rid of me as easily."

"I wouldn't dream of it. But I do think I might need Hania for a while. No one knows who you really are, except me. The element of surprise might be helpful. You can tell me things without others hearing, and your animal senses can pick up things I can't."

"Okay, but you do have a plan, right?" His brow again rose quizzically.

"Sorta."

"Tiponi, maybe we should…"

"No, Sam. The only way to find out what's in there is to go through the door. After that…we'll have to improvise." She deliberately made her voice sound strong and optimistic. Her courage couldn't stand too much scrutiny at the moment. Asking Sam to follow her with no explanation was going to be a hard sell, but how could she tell him what she didn't know herself? She had to see firsthand what was going on before making a plan.

"Here's what I know. There's something evil in there. I don't think it's the dragon, but I'm not absolutely sure."

Sam placed his hand on her shoulder and squeezed. "I believe in you. You don't need to explain your decisions."

"Thanks, I'm pretty new to all this heroic stuff. You give me balance. Ready?"

His voice was rock steady. "Ready."

Tiponi broke the lock and removed it, noting the puff of smoke from the corner of her eye. Her spirit warrior stood on all fours next to her. The door pulled open with surprising ease, and she stepped inside. It looked like a medieval cathedral with limestone formations acting as arching supports for the roof. Scattered around the room, several large flaming pots lit up the area and added even more heat to the already heavy air.

She took a cautious step then another, slowly making her way to the pool. Yamka had said the dragon was here, but at the moment the surface of the pool was glassy and still—just like a mirror. At the edge she looked down at her own reflection. Just behind her head a faint shadow coalesced into a large blurry form—the dragon—had found her!

Chapter Nineteen

Final Confrontation

In her mirror image on the black pool, Tiponi's eyes grew wider as the horrifying image of her adversary expanded. Her blood chilled while her skin heated from the dragon's breath.

The dragon continued to rise behind her, filling the pool with its reflection.

Her eyes remained fearfully glued to the reflection in the pool as she appraised her enemy. Imagination tends to either embellish or diminish that which we fear the most. In this case, she hadn't imagined nearly frightful enough.

The dragon had only one head, unlike the creature in her vision. But it was enormous, sporting tall, pointed ears which moved forward now, listening. Could it hear the wild beating of her heart? The monster's eyes glowed like red hot embers, eyes which stared down at her reflection in the pool, as if deciding how she would taste.

Obsidian—shiny black, was the only color which would come close to describing the dragon's scaly skin. Without warning, the staring contest ended, and the dragon blew a long stream of fire over her head and lit the pool in a hot blaze.

No time to think, Tiponi tumbled to the left, head

over heels to escape the scorching flames. The pool became a burning inferno, with flames rising to the ceiling. The water emitted an odd metallic smell as it burned and vaporized. She stood, her back to the wall, and watched the reptilian form turn toward her.

The oblong snout had long, thin flaps of skin, purplish in color, hanging beneath the mouth and throat, creating a hairy appearance. Large diamonds glinted among the flaps and encircled the neck like a necklace—a feminine touch to counteract the deadly look.

"I am Tiponi of Kahoti." She made her voice as strong as possible, striving to give the impression of bravery. "What is your name?"

At first, she thought the dragon was going to ignore her words as it took a step in her direction. She countered with a step back and found she could go no farther.

Move to your right, don't let her pen you down. She felt Hania's words in her mind and shifted direction, her movements bold to show confidence.

"I am called many names, Tiponi of Kahoti. Some—even call me *death*."

The dragon's voice came out loud, but distinctly feminine. The tail flicked, displaying triple rows of six-inch purple spikes to match the skin flaps. Black and purple—the colors of a bruise.

Tiponi reached out with her mind and tried to touch the animal's aura and felt nothing. "I asked your name, not what you are called," she retorted and took a bold step forward to lend credence to her show of confidence.

"Smart—smart indeed. One's name holds power;

do you wish to have power over me, Tiponi of Kahoti?" Sarcasm, along with spittle dripped from the large mouth.

The dragon moved closer, and Tiponi jumped sideways, putting some distance between them and the pool. The beast stood on two massive legs ending in sharp clawed feet, which could easily step on Tiponi, ending this conversation and her life quickly.

"No, I don't seek your power, and I gave you the power of my name, didn't I?" She held her ground and forced her face to remain calm as the large head lowered, nearly even with her own. This close, she smelled the fetid breath, blowing from nostrils as big as her hand.

One quick snap and it would be over.

The hot wind from the words blew Tiponi's hair as the dragon spoke. "You did indeed. Have they no one smarter or stronger to come after me?"

In a surprise move the dragon jerked upright, twisted in what looked like agony, and released a roaring screech. Tiponi dodged the spiked tail as the animal thrashed and used the opportunity to race across the room. The smoldering pool now lay between them. Her eyes were drawn to the stones around the animal's neck. The stones glowed bright red as the small arm-like claws scratched at the jewels as if they were offensive. Fire burst from the dragon's mouth, nearly searing Tiponi before she erected a psi shield. Blown across the room, she knocked over chairs and tables, as her body cleared a path like a snowplow removing obstacles in its way.

Stunned from her brief flight, it was harder to get up this time. No—not the flight, the landing had been the problem. A growl sounded in her mind that had nothing to do with mirth. Hania was worried, more importantly—*she* was worried. She'd been in the dragon's presence mere minutes and here she lay on the floor in a heap.

I'm okay. She sent the brief message to him. Now she had to prove her words. She pulled to her hands and knees, checking the dragon's position as she did so. Before she could stand completely, the dragon flew at her, like a falcon, homing in on its prey. She dropped to the floor, and rolled to her back, channeling psi energy through her fingers as she rolled. Twin bolts of lightning shot from her fingertips and struck the animal, stopping its headlong flight and flipping the powerful beast backward into the pool.

Tiponi dodged the wet flames that splashed from the pool where the dragon fell. She watched it disappear beneath the watery inferno for several long moments— long enough for her to catch her breath and send healing energy to her back and limbs where she'd fallen earlier. The dragon wasn't dead, merely hiding and probably doing exactly what she was doing.

Rest, review, and respond.

What would it do next? The pool must be very deep to allow such a large creature to submerge and remain completely hidden. Something niggled at the back of her mind. The cavern…too late.

Behind you!

Hania's warning flashed through her mind seconds before the huge tail slapped her in the back, flinging her forward into the pool. She had no time to register pain as she gasped a mouthful of air and struck the surface of the hot water. The flames had subsided, saving her skin from burns, but not the heat. The water was extremely hot, searing her flesh as it engulfed her body. Instinctively, she allowed herself to sink lower where the water seemed cooler and had no chemicals. The pool connected to the cavern pools—that was what buzzed at the back of her brain.

Tiponi—are you all right?

She sent out an *I'm sort of busy* message.

Use your gifts. Grandfather had reminded her. *Well*, she thought as her lungs burned from lack of oxygen, enough was enough. She reached out with her mind, pulled energy from her center, and then gathered more from the surrounding water, then the living mountain. She made her body spin faster and faster, forming funnel of water around her. She focused the energy, slinging her body upward out of the water. The spout rose from the surface like a living thing. Standing atop the cyclone, Tiponi threw psi energy in the direction of the dragon, catching it unaware. This time, the dragon was the one to be flung against the wall. Rocks fell, and the mountain trembled at such a release of power. The cyclone bent, allowing Tiponi to gently step off onto the rock floor.

"Strength and intelligence are not always apparent but can still coexist." Tiponi paused, sucking in large gasps of air. She waited for a response from the animal, lying against the far wall. "Like you—you're intelligent. Most people think dragons are stupid killers—yet here we are talking together."

A humorless laugh escaped the serpent's lips. "I may have underestimated your power, but don't you do the same. Make no mistake, Tiponi of Kahoti, I am a killer. In my lifetime I have killed hundreds."

At that, the dragon's neck jerked back, eliciting a pain-filled roar. Flames shot to the ceiling. The jewels around her throat lit up like neon lights. Waves of pain bombarded Tiponi's mind as the animal screamed. Someone was using pain to control this animal. For just a moment, she sensed the evil one, the one who had tried to scare her away before. *The necklace*—it hadn't been glowing when she'd first seen it. There must be some sort of pain stimulus in it.

The dragon wasn't evil.

The dragon was in pain.

"My name…is Kuwanyauma."

Hanging her head after she spoke her name, its body language was one of shame—or regret. Immediately, the necklace glowed again, and the dragon roared, spread its wings, and flew tight circles around the room. She landed on the opposite side of the pool.

Tiponi watched the tortured creature, noting the engorged blue lines running through the wings, pumping blood for the extra energy she needed for flight. When the frantic circles ceased and the dragon landed, she spoke gently. "Thank you," she said, sending soothing energy toward the dragon. If her assessment was correct, the dragon had no control…

No! She mentally slapped herself. The dragon *was* using control. She could have killed Tiponi the moment they entered the room.

"For what? I must still kill you." The dragon's shiny black skin turned an ashen gray after she uttered the words. "I should have done so already."

"Thank you for sharing your name, giving me that power. You *do* look like a beautiful winged butterfly."

Tiponi hoped she was translating the name correctly. It wouldn't do to get it wrong and insult her. At her words, the dragon's head lifted with something approaching pride, and the purple fringe beneath her snout turned green. "And why haven't you tried to kill me yet? Could it be you feel emotions like people—maybe even love like people?"

"There is no beauty left in me. What love or emotion I may have had once is dead—or buried." The serpent's face took on a defiant look when she asked, "Do you see other dragons here?"

Tiponi's response was honest. "No."

"All that is left is death—the giving or the receiving." The dragon looked defeated, tired, and the ashy gray color became mottled, taking on a bluish color—like the veins on her wings.

Tiponi watched the change in color—obviously a direct result of her feelings. "Kuwanyauma, you once flew freely and lived harmoniously with the Lahapi people. What happened to change that?"

It was time to hear the other side of the story. Hania walked through the shadows to sit a few feet away from her. His mind brushed gently against hers, and she gained strength at its warmth.

Kuwanyauma perked up as Hania entered. "And what is this, your pet? Or did you think to feed me before killing me?"

Tiponi felt the growl in her head and chuckled. The dragon really had a sense of humor. Too bad Hania didn't. "This is my friend. He doesn't appreciate being referred to as a pet or food." She closed the distance to stand at the wolf's side. Just in case the dragon had hungry ideas.

Blue and green color washed across the dragon's skin. "What a shame, he looks to have some meat on his bones. I do so hate it when they're bony."

"Are you trying to be funny or intimidating?"

Tiponi tried to read the creature's mind. All she got for her efforts was a blank. She hadn't been able to sense anything from the dragon, or the other entity, since entering the room—just that one instant of pain when the necklace glowed. Something must be blocking psi waves. She was still able to feel and hear Hania though.

Kuwanyauma's tail twitched restlessly. "Neither funny nor intimidating. "I've missed conversation lately."

"What about your mate— doesn't he talk to you?" Tiponi asked and darted a questioning look at Hania.

She's stalling—waiting for something.

Maybe she's just resting—we've both used a lot of energy. Tiponi sent the words to him—then quickly thought of something. *I think she knows what the others are doing.*

I'll have a look around—be careful.

Hania's words weren't needed. She intended to not only be careful but also successful.

The dragon's eyes followed Hania as he disappeared into the shadows. "I hope it wasn't something I said. No matter—he will find nothing to save you. We will all die."

"It doesn't have to be that way. Let me talk to the *other*. There's no reason for anyone to die."

Shades of black and purple flashed across her skin. Her body jerked upright. "You know of the *other*? That's not possible."

"I have felt his presence from far away. I can't feel him now so he must be shielding himself. He is the true evil one, Kuwanyauma. What you have done was at his bidding. Help me to get rid of him so everyone can go free."

"No. Stop. You can't—"

The necklace lit up, and this time when the dragon roared, spitting fire across the pool, anger accompanied the flash of pain. Tiponi barely had time to form a psi shield to block the flames. As it was, they pushed back with such force, she was knocked to the floor. Still, the flames came, and the dragon's roars grew even louder. The stones surrounding the fleshly neck lit red like her eyes. Kuwanyauma spread her wings and flew in destructive sweeps around the room, spraying everything with fire. Her pain had to be excruciating. Finally, she landed, her sides heaving for breath and her color turned a dull gray.

In an attempt to contact the real evil one, Tiponi said, "Chua Nukpana, I call you by name—show yourself."

"No. I—" The dragon's words were cut off as the necklace turned emerald green and tightened.

"Stop it!" a male voice yelled.

Tiponi whirled as the voice spoke behind her—Qaletaqa. "I told you to go directly to…" Her words were cut off by a gasp of surprise from the dragon.

"Togquo…my love?" Voice raspy, the dragon spoke to the man, her skin turned bright blue and green as she did so.

Surprised, Tiponi took a closer look and realized it wasn't Qaletaqa, but his brother, standing beside her. As she watched in horror, the dragon let out a roar and a blaze of fire directly at them. Tiponi leaped in front of Togquo, raising a psi shield against the firestorm. The flame was stopped, but the force of the impact slung them high against the wooden doors.

She picked herself off the floor as the man lay stunned by the force. "Kuwanyauma, you must stop— you'll kill him."

The dragon stared back at her with pain-filled eyes—eyes which begged for death. "I can't help you, Tiponi of Kahoti. I can't help any of us. He is far too strong. Please—for the sake of the one I love—do what you must."

Tiponi now understood why Kuwanyauma had been stalling—she'd guessed they would release the prisoners. She had been waiting for one last look. One last glimpse, of the Lahapi man she—a dragon—loved. Pain filled Tiponi's heart at the tragic events torturing these innocents. The thought of the manipulation which had ruined or destroyed so many lives brought her chin up. There was no time for pity or self-doubt. There was a job to be done—a job only she, Tiponi of Kahoti, could do.

"I'm sorry, Kuwanyauma. I did not wish for things to happen this way. Trust me, this is for the best."

Tears rolled down her cheeks as she removed her bow and pulled an arrow from the quiver. She touched the turquoise and silver arrowhead Qaletaqa had made from her necklace. If her vision was correct, this was the only way. It didn't make it easier. She'd never killed before, and this was especially hard. Kuwanyauma was a worthy adversary and she suspected, a wise woman. The lives of so many depended upon the right outcome to this. Grandfather had said to use her gifts, think the unimaginable and do the unthinkable. Well, the turquoise necklace was a gift, and killing was unimaginable. Now, she had to do the unthinkable, kill a sentient being. She had to trust in Grandfather's wisdom and her own powers.

"Forgive me." She grasped the arrowhead with her fist, drawing her own blood, bright red against the turquoise stone. "Sky and earth—tears and blood—life and death," she chanted.

She pulsed a rush of healing power into her palm, making the arrowhead glow. She infused the stone with her power. Placing the arrow properly against the bow, she took aim and drew the string taut. She couldn't look into the knowing eyes which stared back at her. The beautiful eyes forgave her but broke her heart at the same time.

"I shall make it easier for you, Tiponi of Kahoti." Kuwanyauma blasted the room with a thunderous roar, spread her wings, and prepared to fly. Her chest was now exposed along with her heart.

Just behind her, Togquo screamed, "No! You can't kill her."

Tiponi closed her eyes and let the arrow fly. Her mind guided the arrow as it soared over the pool toward its target. She heard the growl and was knocked forward as Hania and Togquo toppled into her. The man's attempt to stop the arrow was in vain. The roar changed to a piercing screech, as the arrow found its mark, just to the left of the heart. Tiponi open her eyes, in time to see blood the color of turquoise pouring from the dragon's chest. The arrow had not exploded as in the vision, but the wound kept enlarging. Pain, fear, surprise, and anger rushed into her mind. Of all the emotions that struck her mind—regret seemed to be the strongest.

"Let me go to her, please," Togquo begged from the floor.

She hardened her heart against his pleading. Without blinking, or pause, her hand removed another arrow. This time she added no blood or healing energy. Her eyes never left the dragon, writhing on the floor. She answered him. "Not yet, she isn't free. We must wait until he's gone."

"I don't understand what you're talking about. Please, she needs me. Let me go to her. I love her."

Hania, is he wearing Qaletaqa's medicine bag?

Yes. The word entered her mind.

Good, we'll need it.

As they watched, Kuwanyauma's movements stilled and she breathed out her last breath. The huge head lolled to the side and faded to ash gray.

Togquo was loud in his anguish. "You killed her."

Still Tiponi waited, arrow straight, string taut.

"Lapu Chua Nukpana, I call you by name. Come forth and show your true form." Tiponi spoke the words, evoking the power of the evil one's name, something any magical being could not ignore.

Slowly, a black gaseous form rose from the gaping wound in the dragon's chest. When completely out of the dragon's body, it took the hazy form of a man. Decades of evil had morphed the shaman into something barely recognizable as a man. The heart in his chest was a shiny, obsidian-black spot, pulsing with an inhuman rhythm.

Without a qualm, Tiponi released the arrow which made straight for the pulse. Piercing the heart, turquoise met obsidian—the pure, blue sky stone wiping the black slate clear of evil. For one single moment, Lapu solidified into a true man, just long enough to feel the pain of the shaft in his heart. One moment later—his atoms became gas in the cosmos.

Hania released Togquo and changed into his man form. Together they raced to the other side of the pool.

Tiponi knelt beside the sobbing man and reached to touch the dragon. Such a beautiful creature—to touch it was indeed magical.

"Why did you come here and do this?" Togquo was inconsolable.

The rights and wrongs of what had occurred were probably unfathomable to him at the moment, but Tiponi tried. "Do you remember the legend of how the shaman climbed out of a hole in the dragon's chest?"

At his nod she continued. "Lapu, the shaman, decided to steal the dragon's power for his own. He used black magic to put her under a spell and then used the hole in her chest to go in and out of her. That way, he could see and feel the terror of others while continuing his wicked research on all those poor animals."

A sobering thought occurred to her, and she paused in her explanation before looking at Sam. "They were all albino, Hania." It was the first time she'd called him by that name in his man form, and it felt strange.

With a raised eyebrow, he looked back at her. "Yes, just like you."

Only four words, but they conveyed volumes. Tiponi bit her lip as she thought a moment more. "I was to be his special prize for the collection. He would have used me, just like the animals."

"No, Tiponi, I would never have let him touch you. I would've killed him myself, if need be." His words though truthful, seemed to bring her little comfort.

"So, the dragon wasn't the quest after all. It was Lapu?"

"I can't say. Grandfather has his ways. Maybe both were." Hania bent to place a hand on Togquo's shoulder, drawing her attention back to the dragon and the situation at hand.

Togquo hadn't noticed she and Sam had been sidetracked by other things. His attention remained fixed on the body of his love as his chest heaved with sobs.

Tiponi picked up her explanation where she'd left off. "When you and the others moved to the mountain, he used you as well. He controlled her with pain, using the necklace. You should be proud of your wife. Even through all of her pain she tried to defy him. She must love you very much. She was willing to die for you."

Tiponi gave up trying to explain when his eyes remained glassy and glazed. "She isn't dead."

"I saw you kill her," he gasped between words. "She's not breathing."

"No, you saw me shoot her with an arrow. It isn't the same thing." Logic wasn't working because Togquo wasn't paying attention. Tiponi took a more direct approach. She took his hand and placed it over the dragon's heart.

His eyes widened. "Her heart still beats—how can this be?" He placed his head where his hand had lain—his sobs turned to sighs.

"The arrow was made from turquoise—tears from the sky which fell to the ground. Like your Buffalo

Tiponi, sky stone protects those of pure spirit. Kuwanyauma was willing to sacrifice her own life for yours and the others. Her heart is pure."

"It wasn't just for me and the others." He sat up and provided an explanation of his own. "Kuwanyauma has been around for hundreds of years. At one time she had a dragon mate. There are eggs from long ago, with her dragon mate. Chua Nukpana wanted her to hatch them, giving him control of many dragons. When she refused, he took them and locked them away in a special room held secure by magic. He told her he would destroy them if she didn't obey. It was a standoff between the two. She couldn't kill him because he had the eggs—he couldn't kill her because he needed her to hatch the eggs." Togquo ran his hand gently over the dragon's face and then reached for the arrow.

"No—it is not finished yet." Tiponi stopped him from removing it. "The tip of the arrow has spirit blood and healing power in it. It will cleanse her of the last of Lapu's magical spell."

His hands continually stroked the dragon's scaly flesh. "So, you did not plan to kill her?"

"No, but if it had been the only way to rid the evil from this place, I would have." Tiponi certainly hoped it would never come to something like that. She would have done it, but her soul would be marked by such a thing.

"Thank you for releasing us. We came here to start over, and she woke up…"

Tiponi touched his shoulder gently. "Don't berate yourself, Togquo. There was no way to overcome Lapu's hold without help. Grandfather sent me to help."

"Will she be the same?" he questioned.

"Do you mean, will she be able to turn back into a woman—the one you love?"

He nodded.

"I don't know. Dragons have their own kind of power and magic. Kuwanyauma is one special lady with a strong spirit. I think anything can happen if there is enough love."

"I will love her regardless, and we'll hatch the eggs. I'll love all the little ones, even though they are not my own." His face fell as he said the last words.

"I'm sorry about your child, but what about your brother? He and your father love you, too. Will you try to make peace?"

"I know my daughter's death was an accident, but the pain is still strong, and forgiving is hard."

"Most important things are hard, but they are usually worth it. Now, I think it's time. Sam, could you cut the necklace from her neck?"

When the stones from the necklace scattered to the floor, air whooshed into Kuwanyauma's lungs and her chest rose. Her skin turned from gray back to a bright blue and green.

"Take the medicine bag from your neck," Tiponi said.

"But my brother said I must keep it on."

"That was to keep Chua Nukpana from controlling your thoughts. It's safe now, and your wife needs it. When I remove the arrow, you must hold the bag tightly against the wound so it will heal."

Gently but firmly she pulled the arrow from the dragon's chest. The blood, pouring from the wound, was purple in color. Their two bloods had mingled— one spirit to another. They were bound now as if born sisters. Tiponi smiled at the thought. She'd never had a sibling to love, and it couldn't hurt to have a dragon in the family.

"Togquo?" The big eyes fluttered open. "You are safe, my love."

Tiponi felt odd as she watched the emotions the two shared. Man and dragon—it didn't matter. Their love was strong and would flourish.

"Tiponi of Kahoti, thank you for all you have done." The dragon sat up and stared down at Tiponi. "You came here with a purpose. Togquo, please get the Buffalo Tiponi so it may be returned. We will visit your father and your people immediately to ask their forgiveness."

Togquo started to object. "But—"

"No buts. Wrongs were done on all sides, but now it is time to put all these things behind us." The dragon rose up to her full height. The medicine bag along with a little dragon magic had closed the wound completely.

Togquo walked to an alcove at the back where he pushed aside a curtain. He turned back to face the others. He held a huge single piece of turquoise, delicately carved into the likeness of a buffalo. He placed the heavy piece in Tiponi's hands before moving to stand beside Kuwanyauma. Drawn to her like a magnet, he couldn't stay away.

"I wish you much happiness." Tiponi smiled at the beaming couple. "I must return this and continue my journey."

"Fly with the wind, Tiponi of Kahoti. We will meet again." Kuwanyauma stood in woman form beside the man she loved.

"I think I'm going to cry." Tiponi sniffed as she

walked up the tunnel with Sam. Rich laughter greeted her statement.

"I see you have a soft spot for lovers," Sam responded.

"You have to admit, they're quite a couple. Can we come back when the eggs hatch? I think I'd like being an aunt."

"Now, just how do you get to be a dragon auntie?"

"Well—our blood mingled—so…we're sort of sisters, and that would make me an aunt."

"If you say so, but just think of the problems."

"Whatever do you mean, Sam? Aren't babies just babies?"

"I don't think so. Most babies don't burn down the house when you burp them."

Tiponi laughed all the way to the opening at the top of the mountain. A warm breeze met them as they exited and stood, gazing out over the desert below.

"Your hair." A smile broke out on Sam's face as she turned to look at him.

"My hair?" Tiponi reached up and pulled a swath of her locks in front so she could see.

"Red. Sam, my hair's red." Excitement filled her voice. "How does it look?"

"It suits you. I must admit red hair is intriguing."

"Is that a roundabout way of saying that you like redheads?"

Sam paused and took one of Tiponi's silken red locks. "It's like fire in the light. Yes, I think I like redheads."

The two laughed.

"We did it." She grinned triumphantly. "The quest is over."

"You still have a delivery to make, and it's a long way down." His words did little to dampen her revelry.

A noisy bellow came from the path below. Qaletaqa appeared, trailing behind the white buffalo, prodding it forward. A heavy scowl painted his face as he approached them.

"All the others went with Meda and Yamka down the mountain. This one—" He threw a foul look at the beast. "—refused to go. He kept turning around and coming back up."

She walked over to the huge buffalo. "Thank you, Qaletaqa. Did everyone get out safely?"

"Yes, Sakwa Posi, they will return to the village for a while. My father and I have much to talk about. Maybe with the dragon's permission, we could use the cavern and other rooms during the winter. It would always be warm."

"That sounds like an excellent idea, brother. If it is agreeable, Kuwanyauma and I will journey with you to the mesa." Togquo spoke from the mouth of the cave.

Everyone turned in surprise as the couple exited into the light.

Qaletaqa immediately went to his brother, placing one hand on his shoulder and clasping his forearm with the other. "Brother, I have missed you. Please, forgive me and be my brother again."

Togquo stared back momentarily, then when nudged from behind by Kuwanyauma, he spoke. "Only if you accept our differences and my wife, regardless of what form she takes." Strength resonated in his voice as he gazed intensely at his reflection in flesh.

"Agreed," Qaletaqa answered, then turned to give a slight bow to Kuwanyauma. "Welcome to our family, and please forgive the way we have acted in the past."

"We cannot change the past, Qaletaqa, but we can work toward a new future."

The buffalo bellowed again, as if tired of all the talking. Laughter at the beast eased the tension. Tiponi rubbed his nose and cheeks, then spoke to him softly. "I have a feeling you are part of the quest. According to legend, I'm supposed to fly over the village to declare victory. Would you do me the honor of giving me a ride?"

The buffalo bowed, lowering its head and spreading its wings. Moments later, she was airborn, red hair flying behind her as she headed toward the mesa to deliver the Buffalo Tiponi. Her hands flexed in the soft fur on the animal's back, enjoying the wind blowing in her face and hair. "I think I'll call you Omawnakw or Cloud Feather."

A grunt came from the huge chest which she took for agreement.

Chapter Twenty

Last Quest

The trip which took days for the group on foot
lasted only minutes by air. Tiponi soon landed at the
campsite of the Lahapi people. The entire tribe gathered
outside, waiting for her arrival. Cloud Feather landed
lightly, and Tiponi thanked the buffalo, with a whisper
for his ears alone. "You are a noble friend, and I thank
you for your help."

She slid from the animal's back and approached
Chief Yuma, who stood dressed regally in ceremonial
head feathers and a breastplate made from bone, beads,
and sky stone. The elaborate pattern on the breastplate
was intricately interspersed with what looked like
sapphires.

"Chief Yuma, I have fulfilled the prophesy of your
people, and I now return the sacred Buffalo Tiponi."
She gently placed the heavy turquoise statue into the
chief's hands.

"Sakwa Posi, you have indeed fulfilled the
prophesy, but have done so much more for me and my
people. You have returned my son and helped to reunite
those lost to us. This day will be remembered in dance
and song as long as our people shall live. Thank you
with all our hearts." He held up the Keresan Tiponi for
all his people to see. Cheers erupted from the crowd as

a celebration with drums and dancing quickly ensued.

Tiponi was happy for the Lahapi people but felt saddened and a little unsure. She'd completed the quest and made the change. What now? How would she know what the next quest would be?

Chief Yuma's voice brought her out of her introspection. "Sakwa Posi."

"Yes, Chief Yuma." She looked at the old man's weathered face.

"While you were away, I had a dream. This dream was like no other, and I believe it is important." He paused and removed the beautiful breastplate and bowed. "In my dream, a waken woman came to me and said you might have need of this, in the place where giants sleep. She said it would guard your heart and unlock the unknown." He held the breastplate out for her.

Tiponi had no idea what the old chief meant, but respectfully took the breastplate from him, put her head through, and tied the buckskin strings at her side. "I thank you for your gracious gift, Chief Yuma. Did the waken woman have anything else to say?"

"Yes, but I did not understand what it meant. I will try to speak the words exactly if you consider it important."

"Indeed, it is very important." Tiponi waited anxiously for the old chief to pause and think.

"It was like a riddle."

Follow the star, to find the pipe,
In the city of the dead, the star shines bright,
The star is the key that opens the lock.
Enter the room, a giant will block
Release the power, but beware its lure.

To save the world, you must procure
The serpent's eye, a glassy sphere.
Guard your heart, the time is near.

"Those are the exact words?" Tiponi asked when the chief ended his recitation of the riddle.

"It is. I hope this helps."

"What can you tell me about the breastplate? Does it have a special history?" Tiponi hoped to gather as much information as possible before she left the planet.

"It belonged to each chief of this tribe and was made by Htrae Mother. Much of the history has been lost as many of our story tellers died without passing on the stories."

"That is a great loss, Chief Yuma. I am honored you would give this piece of your history to me."

Tiponi turned to look at the crowd as the sounds they were making changed. All eyes were focused upward, and the joyous revelry subsided. In the distance a bright blue and green shape soared through the sky, moving ever closer to the group.

"The rest of your family is coming to join the celebrations. You have proven yourself a wise chief to your people, Chief Yuma. May I suggest you extend the same wisdom to your family?"

"It is good wisdom comes with age, for today I feel very old but also very happy. Will you stay for the celebration?"

"Thank you, but no, Chief. Today is about you and your people. Enjoy this reunion with your family and friends. I have a riddle to solve and another journey to make."

"Will we see you again, Sakwa Posi?" he asked as Qaletaqa and Yamka joined him.

"I hope so, but think of me each time you touch the sky stone. Peace be with you, Chief Yuma of Htrae." She turned to walk away, only to be confronted by Cloud Feather. He bowed and waited for her to jump onto his back. The white buffalo gave a snort and leaped into the air.

She waved to everyone and watched their attention shift as Kuwanyauma landed, her husband perched upon her back. She would miss them, but according to the riddle, time was running out. She allowed Cloud Feather to fly in the direction where she had first awaked on the planet. How was she supposed to get back to Earth and the city of the dead?

And where was Sam?

Her eye was caught by a horse speeding across the plain, muscles bunched, mane flowing in wild array. An equally muscular rider sat upon his back, his long black hair flying loose in the wind. He was the perfect image of Native American freedom. A brave and his horse—the wind and the plain. Cloud Feather flew lower and touched the ground. His wings folded in as he ran beside the horse and rider. They stopped on the rise above the water. Exhilaration quickened her pulse as she watched thousands of buffalo feeding. This was what it must have looked like on Earth hundreds of years ago.

"I see you've acquired another gift." Sam turned to look at her, his eyes sparkling with something she could only guess at.

"Chief Yuma gave it to me along with a riddle. I think I've been given my next quest."

A smile blossomed on his face. "I really like the red hair. Maybe we can talk to Grandfather about it when this is all over." He laughed at her look of surprise. "What?"

"I would think Grandfather has more important things to consider than my hair color."

"But he chose to give you blue eyes. Maybe I should ask him to leave your hair red."

"Don't I have a say in this? What if I want my hair to be green?" She looked at him mock seriously.

"No—then you'd have to fight off your buffalo when he's hungry."

Tiponi reached down to gently rub the cheeks of the beautiful buffalo. "Does that mean I get to keep him?"

"We don't keep creatures, Tiponi. He must choose to stay. I think he's already formed an attachment to you."

A loud bellow from her mount made them both laugh.

"I have to go to the city of the dead, Sam." Her voice became serious. "How do I get back to Earth? Are there any spare spaceships around?"

"You must learn to use the Slipstream. You won't be able to completely use it by yourself until you're all spirit, but you'll be fine with my help."

"Tell me about being a spirit, Sam," certain as she asked, her voice betrayed her uncertainty. "Will I be different?"

His face turned serious. "That subject has a time and a place, but not now and not here. I know you have many questions, but some things need to *unfold*— without help or coaching. Anything I say could alter the way you think and may jeopardize your transformation."

"I understand that part, but I'm a little frightened about how things will be. Will I be alone and never see my people again? They're all I've ever known." A sigh escaped her lips.

"I'm sorry; these things must seem insignificant when the fate of my world is uncertain."

"First, Grandfather promised you would never be alone. Instead of losing your people, you will gain many more, like the Lahapi. Second, nothing which frightens you is insignificant. You are only as strong as your biggest fear allows you to be. Many little fears can add up to a major stumbling block. Never be afraid to talk to me, Tiponi. I may not be able to answer, but I will gladly listen."

She gave him a cheerful smile. "I always feel better after talking with you."

"As good as running your fingers through Hania's fur?" He laughed at her dumbstruck look. "You admitted as much in the desert, remember?"

"Well, I suppose I could try running my fingers through *your* hair for comparison." Her voice faltered as she noted the fiery glint in his gaze. *Black fire*.

"Be careful. Fire burns."

She gasped at his words. "Did you just…?"

"Just what?" he asked innocently.

"Never mind. What do I need to do to travel in the Slipstream?"

"You already know how to move your essence through the Slipstream, but until you are all spirit your body is too fragile to transport without precautions."

"That's why Leah used the crystal to protect me, right?"

"Yes, but it's much quicker without the spaceship

and the crystals, though you still must be shielded."

He paused for a moment, and Tiponi got the distinct impression he was choosing his words carefully. "What is it?"

"Do you remember much of the trip here or anything Leah said to you?"

"I remember she said my body was too fragile without the crystal, and when I became afraid, she said she would breathe for me and..." She stopped talking and her heartbeat accelerated.

"It's a very personal experience, Tiponi. We have to be together or joined, so my spirit protects your body."

"Then you'll feel..." Again, she stopped.

"I'll feel what you feel, and I'll know what you think. Does that scare you?"

"I've already shared thoughts with you as Hania; is it different?"

"We've both projected thoughts to each other, but our minds have remained separate. To transport, our minds must be joined so we will know what the other thinks."

Her heart began to race. "And feelings?"

"Yes, our feelings will be shared also."

She straightened. "It's a good thing I'm not shy."

Sam's full-bodied laughter broke the tension. "That wouldn't be my choice of words to describe you. Cautious, maybe. Curious would be more likely. Are you curious about the experience?"

"You're having far too much fun at my expense. Let's get this journey started shall we."

"The fun is yet to come. Now, get down from your buffalo and come over here."

Sam had already dismounted and was standing beside his horse, gently rubbing his hands down its neck and whispering soft words. She slid off Cloud Feather's back and turned to thank him. The buffalo bellowed loudly and pawed the ground.

"I'm going to miss you too, Cloud Feather." She patted the animal and walked over to Sam.

He took her hand, and a jolt of electricity arched through her—like always. She felt bereft when he let go.

"In the past you've felt or heard other voices while in the Slipstream." At her nod, Sam continued. "Those are the ungrounded spirits. They have no body and are just part of the cosmos. They have awareness; that's why you could feel and hear them. When you take your body through the Slipstream you must have a destination in your mind. After choosing a location, focus your energy outward until it is grabbed by the Slipstream and pulled to the destination. Only strong spirits can do this, but any spirit can help another."

"I know you're a strong spirit because you were chosen as my spirit warrior. So, basically you will be shielding my physical body with your spirit and pulling me along with you?"

"That about sums it up. The first time you entered the Slipstream, you gave Grandfather permission to bring your spirit to him while your body remained on Earth. Now, since you've gained power, you are able to move your own spirit through the Slipstream. Before, you went to one destination; this way you'll be able to go anywhere. Are you ready?"

Tiponi sucked in a deep breath and slowly blew it out. "Yes."

"Where do you want to go first? Be as exact as possible because the process weakens you. You don't want to arrive in the middle of a battle with your strength compromised. Let's try someplace safe at first."

"Since a serpent is mentioned in the riddle, I think we should try the serpent mound first. There may be something there to provide more clues."

Sam stood tall. "All right, come closer."

Tiponi hesitated only a second before moving forward to stand mere inches from Sam. She was excited by the trip, but also by his nearness. No way could she hide her attraction from him; the process was too intimate. She looked into his dark questioning eyes and smiled.

****

Sam's eyes never left hers as he reached out and pulled her body up against his own. The electrical jolt as their energies intermingled nearly took his breath away. Before—he'd always released her before she became aware. Now, he tightened his arms around her, reveling in her softness. He ached to do more but restrained himself.

Tiponi was a child when it came to emotions, and he needed to go slowly. She had to grow into her own woman before he could reveal all he'd like to share. She was on the brink of discovery and must be allowed to develop free of his influence. Unlike her, he'd had several lifetimes to become accustomed to the strangeness of being a spirit.

The energy between them changed, from a shock to a subtle buzz of particles moving along his skin. He felt the moment she recognized the change in frequency.

Her body detected minute changes in energy frequencies. She felt energy waves like most people heard words. It was a truly remarkable talent and one of the reasons she'd been chosen for this role.

He leaned down and rested his forehead against hers, another point of contact, a place where their minds would mingle. Her eyes were blue pools of wonder, and he wanted to dive in and lose himself.

She looked up at him, her excitement and trust clearly evident. This child-woman was fire in his veins. Their lips were a mere inch apart, and he could almost taste her—no, not yet. He banked his passion and steeled himself to open his mind to hers. Regardless how much he allowed her to see or feel they both would be changed forever. He lowered his mental shields and allowed her into his memories.

Hania felt Tiponi stiffen with uncertainty as she saw bits of his past fly through his mind.

Anasazi—caves in the canyon. His tribe is a peaceful people of twenty families, living high up on the canyon walls. Young Hania surveys the river valley from the clifftop which surrounds the canyon. The hunt has gone well; he has a nice buck to bring back for food and enough hide for new moccasins for his wife who has just given birth to their first child, a son. Already he has plans for what he will teach his young son. Elohea, is so beautiful and loving. He is eager to get home and hold her in his arms as they sleep. Three days apart, not long for a hunt, but a lifetime to a young husband.

As he climbs down the cliff, he becomes uneasy at the quiet below. There should be children playing and dogs barking. He is met with silence as he drops the last few feet to the rocky outcrop which shades the adobe homes of his family. Where is everyone? His heart begins to beat as fast as that of the deer which ran frantically before the kill. There is no one to greet him as he flings back the hide covering the door—only emptiness. Fear settles into his stomach like rocks at the bottom of a stream. Quickly he runs to check all the other abodes only to find the same emptiness. A few broken pots, some burned hides and poles are the only evidence he finds of his family. They have simply disappeared.

Her question drifted into his mind. "Hania, you're Anasazi?"

"I am spirit, Tiponi. My past no longer matters. We need to focus on the…" His mind words broke off and he chuckled. "Yes, I'm an old man by your standards. Do you think I'll be unable to handle any trouble that might arise?" He'd seen her disbelief at what she'd seen. Now he felt as well as saw her blush.

"I didn't mean…"

"It's all right."

He felt her curiosity, but before he could say more, they were caught up by the Slipstream. Glimpses of her childhood, feelings of loneliness which had been her young life, all drifted between them. Deliberately, he avoided watching her grow up after her birth; he'd known her future role and his involvement in it. Still, he must keep some things from her, when he wanted nothing more than to meld his mind and body to hers and fill all those empty spaces.

Chapter Twenty-One

To Find A Serpent

Tiponi's mind and body pulled away from the Htrae planet as she was swept into the Slipstream. Sam's spirit enveloped her, providing both protection and a feeling of happiness. Warmth blossomed as Hania touched her mind. Hania-Sam, one in the same. She should have known much earlier, had suspected, but now they were both in her mind and she was in theirs.

She sensed her physical body blending with his—at least his body *felt* real. All those times when she'd touched him and received a jolt, now she knew. Their energies had merged. Highly sensitive to energy waves, she had unknowingly seen him on the molecular level. His energy was strong and his aura blossomed crimson and harmonic. Her aura was blue-violet, and when the two mingled, a veritable rainbow exploded around them. The experience was similar to her fall into the sipapu, a vortex of color, energy, and feeling.

She had so many questions. What had happened to his family? How would she find the answers to the riddle? Impatient, she shoved the questions aside. Right now, sensation took precedence. Hania's body was part of hers, almost like sex, but better. His energy vibrated through her cells as his spirit wrapped around her like a cocoon. His features blurred, but inside her mind, she could see him in exquisite detail. The fine contours of his face, dark fiery eyes, and lips curved upward in a wry smile. She wanted to touch his lips with her own, taste him, draw in his masculine scent. Deliberately, she projected her feelings toward him. She wanted him to know—to feel what he did to her.

Abruptly the energy around her changed, became darker and cooled. She felt the ground beneath her feet as the Slipstream moved away. Hania stood, arms wrapped tightly about her as she struggled to acclimate to her new surroundings. For a moment, her body weakened, and she was glad of his support. When he stepped away, she experienced the pain of separation and loss. Her mind struggled to grasp tendrils of his essence from the air. But like her dreams they vanished. Her loss was an actual pain in her chest. A heavy sigh escaped her lips, whisking away any lingering feelings of loss. Her eyes focused and looked up into his stoic face. The moment of shared intimacy was gone. She had to pull herself together.

"Where would you like to begin?"

His question put an end to her emotional musings and solidified her resolve. She looked around the pristine area marked with strict paths and warnings, then nodded toward the west.

"There."

They were in Adams County, Ohio. Now a National Monument, the Serpent Mound had provided scientists grist for argument and years of speculation. The mound had been built by another indigenous people, but according to the four directions legend, all people were related. Over thirteen hundred feet in length, the mound formed a snake whose open-mouthed head held an egg-shaped structure as it rested on a cliff. The body wound back and forth across the plateau and ended in a coiled tail. Tiponi wasn't sure why her journey had to begin here, but it did.

"Over centuries of excavation and study, the mound has provided only a few artifacts," Tiponi said, her voice like a teacher, explaining. "I believe it still has a secret. The head of the serpent aligns with the setting sun on the Sumer Solstice. If we start at the coiled tail and walk the entire mound, we should reach the head at sunset." She began walking toward the tail.

"What are you expecting to find? As you've said, the site is well documented and has shown little of significance."

"I won't know until I feel it. The mound sits on a meteor crater. The residual metals should have different harmonics. I'm hoping to pick up something to point me in the right direction." Tiponi fell silent as they walked the mound. In truth, she was anxious because she had no idea what to look for. She would have to rely on her psi talent and trust in Grandfather's wisdom.

A strange buzzing started in her ears and raised the hair on her neck and arms. They were about midway the length of the serpent at the apex of one of the coils. She stopped, her gaze transfixed by the setting sun.

Sam's question came from just over her shoulder. "What's wrong?"

"Don't you feel it? The air is buzzing with psi energy."

"No. Can you get a read on it?"

"I've felt energy similar to this before, but it's a little different. It's almost like sound combined with psi energy. We need to get to the head of the snake, quickly." Her footsteps quickened before she finished her sentence. Tremendous energy was building in the mound and the air. Pain throbbed in her ears as she neared the head of the effigy mound. Rays from the setting sun struck the mouth of the serpent, causing the "egg" in its mouth to glow.

Tiponi sent a gentle wave of energy toward the egg and jerked when the return wave bounced back at her. Covering her ears, she tried to block the pain as the sound intensified. The high-pitched whine created compression waves which pushed on her body. Her nose and ears became wet. She was bleeding. Strong hands grabbed her, and she flew through the air, landing on the rocky stream bed below the head. An explosion ripped through the fading light, sending a blast of rocky debris high into the air.

Sam's body broke her fall, but she was stunned. She sat up to catch her breath and watched as the smoke dissipated.

Sam handed her his water flask. "Here, this will help."

She rinsed the blood from her mouth, and then drank deeply. His hand stopped hers when she would have wiped the blood from her nose. Gently, he cupped his hands around her ears, allowing his long thumbs to touch either side of her nose. Her eyes met his, and she felt tingling warmth in her ears and nose. Light sparkled from his hands. After a moment, he let go, trailing one hand down her cheek as he moved back.

Awed, she said, "You can heal like Grandfather."

"Not quite like him. I'm much more limited. All power can be used for healing or destruction. It depends upon the way you manipulate it."

Evelyn Timidaiski

"Will I be able to heal people?" She hastened to add, "When I'm a spirit of course."

Sam looked away, avoiding her eyes.

She felt a chill where the warmth had been. He was keeping something from her and wasn't happy about it. The atmosphere between them sharpened with tension.

The last rumble of falling rock stilled and broke the uneasy silence between them. Together, they scrambled up the incline and examined the area struck by the energy surge. The "egg" was gone, replaced by a large crater.

"Remind me to stay a respectful distance from you. You seem to attract explosions."

"Don't tell me you're afraid of powerful women."

"Just one. I think the red hair makes you sassy."

His warmth blossomed in her mind, and she felt relieved. The unease between them was gone. She sent an answering wave back to him, and then directed her psi senses downward at the crater. Nothing. She felt the same energy as before, but nothing new. "I'm not reading anything from here. We need to go down."

She pulled out a chem-glow and peered over the edge. The hole was about thirty feet deep with rubble spread over the bottom. It would be a treacherous in the dark. She carefully picked her way down the incline in the weak light. The rubble looked the same as the material that had been hauled by the indigenous people to build the mound. Jagged spikes of glass formed from melted sand increased the danger. She treaded carefully on the crumbled rocks.

The pull was subtle at first, then more persistent as she neared the east side of the crater. This placed her just behind the head, or what was left of it, at least ten feet below the mound. The energy signature here resonated differently. She opened her psi senses and tentatively pulsed energy at the wall of rock. Magnetic energy pulled at her.

"Here, Sam. There has to be something behind this rock."

"Should I move to cover?"

"Only if you want to miss the fireworks."

He moved up behind her to look over her shoulder at the rock wall. "Fireworks are exactly why I'm afraid. What kind of energy are you reading?"

"It's magnetic. I can't imagine why scientists haven't detected it before."

"Probably some sort of shielding. I can't feel it myself. Maybe it's too low for instruments to pick up."

"Maybe."

"Did *you* detect it with instruments?"

"No."

"Exactly, we're not dealing with science or instruments here. We're dealing with psi power and a completely different realm of natural laws. I'm a spirit, you're half human…"

"I get it." Her words broke into his litany. "I keep forgetting the world isn't the same as I once knew it. Thanks for reminding me. You have a way of making me feel better even when I don't know what to expect next." With a gentle squeeze, she tugged his hand from her shoulder, tossed him an impish smile, and reached out to touch the wall.

The rough surface of the rock gave no indication of a power source, but she felt an increase in the resonance of its particles. A low hum buzzed beneath her fingertips, and the rock began to heat up and glow. The outline of a round door appeared. The magnetic field shifted, and she was pushed away. Tiny green lights appeared in the door and began to spin. Light shot outward from each spot and lined up with one of the emeralds on her breastplate.

She held still but couldn't contain her excitement. "The stones on the breastplate must be some sort of key."

Sam didn't reply. His eyes were trained on the door and the beams of light. Without warning, the beams disappeared and with a loud creak, the door clicked like the tumbler on a lock. Air gushed from behind it in a wave of muskiness smelling sharply of ozone.

Lightning created ozone, but how had it formed inside the cavity?

Tiponi took a deep, cleansing breath and stepped forward.

****

The chem-glow burned out. Surrounded by total darkness in an underground room was unsettling. She should be getting used to this. Her entire journey, so far, involved caves and darkness. The ozone disrupted her psi senses. At the moment, her awareness of things was in stimulus overload.

"What's wrong?"

She had forgotten Sam and hadn't realized she'd been quiet so long. "Sorry, my senses are over stimulated, and I'm disoriented.

His strong arms came from behind and tugged her down. "Sit. The ozone should clear out in a few minutes, and you'll feel better."

"We need light." The words were barely out of her mouth before the ceiling burst into amber glow. Above her, crystals arranged in geometric patterns emitted soft yellowish light.

"I think you were expected. Someone left the light on."

"Do you think they left directions to what I'm supposed to find?" She stood and gazed around. They were in a corridor that curved to follow the shape of the mound. The walls and floor looked like rock, but she suspected they were actually metal. There had to be some sort of shielding or this would have been detected long ago.

They turned a bend, and the corridor ended abruptly, with solid rock blocking their way.

She reached out and ran her hands over the wall, hoping something would open or light up. "Okay, what now?"

"Think. Why are we here? Something about the riddle sent you here. What was it?"

"The serpent's eye." She stood for a moment with her eyes closed. "Sam, what if the serpent isn't holding an egg, but an eye? There must be something here that looks like an eye."

"It's not in plain sight. Let's go back to the front and look more closely."

They moved back to where she had been sitting. Spinning about, she looked for signs to help them. Nothing.

Follow the star, to find the pipe,
In the city of the dead, the star shines bright.
The star is the key that opens the lock
Enter the room, a giant will block.
Release the power, but beware its lure
To save the world, you must procure

The serpent's eye, a glassy sphere.

She recited the words of the riddle aloud. Seconds later, she and Sam both yelled, "Star!"

"That's it, Sam. We have to find a star to open the lock."

Sam leaned his head back to look up. "And where do we find them?"

Tiponi followed his lead and looked at the ceiling. The lights were in geometric patterns.

A circle, a triangle, and a star. "That's it. The light crystals are in the shape of a star. I need a lift, Sam. Help me."

He bent his knee to the ground, and Tiponi gingerly raised her leg. He steadied her as she wobbled and then took the final step to his shoulder.

"I'm ready."

She giggled like a little girl when he stood. She had seen other girls balanced on their father's shoulders, but she'd never experienced having a father to play with her.

"Can you reach it?"

Tiponi pulled her mind back to the job at hand. "Yes, but I have to let go of your hands."

She released his firm grip and wobbled. Her hands quickly found his head for balance. She wasn't sure why, but it felt intimate. Tingles of awareness spread through her arms and down through her legs which lay beside his face. Her calves hugged his cheeks. Awareness charged the atmosphere. His shoulders tensed, and his hands tightened on her ankles.

"Tiponi." His voice was gruff.

"I know, Sam. I didn't mean for it to happen. It's just…"

"The wind has a mind of its own. We can't choose the direction or when it will blow. We can only enjoy the breeze."

"Or we could get blown over in the storm." Her laughter brought the tension down a notch. Suddenly, the room tilted, and the lights dimmed. She held Sam's head as he rocked with the vibrations. "We've been away so long; I had almost forgotten the quakes." She hung on tightly as the room stilled and the lights brightened once more.

Sam straightened, and Tiponi righted herself. "I suggest we hurry. That was at least a 6.0 on the Richter Scale."

She reached up and placed her hand in the center of the star pattern. Nothing happened. "Follow the star," she quoted, and ran her hand around the perimeter of the pattern. As her hand passed over a section, it lit with green light.

Sam moved back, and Tiponi slid down his back. The green light started to spin, then spun faster before coming to an abrupt stop. She could hear her own heartbeat in the ensuing silence. One by one each green light blinked off. A loud click sounded, and the area on the floor beneath the star popped up and slid back.

Chapter Twenty-Two

The Eye of the Serpent

Tiponi looked over the edge into the familiar green glow of crystals. She took a cautious step over the edge and found metal steps leading down into a cavern. Crystals of all shapes adorned the floor and walls. She ventured down, amazed by the natural beauty of the cave. Amethysts, sapphires, and various precious and semiprecious gems grew everywhere. The green glow came from the ceiling which was covered by emeralds.

"There're so many. How will I find the correct one?"

Sam followed her down the stairs. "Are you sure the correct gem is an emerald?"

His question gave her pause. "I guess I always assumed it was, but I'm not sure why."

Sam began to wander around, looking at various stones. "Maybe because of the stones on the breastplate, but what did the riddle say?"

"The serpent's eye, a glassy sphere." She recited the phrase from the riddle. "That means it's round or at least spherical. Glassy usually means clear, but glass does come in many colors. I think we should search for something round and then determine color afterward."

Her words to Sam clarified her thinking. She began to walk through the maze of beautiful formations, on the lookout for a circular gem.

"Any luck?" She looked at Sam who merely shook his head.

"I think I'm doing this the hard way. If I was meant to find the serpent's eye, then I should be able to recognize it without this physical search. All of these shapes and colors were put here to stymie an accidental intruder."

"Don't forget, Tiponi, there are others who would stop you from your quest. I seem to remember a serpent of sorts among them."

"Of course. There has to be a way for only the chosen one to find the gem."

"The chosen one?" His rich laughter echoed off the walls. "Sounds like you're getting uppity."

"And that sounds like something my furry friend would say." She looked at him, and they both stilled.

Sam's response broke the spell that held them. "I think maybe Hania should be helping you instead of me."

"Not unless…unless you really think it's necessary. I draw comfort from your presence and our talks."

His gaze held hers for several moments. "As you wish. Now let's find the eye."

She breathed a sigh of relief and gave him a bright smile. "I'm going to tune everything out and search for crystal energy signals. Something's different about the crystal to set it apart from the others." Without looking at Sam, she found a clear spot among the crystals and sat down. Before doing anything, she looked around her, carefully scanning all the areas of the cavern with just her eyes. The eyes Grandfather had given her to see the world differently.

Her mind quieted when she closed her special eyes and she looked inward. She found her calm center and focused it. Soon her body relaxed. Focused energy radiated from her body and gently probed the cavern. The door above the stairs slammed shut, and her ears popped with the pressure change. The light from the ceiling pulsed once then went out. They were in total darkness.

She heard a low growl, then felt the warm furry body nestle against her side. Wolf eyes glowed back at her in the dark. She smiled; she couldn't help it. Hania had felt her sudden waver when the door slammed. Her hand reached to the massive head and rubbed the spot above his eye.

"Thank you, my friend. I need *your* support after all." She closed her eyes again and found her center. This time she altered the wavelength of the psi energy and gently pushed it outward. A low frequency ping came back. "I touched it." She repeated the process.

At Hania's growl, her eyes popped open. "There!"

A white glow came from across the cave. A stalagmite protruded from the floor and stood about chest high. The end was no longer pointed but had broken off. Sitting in the middle of the formation, covered with mud, was a fist sized glowing sphere. Reverently, she touched it and then picked it up. She wiped the mud away and stared into the perfect pear-shaped diamond. She had it, the serpent's eye.

A low rumble began as soon as she held the diamond in her hand. As the sound grew, the floor began to move, and crystals fell from the ceiling and walls. In the darkness she ran up the stairs, nearly falling as the earth shook. Her hands pounded the opening to no avail. The doorway was not only locked, it was sealed.

"What now?"

The Slipstream.

Hania's words appeared in her head along with warmth. But it was Sam's firm hand which encircled her waist. A tremor ran through her that had nothing to do with the quakes. She was going to be close to Sam again. She quickly freed her hands by placing the eye in her buffalo sack. Emeralds from the ceiling pelted them, and there was no time for Sam to prepare her for the jolt of their joining. She folded into his embrace anxious to be one again.

"We must hurry." Sam's words were ripped away as the currents from the Slipstream ripped them from the cave and out into nothingness.

One moment they were the brunt of falling gems and rumbling floor, the next they were speeding through the Slipstream. Though she felt Sam's aura surrounding her, he did not open his mind to her. No more peeks into his past. He couldn't stop the physical blending of their energies, however, and her skin sizzled with electric sparks. She bent her head back and looked up into his obsidian eyes. There she saw the feelings he couldn't fully hide. *Just one moment of indulgence before we must part.* His eyes narrowed at her thought. She opened her mind to him, allowed him to see what she felt.

His reaction was immediate. Strong fingers tensed against her back, and the lines around his mouth tightened. *We can't.*

The words entered her mind, but still she felt the tremor from those strong hands. *Why?*

Because the world is depending upon you, and I am your Spirit Warrior. It is forbidden.

And just like that, the Slipstream let them go and they were on land again. She knew without being told; they were in the Grand Canyon. She stepped back from his embrace and walked to the water's edge. She knelt and filled her cupped hands with icy water, splashing her face. It went a long way toward bringing her down to earth.

Earth—her home. Her journey had taken her through the galaxy and to a different world. Still, the smell of the Indian rice grass and sage brush made her heart leap for joy. She picked up a handful of the red sand and allowed it to spill through her fingers. Earth—Htrae. It all made sense now. They were sister planets, following the same evolution, but on a different time scale.

How many more were out there? And what would happen if she failed? Would it be the end of not only the Kahoti, but all people? Her head began to hurt, and she rubbed her eyes.

Sam's hands found the back of her neck and kneaded her tense muscles. His platonic touch created a fire in her belly and lower. His fingers stilled and moved away. She stood and watched him walk away from her. His back ramrod straight, he never turned.

"Sam?"

He stopped. The breeze blew his long hair back and she wanted to touch it, run her fingers through it. But no—they had to remain apart. She saw the wisdom of this finally. Since they had touched ground her mind and body had been filled with thoughts and feelings. Her mind had to remain focused. When she faced her final quest, her head must be clear and unattached to anyone. Sam had been right all along.

"I'm sorry I've pressed you so. It wasn't kind of me to push when I knew it was wrong. Please, forgive me."

"There is nothing to forgive, Tiponi. The head knows, but the heart still feels."

She nodded and hugged her arms to her chest. "Can you promise me something, Sam?"

"If it is possible."

"Before I die, I would wish that your lips touch mine."

His head jerked at that. "No one said you—"

Her words cut him off. "Promise me."

"I promise. Now I must ask one of you."

"Anything."

"Remember to fight to come back."

The words might have been vague, but she understood their meaning. "With every fiber of my being"

He nodded and moved to sit on a rock by the river.

"I must cleanse myself and speak to Grandfather before I take on this last quest. I feel the need for a cup of tea."

****

Darkness fell quickly, bringing with it a panoramic sky, studded with stars. Fireflies twinkled in the air, making it appear she was standing in the sky. Heady aromas of cedar and sweet grass wafted on the gentle breeze. Nothing could be more perfect than this moment.

Sam had prepared a ceremonial ring of rocks and built a fire within it. He was gone now, and she heard his achingly familiar howl in the distance. They hadn't spoken, but she knew he would be up on the hillside, standing watch while she completed her cleansing.

Her dress joined her moccasins in a neat pile outside the circle. The breastplate and sky stone necklace lay on top. Last, she removed her headband, then stood naked as on the day she was born. Gingerly, she walked across the rocky soil and down into the stream. She sank beneath the icy water, pulled by the current, but held her ground. She allowed the water to wash away the dirt and taint of uncertainty. Blowing bubbles, she rose out of the froth.

Rivulets of water ran down her limbs as she approached the fire and knelt beside the circle. Arms uplifted, she spoke to the night sky. "Oh, Great Spirit, it is I, Tiponi of Kahoti. With this circle and these gifts, I ask your indulgence. Look on me with favor and help me find the right way."

She stood and entered the circle. To keep out evil spirits, she took the bag of ground cornmeal and sprinkled the outer circle of rocks. She picked up the small branch of sage and placed it on the fire. The cleansing aroma filled the air and she stood, wafting the fumes across her body. She lit the bundle of sweet grass and placed it in the smudge-pot. With the spotted eagle feathers, she moved the smoke around her and then placed a branch of cedar on the fire. All the sacred herbs had been used. Sparks flew from the flames, creating an orange path into the night sky.

Tiponi removed the mother of pearl box and poured the last of its contents into the shallow drinking bowl. With water from the pouch, she mixed the herbs and slowly drank the concoction. She sat cross-legged beside the fire and closed her eyes. The potion burned her belly and pushed fire through her veins. Her head spun, and she fell to her side. Tendrils of the Slipstream found her and took her away.

The fragrance of steeped tea tickled her senses. She opened her eyes, and Grandfather was sitting beside the small table, a wide smile upon his face. "Welcome, my child. It is good to see you again. Come, sit and enjoy."

After he motioned her forward, she stood. "I am happy to see you, Grandfather. So many things have happened since we last talked."

"I see." He paused to look her over. "Your change is almost complete."

Frantic, Tiponi looked down. She'd been naked beside the fire. Happily, she saw a simple white cotton dress covered her nudity. Did she have Grandfather to thank for it?

"Do not be embarrassed, my child. You are beautiful, and the covering is there because I knew you would be shy. I really like the red hair." Grandfather poured tea into their cups as she sat down.

She felt the heat rise in her cheeks as she remembered his words. "Sam likes it as well."

The gaze he leveled on Tiponi was penetrating. "And how are things with Hania?"

She said nothing and Grandfather waited.

Finally, she spoke. "Hania is fine and does his job as my protector without fail."

"He is a good Spirit Warrior. Please, drink your tea."

She took a sip of the tea, marveling at how good it tasted. "This is different. What is it?"

"It's an old family secret made from desert flowers

and a little extra. The extra is supposed to make you courageous. Is it working?"

She caught the twinkle in the old man's eyes. Laughter spilled from her lips. She couldn't help herself.

"If all is well with Hania, then why do I sense a problem?"

Grandfather had a way of catching her off guard. Her smile faded, and she gave a deep sigh. It was time to get things out into the open and clear the air. "I know it is forbidden, but I have feelings for him." She looked at Grandfather anxiously, fearing an outburst.

"Ah, I see," he murmured, one eyebrow rising. "And has either of you acted upon these feelings?"

"No!" she responded emphatically. "But the feelings are there."

"This is why I asked Hania to stay in his wolf form around you."

"It wouldn't have mattered; I felt it in his presence regardless."

"Do you understand why it is forbidden?"

"My life could be at risk if feelings or distractions get in the way. If I die, my world may die also."

He carefully refilled her cup. "There is more. You were born to be Hania's mate. He knew this and deliberately avoided you because he knew what had to be."

"What do you mean born to be his mate?" All of a sudden, things became clear. A memory of cold wind and warm fur. "He came to me the night of my birth. He was my protector even then?

"Yes, Tiponi. You had to live to fulfill your destiny, just as he had to fulfill his."

She sobered. So much responsibility rested on the two of them. "Will we—?" Her words broke off, afraid to ask for fear of the answer.

He repeated the same words Sam had spoken. "When the time comes, you must fight, Tiponi."

"When it comes to Hania, Grandfather, I will fight with all my being."

"Good, all your being will be required."

As if by mutual consent, they both changed the topic.

"I have the eye of the Serpent, and I will be heading to the City of the Dead. Do you have any advice for me? I have only the riddle to go by. Will I truly be facing a giant?"

"You will be facing more than a giant, Tiponi. You will be facing yourself. When you look into the mirror, who do you see? Who you see is just as important. Come, I have something to show you."

They moved from the table and entered a stark white room. Against the far wall was a vision panel. Grandfather passed his hand across the screen, and it became alive with a horrific image.

"This is our final enemy, Tiponi. This is why you must complete the quest and gain all of your powers."

Tiponi's mouth dried, and she tried to swallow. The screen glowed with red, hot, molten lava, spewing from a giant volcano. As she watched, the screen changed, and the view became subterranean. The lava core ran for miles deep and across vast distances east and west.

"We have to stop a volcano from exploding? How will we do it?"

"Not even you and I could stop it. It is far too

powerful. But together you and I will be able to control it and redirect it."

Tiponi struggled to absorb the import of what he'd said.

"What is your will?" He asked her the same words her chief had asked before she started her quests.

Here was her chance to say no and let the world go to hell. Other disasters of this nature had struck the Earth before. The world changed and adapted. Did she really have to go through with this and sacrifice everything?

Her words rang out strong and with conviction. "My will is that of Grandfather."

"Good. Your ancestors will watch over you, my child."

"Thank you, Grandfather."

Chapter Twenty-Three

The City of the Dead

The fire popped, breaking her meditative state. Tiponi's eyes opened just as a burst of orange sparks spiraled upward from the dying fire. The glowing orbs twinkled into nothingness. Her naked skin reacted to the evening chill and pebbled. Quickly, she picked up her supplies and repacked them. She raised her foot to erase the circle of cornmeal but jerked back as vicious growls pierced the air. Hania was on the hill above her, and those were his growls.

More than her skin was cold now—her blood felt like ice. Her heart raced rapidly as the snarls and body blows grew louder in the dark. She was torn between her desire to help Hania and staying within the circle of safety. If the intruder was a spirit entity, she was safe inside the circle, where Grandfather's power protected her. No living animal would dare face Hania in his spirit form. Grandfather and Hania had warned that some would try to stop her. Not all spirit entities were good, and this one was likely here to keep her from coming into her full powers.

Lighting flashed on the hill, illuminating Hania in his wolf form, locked in battle with a grotesque creature. An electrical bolt shot from the claw of what she could only describe as an Insect Person. Shaped like a Praying Mantis, it moved like a man—or was it a Katsina? The head resembled one of the hideous masks worn by the dancers in festival. The dancers, however, didn't shoot lightning bolts out of their hands. Hania could be in real danger. He howled, and she felt his pain rush in waves through her mind. She took a step toward the edge of the protective circle.

Stop, Tiponi! Stay inside the circle. If I fail, you must be ready.

Her mind raced through ideas on how to help. To distract Hania while he faced an enemy was dangerous. The loud sound of blows, growls, and screams made thinking difficult. What had she learned about insects as a child? They reacted to certain smells, like pheromones, temperature, and vibrations. Insects had tympanic membranes which picked up vibrations and translated it into sound. Her psi energy was a form of sound.

If she discovered the correct frequency, she could shatter the membrane and disorient the being. Many large animals tuned into to high frequencies. She opted for lower, longer wavelengths, to disrupt the normal audio acuity of the creature.

Closing her eyes, she channeled energy in the direction of the hill. The battle escalated. She sent wave after wave, praying it would hit the entity's tympanic membrane like a hammer on a drum. Hard enough and it would break.

A high-pitched screech pierced the night air. The wave of energy slammed back at her like a tidal wave. Her hands flew to her ears; she crouched in pain. She had to be close. When she could stand, she altered the pitch and energy signature of the wave and sent it back.

An unearthly cry came from the creature, and Tiponi felt his pain. An explosion of light hit the hill and was followed by silence.

"Hania, are you all right?" Her voice held a tremor as she waited for an answer.

"I am fine."

She hadn't heard his approach, but suddenly he was standing just outside the circle.

"I am glad you didn't leave the circle. That was one of the strongest entities I have encountered. He tried to get to you before you regained your strength.

Aware of her nakedness, she quickly erased the circle and stepped out. She didn't hide her body from him, allowing herself the thrill of watching the heat smolder in his dark eyes.

Hania stood before her, staring at her nude form unabashedly as he held her clothes out to her. "Your eyes have become bold." Husky with emotion, her voice was almost a whisper.

His eyes blazed, the heat nearly searing her skin. "It is but a taste of the feast I am denied."

She wanted to rush into his arms and show him her need. But, no, they were like a planet and its moon, eternally together yet always apart. She grabbed the clothes, careful not to touch his fingers, lest she be tempted to forget the danger and break the rules. She dressed quickly and sat by the fire.

Long minutes passed before either spoke. So much had happened in so little time. Once again, she was reminded of Grandfather's words. There is no past and time is fluid. She pulled herself out of her reverie and broached the subject of tomorrow.

"In the morning, I must leave and complete my last

quest. According to legend, the City of the Dead exists, but no one has found it since 1906." Tiponi spoke hesitantly, feeling her way through the subject.

"No human has seen it since then." Hania's voice was serious.

"Why is that? With all the technology available, surely it could have been found."

"It is protected in many ways. Not just by the spirits, but man also. Those records were kept secret to protect man. It is not wise to know some things before the correct time."

She thought back to his similar words in his apartment. He had been speaking of her then. Now he spoke about mankind.

"From my recent experiences, I have learned there are many peoples and creatures different from Earth. But how could a civilization intelligent enough to build the City of the Dead have existed on Earth without people knowing? Don't worry, I'm not asking for help, Sam, I'm just thinking out loud." She stirred the fire and breathed in the calming smell of cedar.

"On this one thing I can give you help, though only information. There have been times in the past when civilizations grew in power and technology. As their power grew, so did greed, for land, riches, and control of others. You know the stories, the Greeks, the Romans, and Egyptians. Often, they destroyed themselves, but sometimes they fell to more powerful enemies. Their stories were lost to history."

"Like the Anasazi?" she asked gently.

"Even *I* do not know that complete story. It is probably for the best." He sighed and looked off into the darkness before continuing.

"I will guide you to make the journey shorter. There are things there I do not know about. To be spirit is not the same as being all-knowing. I am your Spirit Warrior, and I will protect you, but I don't know what you will face. There will come a point, like the first kiva, where I can't participate. Do you understand?" His face was so earnest, she wanted to reach out and comfort him.

"I understand. I will succeed, Sam. I must. Grandfather showed me our final enemy, and I can't let him do this alone. In the other two quests, I had something to rely on. Like tradition or the arrows of the Lahapi. But for this quest, I feel vulnerable with no such help. I have no special weapons. How will I defeat my enemy?"

"This will be the ultimate challenge. You will only have yourself and your beliefs to rely on. Be true to yourself, and you will do fine. Did Grandfather offer any words of advice?"

"He asked me who I saw in the mirror. He said it was very important, who I saw." She looked down at her hands. "I don't especially like mirrors, but I will think on it." She took out her buffalo blanket and spread it near the fire. "Maybe I'll understand more tomorrow."

"Rest well, Tiponi. I will be here."

Tiponi lay on the blanket and tried to shut out her thoughts. She needed to be well rested for tomorrow, but her mind refused to turn off. She never dreamed, so her mind wrestled with problems while she lay awake. The mirror Grandfather spoke about, what did it mean? As an albino among a dark-skinned tribe, she always felt ugly and avoided mirrors. Had she missed something by not observing her appearance? Or was the mirror a metaphor for her life?

Her body relaxed when the comforting form of Hania cuddled against her back. Her Spirit Warrior, her friend.

Chapter Twenty-Four

Into the Maze

Tiponi awoke to crisp, cool air and birds chirping from their nests on the canyon wall. Sam sat beside the fire, tending a pot of tea and poking at the glowing embers within the ring. He turned, and his eyes met hers. A gentle breeze lifted his long hair, blowing it back over his shoulder and exposing his face to the morning light. Seen through the haze of smoke, he could have been a dream—a delicious dream. But she didn't dream. The thought startled her into action, and she moved to wash in the cold stream. She paused at the edge of the stream to study her image reflected in the water. What had Grandfather meant with his cryptic advice about the mirror?

His image joined hers in the water. "Stop trying to force it."

"So much depends on this last challenge."

"But you can't solve it out of context. This is not the Lost City of The Dead, and that stream is not the mirror. Nothing can come before its time." Sam reached down and took her hand. "Come sit by the fire and enjoy the morning and your tea. Then we'll talk."

She gave him a warm smile and allowed him to pull her up. "When did you get so wise?"

"You must remember I'm an old man. Anyone

would gain wisdom with such advanced years."

She couldn't resist his teasing, and her laughter made her heart feel lighter. She sat and enjoyed her tea.

****

An hour later, Tiponi was packed, and the two began their journey to the City of the Dead.

"What do you know of the Lost City?"

Tiponi gave his question some thought before she answered. "I know there are many myths, and most outsiders don't believe it exists."

"Do you believe?"

"Of course, I wouldn't be here if I didn't."

"All right, continue."

"What is this? Will I be tested on my knowledge of the City?" She couldn't stop her laugh at Sam's teacher tone. Her laughter died as he turned to face her, his face deadly serious.

"Yes, you will be tested. Not by me, but the city itself. You must be prepared for anything. Your knowledge could save your life." He turned and continued to walk on the path.

Tiponi sobered and once again began her description. "The first written account of the city was in an article published in the *Arizona Gazette* in March 1909. An explorer, G.E. Kincaide, claimed he found a cave containing artifacts and mummies with Asian or Egyptian characteristics. He described the cave in great detail and drew a map of the portion he explored. He said that he sent materials from his expedition to the Smithsonian Institute who sponsored his trip. When contacted, the institute denied any knowledge of Kincaide or the artifacts." She paused and took a deep breath.

"I've memorized the map and studied every scrap of information about the place. The city is made up of hundreds of tunnels and rooms. It could house nearly fifty thousand people. His story adds credence to the Kahoti story of how our ancestors lived underground with the two deities. The two deities of creation, Hurung Whuti East and Hurung Whuti West, created life and set it upon the land. Some believe this city belonged to an advanced ancient race and the Kahoti are descendants of the slaves or serfs who served these people. The elders speak of being brought to this place from far away." Tiponi stopped talking, lost in thought.

Could this race have brought the people from another planet like Htrae? Were the Kahoti and other tribes brought here to serve as slaves? The possibilities were endless.

She turned and took a look at her surroundings. They were in Marble Canyon, a section along the Colorado River named appropriately for its marble walls. It abutted the Hotek Nation and the Kwagunt Rapids. The stark beauty to the place squeezed at her heart.

The place was protected by its inaccessibility. They walked down the old Kahoti salt trail known only to her people. The climb down to the outer opening was arduous. Sam insisted they climb rather than use power to appear at the opening. She suspected he'd done so to give her the perspective of all past visitors, few though they may have been. Or maybe he wanted to allow her more time to expend energy and not think about the danger she was to face. One never knew with Sam. She could ask but decided to respect his reticence about the city.

Tiponi pulled her body over the last rock ledge, her breath coming in quick huffs from her climb. As she sat up, her breathing stilled. Before her was a cave opening, blocked by heavy metal bars. Well—so much for the nonbelievers. This was definitely the opening to the City of the Dead.

Cold air escaped the tunnel, passing over her like frozen fingers, or—*the breath of death.* She sat still and allowed the breeze to touch her essence, reading her spirit. When it had passed, she opened her bag and removed several items. Sacred cornmeal, ground from the first ear of the harvest, rain tobacco representing the breath of the creator, and water to create the smoke and act as rain. These items were wrapped in a square of hand loomed cotton. She was thankful Kaya had taught her about all the ceremonies and offerings.

The cornmeal was carefully poured, creating a circle. The tobacco was placed in the center of the circle. If she had been male, she would have smoked the tobacco, instead, she would burn it. The dry tobacco lit quickly, sending swirls of aromatic tendrils upward. She sprinkled water over the fire to create smoke. The cotton cloth, an offering of her labor, was placed over the fire and then quickly lifted to release the smoke. Wafting it to her face, she inhaled four breaths. Now she was one with the spirits of the place. Carefully, she doused the rest of the flames and erased the cornmeal circle.

Sam gave her a hand up. "Are you ready?"

"Yes." Moving forward, she touched the bars that blocked their way. "Close your ears, Sam. I'm going to create some high frequency waves."

"You know it won't harm me."

"Sorry, one part of me still sees you as a man, not as spirit."

When Sam made no comment, she looked over her shoulder at his face. He looked like a man with more to say and no time to say it. He merely shook his head, and let her last remark hang between them.

She turned back and placed her hands around the center bars. Metal was strong but could be brittle under the right circumstances. She was going to use sound to increase the movement of the internal molecules and shatter the metal. Closing her eyes, she concentrated on the metal, feeling with her senses until she had the resonance frequency of the molecules. Pulling in energy from the abundance of rock, she raised the frequency. Birds in the area startled and flew wildly away from the canyon. High-pitched screams came at her, and she flinched as thousands of wings flew out of the tunnel. Bats! She had disrupted their echolocation. She ignored their flutters and increased the frequency.

Slowly, the bars began to visibly shake from the vibrations. Small rocks, loosened by the shaking, fell over her neck and shoulders. Ignoring the sharp jabs, she continued to concentrate her psi energy on the metal. Finally, with a wrenching creak, the bars shattered.

Sam came up behind her, chem-glow in hand. Together they started down the wide corridor. According to legend, the city had been hewn by hand from solid rock. It was an amazing feat of engineering and craftsmanship. The walls and floors appeared polished and were straight as if laser measured. About one hundred feet inside they came to a cross hall and saw the first piece of evidence confirming Kincaide's story. Forty feet into the cross corridor sat a gigantic statue.

Tiponi took the light and circled the carved stone figure. "It's the Primordial Buddha. The beginning of everything." The large statue, along with the many smaller statues, was carved from marble. Whoever had done this was a master craftsman. It looked Tibetan. The Kahoti believed the Tibetan people were the fourth race, and their different languages shared many of the same words.

"I'm not sure it's the custom, but I'd like to leave a gift." She removed a small Katsina doll carved from turquoise and placed it on the lotus leaf in the Buddha's hand.

They moved back into the corridor and continued forward. Ventilation holes lined the tops of the walls, and the air flowed freely. The air flow had to be created by another opening on the surface which drew in fresh air. Another opening meant another way out—or in. Others could have discovered what Kinkaide had found.

After walking twenty minutes, they reached a huge open room, the ceiling over thirty feet in height. Off of this room corridors led in every direction like the spokes of a wheel. How big was the city? Turning left, the sight of one of the corridors caught her breath.

This was the crypt room she'd read about. Nothing could have prepared her for the feeling of sacredness that seeped into her at the first sight of the mummies. They lined the walls, lying on stone slabs, accompanied by gifts of goblets, tools, and weapons. Helmets and armor sat beside some of the departed as accolades to those now gone. These people had been soldiers and had been honored in death. She was taken aback by the size of the bodies. They were large unlike her ancestors. She left the room quickly, overwhelmed with sadness by the presence of so many dead.

The room she sought Kinkaide had described as unvented and emitting a foul, reptilian odor. It sounded like the most dangerous room in the city and a likely place to face a challenge. They passed hundreds of rooms, and not one of the rooms emitted psi readings. They entered a corridor directly across from the great hall. Her psi energy immediately began to resonate differently. It was the metaphysical equivalent of hair on your neck and arms rising—though this also happened. She stopped, reaching out with her senses to garner any information. Nothing—just uneasiness, and that could be her nerves.

Another hundred feet down the corridor she stopped outside a small room. The chem-glow would not penetrate the darkness, and no ventilation holes were carved in the walls. Was this the place? She moved to the very edge of the room and was taken aback by the smell. Kincaide had described it perfectly. As a child, she'd helped tend the snakes for the dances. Their smell was unique, and this was definitely a snaky smell. It was pungent, with an oily rankness difficult to describe, but hard to forget. She and Sam looked at each other in the dim glow of the light.

"I think this is it, Sam. I'm getting all kinds of energy vibes."

"What can I do to make this easier for you?"

"Just knowing you have my back is a tremendous help, but I could use the moral support of your presence by my side. Snakes haven't been very nice to me on my journey so far."

Sam laughed. The sound went a long way toward calming her nerves. And then he did something totally unexpected; he stepped up beside her and took her hand. Her heart skipped a beat and then settled into a slower rhythm. Warmth invaded her mind, and she sensed her friend right beside her. *Be at ease, I am always here.*

She replied the same way. *Thanks, Hania.* He had reassured her by touching her mind, reminding her she would never be alone.

Taking a deep breath, she tried to ignore the odor and stepped forward. There was a loud scraping noise, rock on rock, and the opening behind them was now solid wall. They were locked in, no turning back.

Chapter Twenty-Five

The Holy Wall

The stillness engulfed them. Eerie quiet made her heart beat quicker. Tiponi took a moment to center herself. Her rapid heartbeat slowed, and calm entered her mind. The words of the Htrae chief's poem drifted through her mind. There had to be a clue as to how to continue.

Follow the star, to find the pipe,
In the city of the dead, the star shines bright.
The star is the key that opens the lock
Enter the room, a giant will block.
Release the power, but beware its lure
To save the world, you must procure
The serpent's eye, a glassy sphere.
Guard your heart, the time is near.

Tick tock. Time was running out, and she stood here worried about the locked door behind her? The smell intensified, and her senses detected an increase in psi energy. The corridor narrowed, and Sam moved closer behind her. She squared her shoulders and bravely stepped forward. The darkness absorbed the light, allowing limited visibility.

If something or someone wanted to attack, she wouldn't see it coming. *Stop it.* She chastised herself. Grandfather hadn't placed his trust in her because she was a coward. He and all those she loved needed her to be strong.

Tiponi put her pack on the floor and searched through it. Her hand touched the serpent's eye and she removed it. As soon as the gem met with the darkness of the corridor, a powerful light burst from the crystal. It was like holding a miniature sun that eclipsed the darkness and illuminated the hallway.

What she saw ahead gave her pause. The hallway ended in a wall. The entire structure was covered with holes about two inches in diameter. The center hole was larger and located in the middle of an ankh symbol. The Egyptian symbol for life was like a cross with a loop at the top.

The rows of holes looked nothing like ventilation openings but more like openings for something to pass through. Something cylindrical and skinny. A lump formed in her throat, and her heart dropped to her stomach. She had a bad feeling that she wasn't going to like this.

Movement behind the wall drew her attention. With an ominous slither against the rock, a snake appeared in one of the holes and slid out onto the floor in front of her. It took a very long time for its body to completely exit the opening.

The reptile, at least eighteen feet long, rose from the floor and stood several feet high. Even more frightening than its length or height was its head: the massive hooded head of a King cobra.

The snake moved its head as if searching all corners of the room. The royal markings on the back of the large hood were meant as a warning, to frighten predators or in this case prey. They worked. Ice formed in her veins, and her fight or flight instinct was definitely leaning toward the flight end of the spectrum.

Any ideas? She projected the question with her mind while her body remained frozen in place. Cobras were very fast and reacted to both movement and vibrations.

Is it sentient? Sam's warm thoughts came back to her.

I'm not reading anything, but I'll try psi waves.

Do it gently, Tiponi, our friend looks a little edgy.

He's not the only one. She summoned some calming energy and sent a gentle pulse toward the serpent.

The snake reacted immediately, raising its body higher. The hooded head turned back and forth as if searching for an enemy. Finding none, it struck out at the one it could see.

Tiponi had little time to raise a psi shield before the animal was inches from her face. Terror seized her limbs as she stared into the hypnotic gaze of the cobra, its hood creating a vivid picture that would be forever etched in her memory. According to legend, an image of the person who killed a cobra would remain in the serpent's eyes. The slain snake's mate could read the image and track down the murderer and extract revenge. As frightening as the cobra was, she had no intention of killing it. It guarded the secrets behind the wall, and as such, deserved respect for standing strong against an enemy.

Fangs dripping with venom, the snake struck at Tiponi's face and was flung backward as it hit her shield. Her resolve was shaken for a moment. It would be so much easier to kill the snake instead of circumventing it. One little lightning bolt and she could fry the thing and move on. No.

She shook her head and cleared the thought from her mind, remembering as she did so the line from the riddle. *Release the power but beware its lure.*

It wasn't the right thing to do. Tiponi looked at the wall with the numerous holes. No. She suspected, if she killed one, the holes would bring others to help defend the wall.

"Sam, do you see the ankh?" She rushed on before he could answer. "That hole looks like an exact fit for the serpent's eye."

"Yes, but how do you plan to get there without a bite from our friend?"

"Well, I hope Hania is a fast runner. If you shift, the snake will be distracted, and I can run to the wall and place the gem in the hole."

"And if nothing happens?"

"I...I guess we'll just wait and see." Tiponi didn't have another plan, so she hoped she was right. "When I say go, do it, Sam."

The snake had recovered and once more guarded the wall. Its body weaving back and forth as it kept an eye on both of them.

She erected a strong psi shield around her body. "Go, Sam."

Sam shifted into wolf form and ran down the corridor away from the wall.

The snake bobbed in his direction, then shifted to Tiponi. Her shield held when it struck, and the snake darted after Hania.

She had only seconds to complete her part and leaped the distance to the wall. Carefully, she placed the gem in the hole of the ankh. It was a perfect fit. When her hands let go of the gem, it went dark.

Hania howled from down the corridor. In warning or victory, she wasn't sure. The wall shook, and she heard a loud click. She had activated some sort of mechanism. Hopefully, it wasn't defensive like the cobra.

The sound of rock grinding against rock had her complete attention. The wall rose in front of her, and she panicked. She needed the serpent's eye to complete her quest. It was rising with the wall and would soon disappear.

What would happen if she removed it? Hesitation could cost her the serpent's eye. She needed to be on the other side of the wall and the serpent's eye in hand.

Tiponi dropped to the floor and rolled under the rising wall. Before she could think about the ramifications, she reached up and felt the center of the wall. Her hand touched the ankh, and she swiftly removed the gem. The serpent's eye lit up in time for her to watch the wall fall into place. She was alone. Sam had warned this would happen at some point, but without his presence, she felt bereft.

She took a deep breath and looked around. There was no den of serpents as she might have suspected from all the holes in the wall. Instead, the corridor continued. As she walked, the walls and ceiling became taller.

Minutes later she came to a large door. The top of the door frame stood a good eight feet above her head. The only ornamentation was another ankh in the center of the stone door. She held the gem up and searched around the door frame for other markings. None. She inserted the eye into the hole of the ankh and waited for the door to open. That was odd, the gem still glowed and the door remained closed.

She searched the door frame again looking for symbols. Finding none, she knelt and began at the bottom of the door, searching as far as she could reach. Discouraged, she moved away from the door and sat cross legged on the floor. Her eyes closed, and she cleared her mind, allowing the quiet to seep into her being. In her mind, she focused on the gem. She saw the rays and felt the harmonics of its frequency. The sound played in her mind, and her eyes popped open. That was it. Sound was the key. She was about to be tested.

Chapter Twenty-Six

A Giant Battle

Tiponi absorbed energy from her surroundings and sent out a gentle crystalline frequency. She had to be careful, if the frequency was too strong, the gem could shatter. In response, the gem started to pulse with light. The light intensified, nearly blinding her, and then returned to normal. She jumped up and touched the door. Surrounding the ankh, a series of symbols had formed. There were four symbols, each depicting an animal. Animal symbols had so many different meanings depending upon the tribe and the region. Because this quest was about her, she would have to decide which fit her current situation.

The first symbol was an owl, which represented wisdom or death. She needed wisdom, but she wasn't seeking death. The second symbol was a snake. The snake or serpent was a powerful symbol for healing or rebirth. The third symbol was a turtle which represented water or Mother Earth. It was also the name her people used for America, Turtle Island. The fourth symbol was a butterfly. Tiponi smiled when she saw this symbol. Butterflies were her favorite animals. She remembered her delight at seeing them clearly for the first time when Grandfather healed her eyes. Butterflies represented transformation.

With a light heart, she touched the butterfly. She needed to complete her transformation and gain her full powers. Only then would she be able to help Grandfather save the world from destruction.

She heard no sound, but the floor beneath her feet moved and the door moved with her. It rested on a center pivot, and the entire door turned around. She marveled at the engineering behind making a several ton door spin effortlessly. The serpent's eye still shone brightly as she removed it from the ankh. The hallway ended in a large vaulted room. No light was needed here where the entire ceiling was covered with crystals emitting a green glow.

A pool, complete with a statue of a soldier and pouring water, filled the center of the room. In a dry landscape like the canyon, this pool must have been prized by the former inhabitants. Yes, they could have gone to the river, but depending on when and where, the water level varied. Water was such a precious commodity, this pool seemed irreverent in its wastefulness.

She replaced the serpent's eye in her bag and bent to refresh herself. The water was cold as if it came from a spring deep within the earth. Cupping her hands, she scooped up water and drank thirstily, splashing the last drops over her face and neck. A loud creaking broke the silence. Tiponi looked in all directions but saw nothing.

"Hello?" Her voice reverberated in the vastness of the space. "I am Tiponi of Kahoti. I am on a quest for Grandfather."

The creaking became louder, and her eyes riveted on the statue. It moved. The metal and stone soldier was alive. He stood at least fifteen feet tall and was easily five times her girth. An image of the mummies flashed through her mind. They had all been very large. They must have selected this one for this job because he was the largest. He was a giant compared to her. *Enter the room a giant will block*; she recalled the words of the riddle. Well, here he was. Now what was she going to do with him?

The soldier had completely reanimated but looked like he was encased in unset mortar. His eyes opened and she was taken aback. Life-like vivid blue eyes stared back at her.

"You drank from the sacred fountain. It is forbidden." His voice echoed off the walls.

"I'm sorry. I didn't know it was sacred or forbidden. I come from a different place where such a vast amount of water is a luxury."

"Ignorance is not an acceptable excuse. You must pay for your transgression."

"Could I have the honor of your name?" Tiponi didn't want to call him sir, or soldier.

"I am called Tohpka."

"Please forgive me for breaking your rules. How can I atone for my error?"

Tohpka twisted his feet, unhinging them from their stand. The loud rending of metal made her skin crawl. With a bang, he stepped onto the stone floor of the room. The sword at his side grated against the scabbard as he pulled it free.

"There is no atonement, only right or wrong and life or death."

"Please listen, Tohpka. I was sent here on a quest. I don't want to hurt you."

Loud laughter interrupted her. "Hurt me? You are

but an ant to be stepped upon."

"That is no insult," she said. "Ants are respected by my people, and the Ant People saved us during a time of flood. And if you're referring to my size, I…I…Yes, I'm small, but I can still best you in a contest of—"

"A contest? This is not a game, little one."

Tiponi decided to change tactics and try logic. "How many people have you stopped drinking from the fountain?"

"You are the first."

"And what are your orders?"

"I am to stop all who enter and keep them from going farther."

"Everyone? How did I get through all the obstacles before this room?"

Tohpka rested the tip of his sword on the floor. "The chosen one can come through, but no other."

"And how do you know I am not the chosen one? What test must I pass to be allowed through?"

"You must pass the mirror of time test."

Sweat formed on her palms. This was the part both Grandfather and Sam had warned her about. She felt so unprepared. Hiding her fear, she spoke up bravely. "All right. Where is this mirror, and what must I do?"

Tohpka looked down at her and laughed. The sound was not pleasant and reverberated off the walls, creating a cacophony of sound waves. Tiponi refrained from grabbing her ears, barely. She did not want to expose any weakness to the giant. He appeared to have enough advantages.

Bending swiftly brought his face close to hers. She watched his pupils shrink as wrinkles of anger formed between those bluer than blue eyes. "First, little one—"

The soldier's breath covered her face like a storm blowing from the north. His voice produced waves of acoustic turbulence which echoed from the walls in the cavernous room. He gave her ample time to flee or stand her ground. "You must first defeat me. Only then will you be allowed to take the test."

Her throat tightened as she swallowed without the benefit of spit. Fear dried her mouth and addled her brain. How was she supposed to defeat a giant? Why had she ever thought beating this giant was within the realm of possibility? He wielded a broadsword as long as she, and most likely as heavy. Her ceremonial knife, with its ancient designs and carved horn, was a pitiful weapon against such a foe. Her psi power had helped her with the dragon and the wolf. Would it work on this monstrosity?

She sent out a gentle psi wave, testing Tohpka's susceptibility. The wave bounced off the man's helmet and came back to her. The helmet protected against more than swords. His mind was impervious to her talent.

He stood watching, as if waiting for her to make the first move.

She held her fingers in front of her and sent a lightning bolt at him.

For a man so large, Tohpka was agile. He swung the sword up, and the lightning bolt glanced off, hitting the wall behind her. Sparks flew everywhere, and she had to dodge the sizzling embers. He had used her power against her. She would have to be careful. What she threw at him could come back to sting her.

In response, the sword came at her in a horizontal slice. She sprang from the floor, jumped over the sword, and threw a lightning bolt at his side as he leaned into the swing. His armor absorbed the shock, but she heard a grunt. Good, he could be hurt. She just had to find the right spot. The giant stood upright, lunged forward, swinging his sword in a figure eight movement. Tiponi couldn't tell which side he would strike from. She dropped to the floor, rolled behind him, and sent a pulse of high-pitched sound waves in his direction. He stopped and jerked around. "There is no way you can win, little one. Why don't you give in and make this swift?"

"I'm not sure how you were trained, Tohpka, but the Kahoti do not give up easily. We have grown food from bare rock and very little water. We run for miles, just for the pleasure of running. And though peace is always our wish, when pushed, we fight to the bitter end."

Tohpka walked slowly toward her, trying to trap her in the corner. "Those are strong words, coming from one so weak."

"I told you before. I do not wish to hurt you. Isn't there some other way to end this?"

His answer came swiftly. He fell forward, using his body as a weapon. The psi shield she erected barely held against the crushing pressure of his weight. Her muscles shook as his weight pressed them. She reached out with her mind and tried once more to touch his mind. In the quiet struggle, she could only hear the splashing water from the fountain. The guardian of this room was impervious to mind control.

Wait—she could control the water. Why hadn't she thought of it sooner? Her shield would only last minutes if she divided her energies to control the water.

It was the only weapon left to her. She'd have to chance it. Tiponi quickly found her center and focused on the water molecules, felt their fluidity and energy. With a gentle pulse, she sent psi waves to the molecules and made them spin faster. In her mind she pictured the molecules, clinging together and creating a form. Just as she had in the dragon's lair, she created a waterspout which moved at her command. The plume looked alive as it moved from the fountain to wrap around Tohpka's head.

Blinded, he fell back. The spout tightened around his face, depriving him of air. His arms flailed. Where his hands touched, water flowed through his fingers only to reform on the opposite side.

He was weakening, drowning in the vast plume. Her heart ached at the sight. He looked helpless, like the eaglets who were smothered with cornmeal by her people when gathering ceremonial feathers. She could stand it no longer. "Be still and flow freely."

The water obeyed. It flowed off the giant's face and pooled around him. His body stilled, and she moved to look at his face. His eyes were the only thing that moved. The water had caused his metal armor to seize around him. He was frozen in place, just as she had found him earlier.

"Forgive me, Tohpka. I did not wish to hurt you."

You did what had to be done. I will merely sleep until I am needed again.

Tiponi was shocked to hear the words in her mind. He had purposely blocked her. She gently placed her hand on his cheek, glad he would not die. "Sleep well, Tohpka, you are a true guardian. I am richer for having met you."

Slowly, his eyes closed.

Chapter Twenty-Seven

The Mirror Test

Sitting back, Tiponi's chest ached from the intense emotion contained therein. She wiped tears from her eyes. She had defeated the giant, but she did not feel triumph. How could one feel gladness at the defeat of such a noble foe? A noise behind her brought her abruptly to her feet.

The empty fountain began to spin, the bottom pushing upward. It stilled, and the top melted into a silver liquid that held its shape but moved. A light flashed on the ceiling, and a hologram image appeared on the wall.

A woman stood before her dressed completely in white, including a hooded cape which covered her hair. Her face, the color of bronze, was smooth and serene. Topaz eyes stared back at her, and a smile tilted the woman's lips. The shimmer of light was the only detail which verified that this was an image and not a real woman. "Welcome, Tiponi of Kahoti. I am Hehewuti. We have waited long for your arrival."

"Forgive me, holy one. Could you please tell me who 'we' are? I've heard those words several times on my quests, and I'd like to know more."

"Your curiosity does not need pardon, Tiponi. You have earned the right to know." We are the Pleiadians.

Our people visited your planet when it was inhabited by primitive life. We lived in this underground city for thousands of years. Your people are descendants of Pleiadian and Human unions. Though we have long since departed this world, we left protection for our children in times of need. This facility contains knowledge far advanced than your world. For this reason, it is kept secret and protected. You have done well to find it and breech the security measures we have in place."

Tiponi's mind struggled with the information. The people of Earth were descended from aliens. Why should she be surprised after all she had seen and done on her quests?

Hehewuti stood silently as Tiponi assimilated what she'd been told. She now had a test to take and a world to save. She gave a slight nod to Hehewuti.

"Your transformation is nearly complete, Tiponi. Your last test is the mirror of time. Are you ready?"

"I am. What must I do?"

"Time is fluid. There is no past, present, or future. You must look into the mirror and tell me what you see."

"What will happen if I do not answer the question correctly? Will my people die?"

"Your concern for others is admirable but unnecessary. Now approach the fountain and look."

The silver fluid atop the fountain smoothed out into a glassy sheet. Tiponi cautiously stepped forward and looked at the shiny surface. Immediately, the room became dark and cold. The mirror turned black, then slowly an image formed.

****

Tiponi

Shrouded by darkness, the woman walked alone through the sandy desert. Her steps were unsteady as she trudged around boulders and stunted cacti, clutching her belly. The wind screeched, echoing off the mesa walls ahead as clouds swirled in the angry wintry sky. She stumbled and fell hard on the rock-strewn path.

Tiponi watched yet remained part of the scene. She felt the jabs of rocks against the woman's bare legs as if they were her own. She clutched her own belly as it contracted in pain. She felt the coolness of the sand as the woman rolled over and rested on her back. Waves of exhaustion and loneness filled Tiponi's mind. The woman welcomed the idea of death.

Chilled by the cold and buffeted by the wind, Tiponi stood in the desert and watched the woman. She had never seen her but felt she knew her. The burden of sorrow and despair was heavy, and she sank to her knees. Her eyes remained riveted to the image as it continued.

A sob escaped the young woman's lips. "Not yet," she moaned. I cannot die and cause the child's death. She sucked in a fresh breath, lifted her face upward, and uttered words of prayer for strength and forgiveness.

"Oh, Great Spirit—forgive me. I...I did not heed your wishes and have done wrong. For myself, I ask nothing and accept what punishment you decree for my evil ways. The child I carry is innocent and should not suffer for my sins. Please, give me strength so she might live. Do not let my evil taint her soul." She looked up at the full moon and recited a prayer, a childhood prayer.

Tiponi prayed the words along with her. "Mother

Moon, shine down on her tonight, bathe her face with light. Brother Wind, breathe life into her body so her spirit may rise."

The woman's belly heaved as the child within clamored to be out. Moments later she spoke the name Powaqa, kissed the child's cheek, and then died.

She had just witnessed her own birth.

Hot tears heated Tiponi's cold cheeks, and emotion clogged her throat. Her mother had loved her and wanted her to live. She had thought herself unwanted and abandoned. Just the opposite was true. Her mother had struggled for her to live and could not be blamed for her aloneness.

The words escaped her lips. "My mother."

"Yes, Tiponi." Hehewuti's voice echoed around her. "Your mother, Cheropsi, was Human, but your father was Pleiadian."

"Why did she have to die? Why was she punished?"

"She was not punished. She could not reconcile herself to life without your father. Continue watching; there is more to see."

"Why must I see these things? They cannot be changed."

"You must see to understand. These events formed you and the way you think."

Sighing, Tiponi turned with trepidation and looked into the fountain.

****

Cherospsi's body hovered above the desert momentarily, and then with a pulsing flash, it disappeared. In its place, large flakes of snow formed and fell upon the crying child.

Tiponi felt the wetness of the snow and wished to comfort the crying child. Out of the darkness came the excited yips of coyotes. She was alone and cold. Moments before she had been so warm, swaddled in her mother's womb.

In horror, Tiponi watched as a pack of coyotes made their way noisily toward the helpless infant. They were in search of an easy meal. The pack circled closer to the baby who lay alone and wailed. The pack members salivated, inched forward, and closed in for the kill.

Clouds shifted, allowing the heavy moon to peek through, spotlighting a giant gray wolf standing beside the baby. He raised his head, faced the moon, and let loose a powerful blood-curdling howl. Hackles raised, the wolf stared through unearthly glowing eyes.

The timid coyotes cowered, tails between their legs, and slunk away into the shadows.

"Hania." He truly had been there. In her mind, she felt his warmth, sensed his presence.

Silently, Hania moved to lie next to the child, sharing his warmth and shielding her from the wind. He nuzzled the child gently, sniffed at the soft white skin, then bathed the infant with his warm tongue. The child quieted and fell asleep.

The back of Tiponi's hand tingled as she watched the spirit wolf bathe the baby. She could feel the warmth of his fur as it warmed her skin.

A low growl rumbled in the wolf's throat as the wind brought sounds of shuffling footsteps toward him. Out of the darkness, an old woman stepped into the moonlight and hobbled toward him, showing no fear. Her attire was that of a traditional Kahoti religious woman. She spoke to him as if he was human.

"Brother Wolf, thank you for keeping the little one safe. I am called Kaya, and we have met in my visions. Our people have waited many lifetimes for her to come. Born an outcast, this child will someday save the world. It has been written and so it shall be." She finished speaking and stood waiting.

A rush of love flooded Tiponi's veins as she watched a younger Kaya speak to Hania.

Hania bowed before Kaya, who in turn reverently lowered her head. The wolf disappeared. She gently gathered up the child, swaddled it in a Kahoti ceremonial cloth, and then carried the child out of the desert and up the side of the mesa.

Tiponi had known that Kaya had found her in the desert, but watching her Earth mother gather her up and swaddle her was almost overwhelming. Her chest tightened, and her breathing came in short gasps. Scalding tears burned her eyes, then spilled over, washing her cheeks when she closed her lids.

"Thank you, for showing me these things." Tiponi opened her eyes and spoke to Hehewuti. "Is there more?"

"Your whole life is there, Tiponi, but you have seen enough to continue the test."

Tiponi took several cleansing breaths and cleared her mind. *Grandfather, please guide me.* The prayer whispered through her mind. She looked at Hehewuti. "I am ready, holy one. Let the test continue."

"The test is simple, Tiponi. Tell me who you saw in the mirror."

The words fell into silence.

The moment of truth had come. The test couldn't

be as simple as, "I saw myself. Could it…?" No, there had to be more. Hehewuti wanted to ascertain what kind of person she was. Her character, strengths, weaknesses—all from a simple question. She allowed her mind to spin through the scenes again, carefully noting what happened and who she had seen. There were no second chances, and this was life and death. Her life was forfeit, given freely for her people, but she had to save them and all who would come later.

Warmth filled her mind, and the back of her hand tingled. The smell of tea awakened her nose, and the low croon of a lullaby echoed in her ears. Hania, Grandfather, and Kaya. She wasn't alone in this. They were part of her and part of the answer. Suddenly, she felt more confident about her answer.

"When I looked into the mirror, I saw a child of two worlds, forgotten by some, loved by others, and chosen by the spirits to save my people. I saw Powaqa, the past, Tiponi, the present, and White Mesa Woman, the future. Because time is fluid, they are all me, and I am you. I am Human, Pleiadian, and Spirit." Tiponi fell silent. She hoped she had answered correctly.

The hologram solidified, and Hehewuti stepped from the light. She approached Tiponi and took her hand. "You are wise, Tiponi of Kahoti. You are indeed all these things. Your quests are complete, and now your transformation can begin. Follow me and bring the Serpent's Eye."

Joy bubbled through Tiponi. She'd done it. Her people would not die. She hastily picked up her bag and followed Hehewuti behind a silver curtain where the hologram had been.

Chapter Twenty-Eight

The Transformation

The room looked strikingly similar to the spaceship she had flown in with Leah. The white tiled floor absorbed the sound of their footsteps. The glossed tiles were embellished with gold symbols, many of them unfamiliar to Tiponi. Outlined by a large gold oval in the center of the floor lay the sparkling outline of a human form. Once again, the green crystal she'd encountered during her quests glowed within the form.

The crystal ceiling supported an elaborate three-dimensional serpent carved from ivory. Only the tusk of a mastodon could have been used to create the large work of art. Decorated in an ancient, feathered serpentine style, the carving bore elaborate coils and frills. The serpent could have been a dragon, or a giant snake, both representing life and a connection to the earth. The eye socket on one side was empty.

"You must replace the Serpent's eye, then lie on the floor within the outline." Hehewuti studied Tiponi. "There is no way I can prepare you for what will happen. Just accept, and it will soon be over." She touched Tiponi's shoulder, then exited through the curtain. A shiny metal door slid into place behind her, and a lock clicked ensuring she could not leave.

Tiponi wasn't comforted by her words. Was she

trying to tell her that it was going to hurt? So far, she'd fallen from a cliff, been struck by lightning, and slammed around by a dragon. The quests were over, why should her transformation hurt? She retrieved the Serpent's eye from her bag and walked to the center of the room. She reached up, placed the eye into the empty socket, and then nervously lay down on the cold floor.

Darkness invaded the room. Sweat dampened her hands, though the rest of her body felt icy. Nervous butterflies fled from her stomach. In their place, fear settled, creating a cold hard knot. Tension tightened her muscles. Dry mouthed, she whispered, "I choose the will of Grandfather. Let it be done."

The serpent's eye lit up, drawing her attention upward. Rays of light reflected off the crystal ceiling and then bounced around the room. Thick as her arm the light beams curved, mimicking atomic orbits, spinning and pulsating to some unheard rhythm. They slowed and coalesced into one wide beam focused down upon her. The light separated from the eye and attached to the ceiling. The ivory serpent moved. Freed from its structured form, it undulated across the ceiling as if alive.

Beneath her, the crystal heated and molded to the form of her back. The floor began to spin, slowly at first, and then faster. The crystal from the floor moved up and surrounded her body, encasing her in a green sheath. The flexible sheath quickly solidified into a hard shell. Only her face remained uncovered. The serpent glowed red and moved down the wall. Fear raced through her veins. She couldn't move, and it was coming right at her. Concentrating, she sent out a wave of psi energy.

The serpent's words seeped into her mind. *Have no fear.*

Helpless, she watched as the serpent crawled on top of the crystal shell. Held in place by the crystal, she watched with awe as the serpent melted, encased the shell creating a sarcophagus. From the melted socket, the serpent's eye rolled toward her face, softened, and formed a clear covering over her face.

Separated from the room's environment, she at least could see what was happening. Small comfort when there was nothing she could do to alter her situation. Hehewuti had said to accept. That was difficult since she was now completely entombed. Her breathing quickened as she imagined herself suffocating. A whisper of sound like a gentle wind invaded her coffin. It blew across her face, and she breathed deeply. The comforting smell of sweetgrass permeated the tomb, and she calmed.

The floor spun faster creating g-forces on her chest and pushed hard against her body. It was like being crushed from the outside and heated from the inside. The beam of light thickened above her and began a scanning motion over the sarcophagus. She became dizzy and disoriented from the flashing light and the speed of the spinning sarcophagus. She fought to keep unconsciousness at bay. Pain greater than any she had ever imagined sliced through her body. She became aware of each cell of her body in excruciating detail.

They were changing—she was changing. She felt her cells morphing, their DNA rewritten. Once, her body had been like a simple song, she was now being rewritten into a symphony. Power surged through her limbs and then burst into her brain. Her scream could not penetrate her tomb. Only she heard her cries. And then—there was no pain, no sound—nothing.

****

Ho, ho, wa-ta-ne, ho, ho, wa-ta-ne… heyahh heyahh

Sam's beautiful voice filled her ears, whispering the words to the ancient lullaby. She opened her eyes and stared into his smiling face. Dressed as he had been on Thrae, the wind blew the colorful medicine wheel attached to his headband. The colors fascinated her as they spun in the wind. She reached up, placed her hand against his cheek, and felt a tremor run through his body.

"I am yours, Tiponi, now and always."

Her heart raced at his words. She ached to tell him of her feelings.

Suddenly, his face changed, became harsh as he grasped her shoulders and gave her a shake. "Fight, Tiponi. You must fight."

She sucked in a breath of cold air and her eyes popped open. "Sam?"

He didn't answer.

It had to be a dream. No—not a dream, a vision. Her sarcophagus gone, she lay on the floor, totally naked. She sat up, pulling her knees toward her chest in a gesture of modesty. But there was no one in the room, save the ivory serpent. Back on the ceiling, both his eyes intact, he stared down at her—lifeless.

"Hello?" The word echoed off the walls and came back at her.

She scrambled from the floor and searched the room. "Can anyone hear me? I need some clothes."

On the wall, a panel opened and folded down.

Inside, she found a complete replica of White Mesa Woman's clothing. She tentatively touched the lovely white outfit, then picked it up reverently and dressed. Adorned appropriately, she exited the room through the curtain.

The mirror was gone, and the fountain bubbled cheerfully. Tohpka stood in place, guarding against intruders.

"Hehewuti?"

The light came on in the ceiling, and the hologram activated. Hehewuti stood before her in the beam of light. "You look lovely, Tiponi. How do you feel?"

"Thank you. I feel invigorated. How has my body changed?"

"Your cells have always contained Pleiadian DNA. It has now been activated, and your powers are enhanced. Our scans show in addition to controlling psi energy, you now can control any kind of energy. Your empathic skills have also been intensified, so you will need to shield your mind around others."

"And the chanunpa?" Tiponi managed to get the question out. She was overwhelmed by what Hehewuti had revealed.

The light on the ceiling switched off, and Hehewuti stepped toward her. "You will return it to your people today, and tomorrow you and Grandfather will face the volcano."

"Can you please tell me how bad things are? What of my village? Is Kaya alright?"

"Be at ease. All is well with your village, and Kaya will be there to happily welcome you home." Hehewuti's voice sobered. "Many others have not been so fortunate. Hundreds of thousands have been evacuated in anticipation of an eruption, and thousands more have been injured by the earthquakes. All will be for naught if the volcano erupts."

"Is it truly possible for Grandfather and me to stop this from happening?"

"Not completely, but with your help he can divert much of the lava and lessen the damage." She took Tiponi's hand, searching her face, as if she would find an answer to her next question before asking. "Do you understand that all of this comes at great cost?"

The question hung unanswered as Tiponi bowed her head. "I think I knew from the beginning my life would be forfeit. It is a small price to pay for such great ends."

"No life is a small price, and yours is worth many. Your sacrifice will save millions." Hehewuti touched her palm to Tiponi's cheek. "My son, had he lived, would have been very proud of you, Tiponi, as am I."

"You're my—"

"Yes, Tiponi. I am your grandmother."

A strong quake shook the room, knocking the two women down. It lasted several seconds before it abruptly ceased, leaving only dust and shattered nerves in the aftermath. Tiponi stood, helping her grandmother to stand, steadying her before letting go. "That was strong and close. I should hurry home and return the sacred chanunpa. I would cherish a visit with those I love before tomorrow."

"You don't need to hurry. I have arranged transportation for you." Hehewuti pointed to a door Tiponi had not seen before. "Come; let's get you started on your journey."

Tiponi followed her into the corridor and up a

flight of stairs. They entered a room, tiny in comparison to all the others she'd encountered. Arranged as a sitting area, the room had a small settee, a low table, and some marble carvings.

Hehewuti walked to the wall and touched it. A panel opened to reveal a lighted glass case. Inside the case, lying on a white buffalo blanket, was the sacred chanunpa. The red pipestone stood out vividly against the white blanket. She slid the glass open. "Take it. It is yours now. You have earned the right to reclaim it for your people. Once again they will have my people's protection."

Tiponi reverently lifted the pipe and wrapped the blanket around it. "My people and I thank you, Grandmother." Tiponi gave the woman a little bow.

"Quickly, you don't want to waste any time with your loved ones." Hehewuti directed her to another door, another corridor, and then another room.

It looked suspiciously like Leah's spaceship. Hehewuti led her to a small platform. "This will take you to the surface. From there I think you will have no problem finding your way."

Before Tiponi could say a word, Hehewuti pressed a button and her world became light.

Chapter Twenty-Nine

Homecoming

As the bright light vanished, Tiponi found herself standing on the south side of the Grand Canyon. Disoriented, she took a moment to steady herself before moving. A loud bellow sounded behind her, and she nearly toppled over the edge. She tightened her hold on the Sacred Chanunpa. Her heart jolted and then leaped for joy at sight of the white buffalo, snorting and stamping beside a pinion pine.

"Cloud Feather, it gladdens my heart to see you." She surrounded his massive neck with a strangling hug. As usual he made an assortment of grunts and snorts. She raised her head, running her fingers across his bulging cheeks and scratching his forehead. "How did you get here?"

"I brought him."

His voice caused her blood to pulse with pleasure. She spun around, finding him closer than she expected. He stepped even closer, a mere whisper away.

"Sam." Her voice came out in a husky cry. How could one simple word express so many different feelings?

They stood without touching, holding an intimate conversation with their eyes.

His breath fanned her face. "I've missed you."

With her enhanced senses, she felt what he could not say aloud.

"You look beautiful. Your black hair is becoming." His fingers picked up a tendril from her shoulder, letting it slide across his hand. "But I miss the red." He gave her a rakish grin.

"I hadn't even noticed my hair." She tried to keep things light, when all she wanted to do was fling herself into his arms. If only they could put aside all their responsibilities for just an hour. But they couldn't.

"My transformation is complete, and I'm heading home. I—"

"I know, Tiponi, all those things that we cannot speak. Let's not spend our time together in sadness. Would you like some company on your journey?"

Every moment spent with Sam before tomorrow would be precious. Without hesitation, she said, "Yes."

He raised one brow in question. "Do you think you could convince your buffalo to carry both of us?"

She laughed at the reference to owning beings. "He's not *my* buffalo, but I'll ask." She turned to Cloud Feather and rubbed his cheeks. "Would you do the honor of giving Sam and me a ride home?"

The buffalo snorted, and then bowed. Tiponi climbed on, and Sam jumped up behind her. With the Sacred Chanunpa safe in her arms, they took off and headed home.

As the crow flies, the journey did not take long.

"We should land on the plain and let me off. White Mesa Woman should make her entrance alone." Sam leaned close to speak against her ear.

Tiponi nodded, then used her knees to urge Cloud Feather toward the ground. Red dust billowed up as his heavy hooves made contact and continued running. Tiponi signaled with her knees for him to stop. She slid from the animal's back and looked up at Sam.

"Will you join our celebration tonight? I can promise there will be an abundance of singing and dancing."

"Look for me when the sun sets. Meanwhile, I will take care of your beast."

Tiponi waved a quick goodbye, then took the track leading to her village.

With her new ability to manipulate all energies, Tiponi gathered psi power from the earth and altered the gravity below her feet. In accordance with legend, White Mesa Woman began to float above the ground as she moved forward.

She was still a long way from the village when the first sentry saw her. As she approached, the young man flung himself to the ground. He lay prone before her as she spoke.

"Rise and speak your name."

The young man rose to his knees. His face became struck with awe, as he took a quick look at the living Katsina before him. He immediately lowered his eyes, treating her with respect.

"My lady, I am Mochni."

"Mochni, you have treated me with respect, and this is good. Now hurry to tell your chief to make ready. A holy woman is coming and bringing with her a sacred gift."

The young man jumped up and bowed. "Yes, waken one." He immediately ran to the village.

****

The drums rumbled, heralding her arrival into her

village. The sacred tent stood ready, surrounded by her people. Long had the story been told and with her arrival, it would happen again. She drifted until she hovered directly before Chief Honaw, where she lightly touched earth. The drums stopped and total silence reined over the crowd. What they saw was history and prophesy coming to life. Generations to follow would speak of this moment.

"We are honored by your presence, waken sister." Chief Honaw bowed. "May I offer you refreshment after your long journey?"

Tiponi smiled. She wanted to shout out to her chief and run find Kaya, but tradition and protocol must be followed. "Some water and meat would be most welcome, Chief Honaw. I would also have the sacred fire lit."

"It will be done as you request." He indicated the covered poles, festooned with feathers and beads. "Please join me out of the sun."

Beneath the covered poles, they sat on woven rugs and were served water and stewed lamb. These meager foods were traditional offerings for such an exalted occasion. Tiponi washed her hands in the bowl of scented water, held by a young girl, then partook of the meat.

After the meal, she headed to the ceremonial tent. The crowd stood in the plaza, still quiet, and still waiting. She entered the tent where the sacred fire blazed, too hot for the day, but necessary to complete the ritual.

She removed the white buffalo rug from her bag. With respect, she removed the Sacred Chanunpa and filled it with Red River birch tobacco. From the dung chip fire, she took a glowing twig and lit the pipe, breathing deeply of the breath of the Great Spirit. Afterward, she handed the pipe to Chief Honaw. He drew in the breath of the Great Spirit, holding it within his body for a long time. Slowly, he blew it out, then placed the stem in the crook of his arm while the bowl rested in his palm. "Tiponi, your people are proud that you have returned our Sacred Chanunpa. Tonight, we will celebrate its return."

"Thank you, Honored Father. I have completed my quests, and tomorrow Grandfather and I will face our final enemy, the volcano. If it erupts, I fear that few will survive. Our celebration tonight may be our last. Another guest will arrive at sundown. He is my spirit warrior and a Katsina."

"The spirits do us great honor. After I share the good news with the people, I am sure you would like to visit with Kaya."

"Thank you, Chief. The remaining hours are precious."

They stood and parted the tent flaps. The crowd silently moved closer.

Holding the Sacred Chanunpa above his head, Chief Honaw spoke to his people. "Today, that which was taken has been returned. Once again, the spirits smile upon us. Tonight, we will feast and celebrate. In our midst, two Katsinas will walk, and we will be doubly blessed. Now, let the preparations begin."

The crowd cheered and danced freely.

Kaya separated from the cheering crowd and moved toward Tiponi.

"Kaya." Her heart nearly burst with love. "Kaya, I've missed you so."

"And I, you, child." Kaya stopped several feet from her and did not come closer.

Tiponi understood. No matter that Kaya had raised her, Tiponi's new status separated them. She rushed into the woman's arms and held her tightly. "I will never stand on ceremony with you, Kaya. You are my Earth mother and will always have my love."

Kaya's hands kept touching her face as if unable to believe she was home. "Will someone so exalted still enjoy piki bread with guava syrup?"

"*This* exalted person would love some of your piki bread. Let's go home, please."

Tiponi slipped her arm through Kaya's as they headed up the mesa to their adobe home.

Chapter Thirty

The Last Dance

Tiponi drizzled warm syrup over the paper-thin bread. Kaya had used purple cornmeal for the heavenly fried concoction. It felt good to sit and watch her Earth mother work in the kitchen, like she'd done so many times as a child. The place smelled of memories. Sad ones, like the time she'd come home crying from school. The kids had called her a freak. She had taken matters into her own hands to punish the boy—and had gotten punished herself. There were many good memories also, like picking the herbs, which hung from strings beside the cabinets, and learning the rituals from Kaya, some right at this very table.

Kaya poured more herbal tea into her cup. "Why do you look sad, Tiponi?"

"I'm not sad. I suppose…I'm feeling nostalgic."

Her eyes held the sparkle of someone waiting for juicy gossip. "You are far too young for that. Tell me what you think of your spirit warrior."

"You already know him, Kaya, a fact that you kept well hidden."

"True, but it wasn't the right time to speak of him." Kaya's voice was unrepentant. "Now, tell me about him." She sat at the table and poured her own cup of tea.

Tiponi closed her eyes for a moment, picturing Sam in her mind. "He's wonderful." Her voice held a softness, which said much about her feelings without need of words.

"You *love* him," Kaya said in a clear statement, not a question. She looked at Tiponi with the eyes of a mother whose dream has come true.

Her mood switched from nostalgia to sadness. "Yes, I do. I wish we had time to be together."

"Does he know how you feel?"

"It's forbidden, but we speak without speaking." She reached over and took Kaya's hand. "Tonight, is all I have. He will sit beside me in a place of honor. I can do no more."

"I know, child. It has been a burden to carry that knowledge. I've loved you since I brought you from the desert that cold night. I…I knew I would lose you, but it had to be done." Kaya's voice filled with emotion and a small catch. "Do you forgive me, Tiponi?

"Forgive you? I love you. Neither you nor I have reason to regret anything. I freely chose my fate. That I was born for this purpose does not negate the choice."

"You are wise for one so young."

Tiponi took a sip of now cold tea. "You once told me power comes with responsibility. I had a great teacher." She stood and hugged Kaya's slim shoulders. "I love you, waken mother."

"I love you, daughter." Kaya turned and embraced her. She patted the back of Tiponi's head, and then leaned back to kiss her brow. "Now, no more serious talk. Let's speak of happy things. What shall I fix for our guest of honor tonight?"

"Do you have any six-hundred-year-old Anasazi

recipes?" Tiponi laughed at the look on Kaya's face.

"As a matter of fact…"

****

The sun sat low in the western sky as Tiponi walked with Kaya to the center square of the village. Excitement buzzed in the air as everyone bustled about cooking and preparing for the festivities. Tonight, they celebrated the return of their Sacred Chanunpa and the presence of two living Katsinas.

As she passed, men and women cast their eyes downward and stilled. To them she was a messenger from the Great Spirit. She played her part by remaining aloof and nodding her head.

She stamped hard on the small voice inside her head that told her she was unworthy of such attention.

You are more than worthy. The familiar voice filled her mind with warmth.

She stayed Kaya with a hand on her arm. "He's here."

A large wolf appeared, silhouetted against the setting sun. The crowd hushed. Everyone remained frozen, eyes riveted to the figure moving toward them.

Tiponi's heart thumped erratically as she watched him approach. Heat radiated up from the sand, making his form shimmer with an otherworldly look. His steel gray coat glistened in the sun's fading rays as he moved lithely across the hard-packed plaza. Eyes, red as the evening sun, watched them as he came closer. Stopping several feet from her, he bent his front legs and head in a reverent bow.

"Hania, rise. You are my equal and my chosen mate. Come take your place at my side as we celebrate tomorrow's coming."

A puff of smoke encompassed the wolf. From it, Hania arose, resplendent in his feathered headpiece and quill-bone breastplate. Tan colored breeches and moccasins completed his attire.

The crowd gasped, and all sank to their knees. What they witnessed had not been seen since early times.

Hania's muscular arms drew Tiponi's attention briefly before her eyes traveled upward and stared into his dark, fathomless eyes. As before, they spoke without words.

Breaking eye contact, she spoke to Kaya. "This is my spirit warrior, Hania." She used his Anasazi name because he was in Katsina form. The name, Sam, would only be used out in the world or between themselves.

Hania dipped his head in respect for the waken woman. "It has been long since we met, Kaya. Thank you for taking such good care of Tiponi."

The old woman held her hands out in front of her, palms up. "I expect you to return the favor."

"Her safety is my only concern." He gently placed his hands above hers, but not touching. A vow had been made.

Tiponi took his hand and turned to her people. Beaming with happiness, she raised their clasped hands. "People of Kahoti, let us celebrate with song, dance, and food."

The crowd dispersed as Tiponi, Hania, and Kaya walked to the line of chairs beneath the open tent. Chief Honaw greeted them as they took their seats. The two men sat in the center, flanked by the women. A single drumbeat sounded. Two young boys, painted head to toe and naked save a breech cloth, ran through the crowd with lighted torches. The drum rolled as the boys touched their torches to the large pile of wood, erected for the bonfire in the center of the square. The resulting blaze lit up the entire plaza while the drums beat to a vivacious dance. The celebration had begun.

From the crowd, young men jumped up and danced around the fire. They moved first one way and then the next as they circled the blaze. Some moves were more enthusiastic than accurate, but no one minded. Those lucky enough to possess an eagle feather flaunted it prominently at the top of their head. Eagle feathers were a sign of bravery or acts of heroism and must be earned. Tiponi turned and glanced at Hania. His entire head was covered with eagle feathers that continued down his back. Pride in his accomplishments filled her breast.

The music stopped, and everyone partook of the many refreshments laid out on the tables. Tiponi picked at the food Kaya brought to the tent. She tried hard to keep her mind in the present, but it kept rushing ahead to tomorrow.

Hania squeezed her hand and brought her mind back to the party. "No sad thoughts, remember."

"They're not sad, just contemplative. How about you? What are your thoughts?"

His eyes darkened, reminding her of two black holes sitting darkly among the bright stars. "I dare not say. Your cheeks are flushed enough already."

"It's just heat from the fire." She turned away as Chief Honaw stood.

"The flames are indeed hot," Hania mumbled beneath his breath.

Tiponi could have sworn he'd been talking about

something entirely different.

As the chief stood, the villagers quietly gathered, waiting for their leader to speak. The tribe was fully aware of the impending danger. And yet, they chose to celebrate instead of running away. The Kahoti were resilient and tenacious.

"My people, we are blessed tonight by the presence of two living Katsinas. In their honor, we dance and sing. Our world is in great danger, but as promised, they have come to protect us. Tomorrow, they will face the volcano to try and tame it. If they succeed, we will celebrate again, but if they do not—we celebrate tonight." The crowd laughed at the chief's joke. No Kahoti missed a chance to sing and dance.

"As Kahoti, we were directed to this land by Sotuknang. We have followed the edicts of our creator. Now we are in danger and need help. We seek the ear of the Great Spirit through his messenger, the eagle. In his honor we have a special group of dancers who will perform the Eagle Dance." The chief sat.

Four young dancers, two boys and two girls, approached the fire. They were elaborately dressed in eagle costumes. The boys were dressed in black and white. Tufts of eagle feathers stood upright on their heads, and white eagle down covered their heads and formed a vee down the chest. A yellow triangle fit across their nose forming a beak. Around the shoulders and down past the fingertips eagle feathers formed perfect wings. A black kilt and a fan tail gave the costume a very realistic look.

The girls wore white dresses with sashes. In each hand they carried eagle feathers and wore them behind their necks like a halo. Yellow macaw feathers added color to the black and white scheme.

The dancers moved to the accompaniment of flutes and rattles. Like a delicate ballet, they mimicked the flight of the graceful birds high in the sky. Tiponi found herself mesmerized by the movements. She could almost feel the gentle air currents lifting her body, the warmth of the sun shining on her cheeks. She soared higher, above the mesa all the way to the distant mountains. A lone flute played as the eagles flapped their wings and landed.

As the youngsters completed their dance, Tiponi was surprised when Hania instead of Chief Honaw rose to address her people. "Chief Honaw, White Mesa Woman, and Kahoti people. Listen now, for I have a message from Grandfather. A new Katsina shall be named, with a celebration all her own. This Katsina will be your guardian against volcanos and natural disasters. She will have her own song and her own dance. Her image shall bear the face of the moon and her hair shall be adorned with stars. White shall be the color of her dress, adorned with volcanoes and red lava flow. In one hand shall be a spear of lightning, and the other will act as an invisible shield."

Hania turned and pulled Tiponi from her seat. "Because of her sacrifice for her people, the new Katsina shall bear the name Tiponi."

Silence met his pronouncement, the people stunned. A new Katsina had never been named in their lifetime.

Tiponi gasped. The crowd cheered, and the drums began to beat.

From the darkness, a line of dancers made their way toward the fire. The Tiponi Katsina dancers moved to the music, playing out a story of victory over the volcano. Tiponi was sure the dance and music would evolve over time to accommodate other dangers. Like all things, Katsinas evolved with the people or were forgotten. Her heart filled with joy. She would be remembered in song and dance. There could be no greater honor from her people.

She ignored the tears streaming down her face as she watched her last dance.

Kaya's hand squeezed her shoulder, and she covered it with her own. It was time for her to leave.

Kaya kissed her cheeks and gave her a hug. "Go with the Great Spirit, child."

"I love you, Kaya," she whispered, then moved to take Hania's hand.

A bellow startled the observers nearest the plaza edge. Tiponi felt a smile tug at her lips. Her ride was here. Cloud Feather stepped into the light, and everything and everyone stopped. The white buffalo was the most sacred of animals to her people. He walked to Tiponi and waited for her normal attentions. She scratched his cheeks and rubbed his ears, then mounted when he bowed. Sam jumped on behind her.

She knew she was expected to say something before her departure, but what? Hania placed his arms around her waist, and her mind filled with warmth. Suddenly the words were there. "People of Kahoti. I have returned to help in your time of need. I ask that you help each other in my absence. Let no one hunger or go in need. Defend your neighbor and forgive wrongs. Keep your traditions and pride in your culture. You are Kahoti; live proudly."

With a quick wave, they lifted off the ground to

cheers and beating drums.

Chapter Thirty-One

Promises to Keep

They flew into the night, toward the stars and tomorrow's destiny. Drumbeats faded, replaced by cool wind singing through their hair. All thoughts in the here and now, letting tomorrow and all its pain wait for its time. When she sensed Cloud Feather tiring, she urged him toward the sand below. If she had a choice, she'd spend her last night with Hania in the desert.

The great animal touched down in a full gallop. She slowed him for fear he would hurt his legs on unseen rocks. Sliding from his back, she gave him a pat. "Thank you, Cloud Feather, you have served me well. It isn't safe here, so you must go home to your own world."

The buffalo butted his head into her stomach in disagreement.

Her voice shook when she said, "Sam, could you take him home for me, please?"

"Are you sure? We have all night."

"Yes, I need to focus on tomorrow and rid myself of emotional ties."

Silence fell between them. It was several moments before Sam spoke. "Does that include me?"

His question caught her off guard, piercing her heart. "I...yes, I believe it does. If I think of what could be, I might lose sight of what must be. We both knew it would happen, but I never realized how much pain it would bring." Her hands pressed across her heart as if she could stop the hurt or hold it at bay.

"I would never willingly bring you pain." Sam's voice could not disguise his own hurt. "I will take Cloud Feather home." He turned away from her and jumped on the buffalo's back.

"Sam?"

"Yes?"

"Please hurry. I need you." Her words gave lie to her previous ones. Poor Sam. One moment she was pushing him away, the next, she was grasping hold of him like a lifeline.

"Start a fire. I won't be long." His words did not chastise her for her capriciousness.

He blinked out of sight, taken by the Slipstream.

By moonlight, she gathered wood from nearby shrubs and made a fire ring. Ready to start the fire, she realized she had no flint. Feeling a little rebellious, she drew energy from her surroundings and sent a small bolt of lightning from her fingers to the wood—instant fire. It was a gross misuse of power, but it made her feel a little better.

She sat cross-legged by the fire as Sam walked out of the darkness carrying a bag. His words made her smile. "That is one stubborn buffalo."

She looked up at him across the flames. "What did he do this time?"

"He wouldn't move away from me. I was afraid he would get caught up in the Slipstream on the return trip." Sam walked over and sat beside her on the ground.

Evelyn Timidaiski

"He's the first pet I've had, and I love him, stubborn or not. Cloud Feather and I have a special bond."

"I suggest you get a smaller one with less orneriness next time."

"Just listen to us. What are we doing, Sam?"

He threw a stick into the flames, sending a burst of sparks upward. "We're talking about happy, unimportant things. Would you like to change the subject?"

"I'm assuming you know where and when to meet Grandfather?"

"Yes. We'll use the Slipstream and appear where we need to be. He will explain all the technical aspects of what the two of you are going to do." Sam pulled a woven blanket from the bag and spread it on the sand.

She scooted over to sit on the blanket. "You think of everything."

He joined her. "While the dropping temperature will not bother me, you might get chilled."

She lay back and gazed up at the full moon glowing in the dark sky. "There's so much I want to say, yet…" She paused, unable to go on.

Sam turned to look at her. "I thought we'd agreed to talk of only happy things."

"But I am happy. My people have the sacred chanunpa; I've transformed, and now I will help Grandfather save the world."

He sounded almost angry. "Have you ever done anything for yourself?"

"What do you mean?"

"Your entire life has been spent preparing for this event. You've trained and studied, but you've never

278

taken the time to do something for Tiponi and no one else."

She sat up and looked down into his handsome face. "Wouldn't that be rather selfish?"

"No, it would be human. Have you ever traveled and seen some of the world for which you've sacrificed your life?"

"I agree there are places I would have liked to visit. But we don't always get to do what we want. But what about you, Sam? Did you get to see everything you wanted to?"

"No. I would have liked to have seen my son grow up."

Tiponi gasped. How could she have been so stupid? "I'm so sorry. I didn't mean to make you hurt.

"It is *I* who should be sorry. You are merely better at acceptance than I." He sat up and took her hands. "Allow me to give you a night tour of some of the most beautiful things in the world."

"You're not talking about Paris, are you?"

"Not unless you wish it."

"You could do that? Not that I'd want to go there."

"What would you like to see?"

"I've never really thought about it. Why don't you surprise me?"

"You trust me?"

"Always and forever, Sam."

Something in his eyes changed, along with the atmosphere between them. She could feel the charged molecules in the air. Abruptly, he stood. "Bring the blanket; you're going to need it."

Excitement made her blood tingle, or was that Sam? She stood and he wrapped the blanket around her followed by his arms. His head bent to touch her forehead and she felt the Slipstream grab them. It was different this time. Not only could she feel the spirits of others, she could recognize some of them.

A cold blast of air met them when they reappeared. Snow crunched beneath her feet, reinforcing the cold. Sam turned her in his arms; she gasped in awe. The Aurora Borealis.

"It's beautiful. I can't think of words to describe such splendor."

They stood on the edge of a lake, surrounded by fir trees and snowcapped mountains on the horizon. The sky moved with brilliant, yellow-green ribbons. A curtain of light shimmered and undulated like a living entity swimming in Earth's atmosphere.

Reflections in the lake mirrored the beautiful lights as they writhed above. The color shifted, turning blue, pink, and purple. The curtain twisted, forming spikes of light shooting upward like rays from the sun. The constant motion and changing colors and patterns mesmerized her.

"I can feel it as well as see it."

"Then you are doubly blessed." His voice spoke near her ear. "What do you hear?"

"Why, music of course. It's a haunting melody as old as the stars. It reminds me of a quote from Geronimo that I read in school."

"…The song that I will sing is an old song, so old that none knows who made it… This is a holy song, and great is its power. The song tells how, as I sing, I go through the air to a holy place where The Supreme Being will give me power to do wonderful things. I am surrounded by little clouds, and as I go through the air I change, becoming spirit only…"- Geronimo, Apache (1829-1909)

Her words ended with charged silence. She reveled in the song another moment, then turned to face Sam. "Thank you for bringing me to this place. I think it has healed my heart."

He turned her around. "We need to get you out of the cold." His voice was gruff.

Before she knew it, they were once more in the Slipstream. They were caught up in its pull mere minutes before she felt the Earth pulling her downward.

Warmth, sand, and a gentle breeze greeted her. They were in the desert again. Sam took her hand, and they walked in the moonlight on a path up a hill. As they crested the hill, Tiponi dropped Sam's hand and sank to her knees. A natural sandstone arch was illuminated by the moonlight. The red sandstone glowed in the moonlight, creating a frame for the Milky Way Galaxy. On either side of the arch, the galaxy extended into infinity. Millions of stars glittered against the indigo backdrop of the sky.

"Sam, let's stay here. I want to fall asleep with this image in my mind. I never realized there was so much beauty in the world."

Sam cleared a spot on the ground and spread the blanket. They sat for a long time soaking in the panoramic view.

She turned to look into his dark eyes. "Do you remember the promise you made?"

"Of course. Do you remember yours?"

"Yes. I will fight to come back, Sam. You told me once that one spirit could help another. I'm counting on you to show me the way."

His breath whispered across her face. "I will wait forever if need be, and I will keep calling to you."

"I think I'll call in your promise now."

Sam's eyes became black fire. He pulled her close, and his lips touched hers.

An explosion of feeling flashed through her. She was on fire as his lips moved across hers. Her heart pounded so wildly, she thought it would burst with love. Her lips parted and he swooped in, demanding, taking. His tongue met hers in an age-old dance—a dance of mating. Reaching up she placed her palms on either side of his face. Her fingers roamed, discovering, memorizing each angle and curve. She felt his heart racing against her breast and thought she would die from feeling.

Abruptly, he pulled away from her and stood. Bereft, she could only stare in horror as he walked away from her and into the desert.

Chapter Thirty-Two

The Last Stand

Fingers of light crept across the morning sky as Hania's warmth settled against her back. Tender feelings seeped into her mind, and her body relaxed. She had only herself to blame for the pain in her heart. It had been she who had demanded payment of his promise. The small taste of him had been exquisite and worth any amount of pain. Now—she had to put all that behind her and focus on the volcano.

"Good morning." She tried for chirpy, but her voice came out more like a croak. She felt him shift from wolf to man behind her.

"Good morning, Tiponi."

Reassurance, strength, he was her rock. She turned over and sat up on the blanket. Sam's face was as handsome as ever. His countenance showed no signs of emotional distress or a night spent in a game of 'what if's.' She could have spent the night *inside* the volcano, for all the sleep she'd gotten.

"It's time," Sam said.

She stood at his words. Somewhere in the restless night, she had come to terms with her destiny.

Sam threw sand on the remains of the fire and gathered the blanket and bag. Mundane tasks that only served to delay the moment they both must face. When she and Grandfather would combine their powers and pit themselves against the volcano. A time when she could very well die.

She faced Sam, and he took her hand. Electricity jolted where they touched, but Sam kept his mind carefully shielded from her. He couldn't shield his eyes, however, and she saw the sadness in them.

"It's okay, Sam. I'm ready."

He leaned in and touched his forehead to hers. The Slipstream grabbed them, and the vortex of swirling energy carried them to their destination.

****

Yellowstone National Park had once been a source of national pride. An unspoiled wilderness filled with natural beauty and boundless wildlife. A place where people could enjoy hiking among trees and wildflowers, climb majestic mountains, and watch water cascade over naturally carved escarpments. Unique environments such as the geysers and mud pots provided evidence of the subterranean cauldron roiling beneath the serene surface.

Tiponi and Sam set foot on the trembling surface of the park grounds. He steadied her until the rumbling ceased and she got her first look at America's worst nightmare.

The Yellowstone Caldera sat atop a super volcano, asleep for thousands of years. Now the sleeping giant was wide awake, making its presence known with daily earthquakes and rapid ground swelling of three to six inches per day.

She looked around at the bubbling mud pools and fumaroles. Spewing sulfur gases added noxious smells to complete the analogy. "It looks like a biblical description of Hell."

"Hell is a state of mind," Sam seriously intoned.

She cast a quick look at him but didn't ask.

Stepping cautiously around a bubbling mud pot, she continued on the track through Norris Geyser Basin. "When will we meet Grandfather?"

The elevation of Yellowstone had increased over two hundred feet in the last century. The basin, now a mound, looked like a giant boil on the face of the park. With lava only thirty miles beneath the surface and the increased seismic activity, it could 'pop' at any moment.

"He's conversing with a park ranger about evacuations of personnel. We will rendezvous at the mouth of Grand Canyon of Yellowstone."

She stopped as she approached an area of small geysers shooting super-heated water several yards into the air. "I can't believe people are still here. Everyone within a hundred-mile radius should have been out of here six months ago."

"The government kept a skeleton crew here to help the scientists who've been studying the volcano's changes." Sam took the lead, deftly avoiding the spouting flumes.

"And the military? I'm sure they're involved."

Sam stopped and turned at her question. "They are at all entrances to the park and spread over a two-hundred-mile area radiating outward. They're forcing stragglers from small towns in the danger zone."

"Why would anyone want to stay? Surely they must know it's certain death."

"Unfortunately, the volcanic eruption has been predicted, analyzed, and sensationalized by everyone from the media to the Doomsday prophets. Many people have decided it's just another false alarm. Others just want to gawk."

"So many are going to die needlessly. The soldiers are risking their lives to remove those stubborn people," Tiponi said with heat.

"If we're unsuccessful, the death toll will be unthinkable. Not just here, but over most of the United States. Two thirds of the nation will become uninhabitable," Sam said. His words brought a pall over their discussion.

As they approached the canyon village, Tiponi was surprised to see several Native Americans standing around Grandfather and a park ranger. A long black braid dropped past the ranger's shoulders, a contradiction to the crisp uniform and sidearm which identified his position as a federal government employee.

"Good morning, Tiponi. All is well with you?"

"Of course, Grandfather. I had not realized there would be so many people."

"May I introduce Ranger Chanton Bird-feather from the Sioux tribe. He is well versed in the subtleties of the area, having worked here for thirty years."

Tiponi shook the strong brown hand extended to her. "Ranger Chanton. We appreciate all your help."

"It is we who are grateful for the help of the spirits. Many tribes have sent holy men and women to help." He pointed to the assembled group of Native Americans.

About thirty people dressed in tribal clothing from the Dakota, Cheyenne, Crow, Shoshone, Nez Perce, and Sioux among others stood awaiting instructions.

Tiponi had no wish for unnecessary loss of life. "These people, honorable intentions aside, are in great danger, Grandfather."

"How can we deny them the right to help save their homeland?" Sam asked.

"All help will be needed to accomplish our task," Grandfather interjected calmly.

Ranger Chanton harrumphed. "The volcanologists have come on board with our plan after realizing that anything we do will not hurt and can only precipitate the inevitable. It seems scientists have little faith in higher powers."

"It is their job to be skeptical. They deal in absolutes, whereas we deal with things that cannot always be seen or measured. Their knowledge will be very helpful. With our combined resources we may well succeed." Grandfather's words quelled any further discussion.

Ranger Chanton walked over to a wall board covered by a detailed map of the park. With a red marker, he circled several areas on the map. "The idea is to take advantage of natural weaknesses in the subterranean fault to release lava and reduce the magnitude of an eruption. We hope to guide the lava into the canyon and the lake. First we need to drain the lake to prevent the lava from cooling and damming the flow."

"That is where we help, Tiponi. We will drain the lake and control the flow of the lava." Grandfather gave her a questioning look. "Are you ready?"

"Yes, I am ready. How will we initiate the lava flow?"

"The Army has placed explosives at the places

pinpointed by the volcanologists. I have marked the areas on the map," Chanton explained. "Each of the explosions will be sequenced to help the lava flow in the correct direction."

"But the river in the Canyon flows northwest," Tiponi interjected.

"Yes, but the elevation difference will aid in the flow. You and Grandfather will have to do the rest." The ranger moved over to the group of Native Americans. After speaking with one of the older men whose headdress was covered in eagle feathers, the two walked to the map.

"Chief Hiamovi will explain the detonation points." Chanton stepped back from the map.

Tiponi was surprised to see the renowned scientist here. He had often spoken out against the park's handling of the volcano's progression. She knew he was Cheyenne, a fact supported by his beadwork and face paint. He had always been a role model to her. He maintained his Native American beliefs, yet successfully worked in the White man's world as a scientist. The two seemed to contradict each other, but he was living proof that it could be done.

"*Pâhávevóonä'o*. Good morning. Many of you are familiar with my work as a scientist, but few know my Cheyenne heart."

Tiponi's eyes burned as tears rolled down the proud chief's face.

"This land is sacred to all of us." He moved his hand in an arc to in include all the Native Americans. "My Cheyenne heart weeps for the destruction that must be done. We will deprive our grandchildren of their heritage—their birthright…but I would rather see my children's children shed thousands of tears, than the alternative—no children, no grandchildren, and no Native Americans left to teach those who survive." He paused, and then let loose a chilling Cheyenne war cry. The other tribes joined in, and the resulting shrieks raised goose bumps on her flesh.

"Now," he continued solemnly. "The first explosion will take place just south of Norris basin which will deflate rather than burst the land bulge. The lava will be directed south toward the lake." His fingers snaked down the pathway on the map that led to the lake.

"Next, there will be simultaneous detonations at West Thumb geyser basin and Sulfur Cauldron. Lastly, the upper falls of the Canyon will be blown and the lava directed down through the Canyon." The Chief looked around at the serious faces. The ground rumbled beneath their feet, the only reply to his words.

Grandfather moved to stand before the group. "I am sure all of you are aware, this could fail. We could very well cause the entire volcano to blow. We must go into this with the conviction of success in our minds. Tiponi and I will begin to drain the lake as the rest of you take up places of safety along the lava path."

Grandfather nodded to Hania, who took Tiponi's hand, preparing to transport them to the lake. Around them the tribal representatives began a prayer chant with rattles. Grandfather and Hania joined their voices with them.

Hania's voice resonated in her ear as she placed her head against his chest. The Slipstream grabbed them up, only to deposit them seconds later at the edge of the vast Yellowstone Lake.

Chapter Thirty-Three

Ground Zero

A hot breeze, along with the stench of rotting meat, blasted her face as her feet touched down beside the lake. Dead fish floated around the edge, their corpses cooked by the boiling temperature of the water. Heated by the cauldron from below, the water escaped into the atmosphere as thick vapor. The mist gave the lake an eerie appearance like an omen of things to come.

Tiponi shook her head to rid the fanciful thoughts from her mind. She could feel Grandfather high up on the mountain top, standing on the continental divide. They were going to move the water up and over the divide, creating an empty basin here and a damp desert on the other side.

Hania's voice sounded in her mind as he positioned himself behind her. *Grandfather is ready to begin.*

She nodded, straightened her back, and concentrated on the water. She imagined pressing down on the top of the water and caused a circular current to form in the center. Waves swirled as if happy to dance at her command. Kinetic energy increased, pushing the molecules about in a frenzy of movement. The top of the water jumped in arcs as if rain had plopped down and displaced it. Energy from the water seeped into her body making her more powerful. A thrill ran through her body as the energy surged higher.

She threw her hands up, pushed with her mind, and forced the water to obey. Suddenly, she felt the breath of Grandfather blowing against the water. The water twisted tightly together, and a huge waterspout shot upward. She staggered from the strain of holding the water. Hania moved up against her back, supporting her with his strength. She couldn't acknowledge him as she pushed even harder, raising the water thousands of feet into the air.

Her arms shook with the effort of holding the water. Strong arms held hers upright, and warmth filled her mind. He was with her, in her—her rock, solid and supportive. When she thought her strength would give out, she felt a forceful jerk on the geyser. Grandfather had the other end of the swirling mass, pulling it up and over the divide.

Relieved of some of the strain gave her impetus to continue drawing water from the lake and up to Grandfather. Millions upon millions of gallons flowed through the air as if sucked up by an enormous siphon and transported through an invisible pipe. She held the swaying vortex, continuing to pull more water into it. Her energy steadily depleted, and she worked hard to hold the stream of water steady. The lake was large, and the process to drain it was a mere hour old.

Two hours later, her legs and arms numb with fatigue, the water funnel dried up. The lake was nearly empty, but some of the deeper parts remained. She lowered her arms slowly, wincing at the sharp pins and needles stabbing her muscles.

Hania turned her body toward him and rubbed each of her arms to force blood into her extremities. Aware of her surroundings now, the sound of ancient prayer chants drifted to her ears on the wind. Her spirits lifted at the sound. They could do this. Together, using all their talents and powers, it would be done.

Grandfather appeared a few feet away. "You did well, Tiponi." He touched her shoulder, and healing energy pulsed through her.

Closing her eyes, she allowed the restorative surge to rejuvenate her aching muscles. Nothing could ease the tense nerves in her head. The strain of concentrating so intensely made her head throb as her neurons struggled to reconnect with synapses.

"I'll take care of the last few spots. You go to Observation Peak and prepare for the detonations."

Hania pulled her against his chest, wrapping her in his protective aura. Moments later, they stood high above the canyon at Observation Point. The view was breathtaking. From this vantage point, she could see the canyon and to the other side of the lake.

Grandfather was ridding the lake of the last of its moisture, by evaporation. His hands before him, tremendous heat shot from his fingers. She could see the heat waves as they struck the water and instantly changed it to vapor. Clouds of steam rose above the lakebed, looking normal in this place of steam and geysers.

She tried to shake off the unease swirling through her mind as Grandfather completed his task. Hania stood beside her, keeping his thoughts and comments to himself. *Her* thoughts were scattered. Could she really help Grandfather defeat the volcano? Would she survive the process, and if not—did it hurt to become spirit? She had seen pain in Hania's eyes and felt it in his heart. Did he feel physical pain?

Hania's voice brought her back from her reverie. *One minute before the first detonation. Prepare yourself; the explosion will rock the landscape for miles.*

She spread her feet apart for balance and took the hand Hania held out to her. The sound of the explosion was enough to shake her without the shock wave that pushed through the crust and rocked them both on their feet. Rocks, truck-size to small pebbles, blasted upward along with a plume of dust and smoke. Heat rose from the blast site and spread with volcanic gases—poison to humans and animals alike. That was why all but Grandfather had been placed so far away.

The cloud of dust and smoke disappeared to be replaced by lava, oozing from the hole at the bottom of the land bulge and pouring down the hill. This was exactly what they wanted. The precision explosion had opened the lava stream from below the bulge and not exploded it from the top.

She opened her mind to the energy from the blast. Her body recoiled as her mind penetrated the heat and met the lava flow. Once again, she lifted her arms and pushed energy from her hands toward the molten rock. The viscous mass bubbled and popped like water droplets in hot grease. Bright orange beneath, the outer edges of the flow cooled to grey and then black as it moved through the atmosphere. She worked the molecules to keep them fluid and moving down the slope. The water had been easy compared to this. It was as if the spawn from the volcano had a mind of its own. Like a living entity seeking its own path, not content to follow the whims of a human choreographer.

Her concentration veered momentarily as the sound of one, then two explosions occurred within seconds of each other. West Thumb geyser basin and Sulfur Cauldron spewed more lava from the belly of the volcano to join the other stream heading for the lake.

She split her attention between the three areas. Controlling the massive flows caused a tremendous energy drain. Grandfather's presence entered her mind. She felt his power moving the flows with her. She had no time to be awed by his presence in her mind. The drain on her powers took a toll on her physical body. Arms wrapped around her from behind. Warmth entered her mind. Again, Hania lent his support.

Her psi senses picked up a mammoth increase of pressure beneath the Norris basin bulge. The exploded opening wasn't draining the lava pool fast enough, and the excess was building up quickly. If they didn't act fast, the pressure would cause the volcano to erupt. She was torn. She and grandfather were controlling three flows, and the next detonation was about to occur, right beneath high falls where she stood.

The falls.

She heard Grandfather's words as if he had spoken them face to face and not a mile away.

"Hania, it's time to move."

She released her hold on the lava, allowing Grandfather to take over. Hania already had his arms around her, and the Slipstream grabbed them, spiriting them off to their fallback position, Roosevelt Tower. The site was located at the downhill end of the Grand Canyon at Yellowstone. She'd be safer here until after the falls were blown.

The canyon was small compared to the true Grand

Canyon and had been formed by water erosion and subterranean geysers. It had filled once before during a lava flow thousands of years before. Wind and water had re-forged it over the millennia. Now they would use it again to hold a large portion of the overflow of lava.

She stepped reluctantly from Hania's embrace and set her stance to wait for the next explosion. It didn't take long. The explosion was long and loud. From her vantage point she could see the plume of debris and smoke. Something was wrong; she felt it on an elemental level. As she watched, the smoke cleared enough to see that the lava wasn't flowing downward. The explosion had not blown the falls, merely created a hollow stack to channel the molten rock straight up into the air. The scientists couldn't be faulted; no one really understood all the geological nuances of this area. It was like no other on Earth.

"Quick, Hania." The words barely left her mouth and they disappeared into the Slipstream. Heat blasted them as they landed back at Observation Point. Most of the volcanic gases had dissipated, but she knew she couldn't last long under these conditions. She was far too close to the disgorging monster.

You can do it, Tiponi. Grandfather's voice calmed the panic forming inside her brain.

Warmth from Hania also infused her with calm and...*love?* Yes, it was there for her to read. She sent her feelings to him and then took a calming breath.

Deliberately, she cut off her mind from the two and focused inward. From deep within herself, she pulled every ounce of energy and strength. Ignoring the heat, gases, and rumbling ground, she focused on the spot which should have been blown. Inside a crevice nearly forty feet down was a weak area faced by granite. She had to remove that granite and divert the flow outward.

Denser than the surrounding rock, the granite gave off a different psi reading. It was hard to read anything in the spewing mess. The intense heat distorted frequencies and made it more difficult to separate the granite from the rest. Concentrating, she reached out with her psi senses, probing for the correct area. *There!*

Her hands stretched outward and down, and she released lightning bolts from her fingers. A small explosion occurred, but the granite held. She was going to have to sustain the bolts like a laser to cut through the solid rock.

Her body was weakening, held up mostly by Hania's arms and her own will. She had to do this— couldn't let her people down. This was the reason for her birth. She gathered the last of her strength and sent out a gigantic pulse of lightning, holding it steady. Minutes passed as she held the stream of electricity directly on the granite. Just when she thought she'd have to stop, she heard chanting. Real or in her head, it did not matter. The prayers of the people gave her strength to hang on. Finally, the rock exploded, and the falls collapsed. The Yellowstone river was replaced by a stream of red lava, flowing to the end of the Canyon. They had done it. The Volcano had been lanced and would purge itself, then heal its wounds by sleeping.

Relief filled her as her hands dropped, and she collapsed against Hania. His arms surrounded her, and feelings of love encased her in a bubble of time. The volcano receded from her mind. There was just the two of them. She felt no pain, just emptiness. Her body and mind had been drained of all energy.

"Tiponi, my love." Hani's voice rasped from his lips.

She saw the pain etched on his face—barely recognized the hard visage looking down at her. Her hand reached up to touch his face. Those hard lines relaxed, and she wiped the tears from his cheek.

"Don't cry, Hania. I can't bear it if you cry."

"It would be as difficult to stop my tears as it was to stop the volcano." His voice choked.

"I promise, no matter how long it takes, I'll find my way back to you." Her voice was weak, and he had to bend closer to hear her words.

"Kiss me, Hania, and then let me sleep."

Their lips touched in a soft caress, and her last breath escaped into his mouth.

Chapter Thirty-Four

Spiritual Awakening

Tiponi sagged in Hania's arms. Pain, sharp as a knife, ripped through his body and pierced his heart. From the depths of his soul, a scream welled up and spilled forth. It was the cry of a wolf that has lost his mate—a warrior whose heart has been ripped out by cruel hands. It became a chilling war cry—eerie, unearthly, meant to terrorize his enemies. Had there been any animals left in the area, they would have fled for their lives at the harsh wail.

"Hania, let her go. She must find her own way." Grandfather's quiet voice broke through his anguish.

"What if she can't make it back?"

"The journey and the choice to return is hers to make. For now, you must release her spirit and let it seek its destiny."

"You are right." He sighed and gently placed her on the ground. He ran the back of his hand down her cheek. "Remember your promise, Tiponi. You must fight to come back. Only strong spirits can come back. Be strong, my love."

"There's an old poem by Mary Elizabeth Frye that is appropriate," Grandfather said gently.

Do not stand at my grave and cry;
I am not here,

I did not die

"She's not dead, Hania, as long as her spirit lives. If you release a butterfly and it returns to you, then it is yours. Let her fly, my son."

Hania placed his hands upon her stomach, and her body began to sparkle like fireflies twinkling in the desert sky. He watched as her form disappeared and then turned into his animal form. He gave vent to his lost love with his wolf voice and vanished.

****

Hania's face blurred as grayness dimmed her vision. Her last glimpse of him was of anguish—tears flowing down his face—unashamed in his weeping. Her breath caught, not in pain, but awe. This great warrior was crying for *her*. She wanted to take him in her arms and comfort him, but she couldn't. Her body floated above the ground, twinkling like miniature stars. He and Grandfather watched as she rose toward the heavens. She no longer controlled her body; forces were pulling her away from her love.

Darkness overtook her, she became cold, and then…she felt nothing.

Tiponi.

She felt a tingle of something in her mind. Where was she?

Please, come back.

There was the sound again. Disoriented, she had no idea of up or down. The sound was indecipherable—just a buzz.

THUMP-thump-thump-thump,
THUMP-thump- thump-thump

Drums. She sat up, or at least she thought she did, and opened her eyes. In the distance was a small light.

It flickered, and an image of fire came to her mind. She flowed closer to get a better look. She had no form. She was an untethered spirit, moving at will, but with no place to go. Warmth surrounded her body as she came near the fire. She hovered, enjoying the heat as it radiated from the flames.

THUMP-thump –thump-thump,
THUMP- thump- thump-thump

The flames danced with the pounding drum. She watched in fascination as a man's face appeared in the fire. Like steam wafting from a hotcake, the face rose and formed a body, drifting from the fire. Staring into nothingness, the man continued beating the drum. He came to the end of his piece and stopped. The drum faded and disappeared. The man, neither young nor old, sank to the ground, his legs crossed as he sat.

"You saw the flame, this is good."

"Actually, I heard your drum first."

"Ah. Many do not hear or see. They drift without thought or worry."

She studied the man quietly for a few moments.

"There was something in my head, but I did not understand."

"That was someone calling to you. They wish you to return."

"Who was it?"

"Did you not recognize the spirit who called you?"

"No, I did not even hear the words."

"Then, you are not ready. Something or someone holds you here."

"But I saw the fire and heard the drum," she reminded him reasonably.

"There is time. You will see and hear more before

you are ready."

"What must I do?" She felt like a child, anxious to play but not understanding the rules.

"You must do what you must." His form wavered briefly, then disappeared.

His words made her curious. If there were others, she would find them. Maybe they could help her. Streaks of lights flashed in the distance. Familiarity swept across her as she approached the lights. Voices sounded around her as the lights swirled past. She heard them, but they did not speak to her.

Tiponi, fight.

This time, she heard the words, but the voice still eluded her. Someone was out there and knew her name. They wanted her to fight, to come back. How was she supposed to fight? There was no enemy.

A ripple in the stream of light caught her attention. She followed it and found an old woman outside her home. Knees bent, the woman poured dry kernels of corn onto the metate, the grinding stone. She picked up her mano and skillfully ground the corn into powdery masa.

"Would you like some piki bread?"

"Yes, please."

The smell of corn rose from the heated cooking stone, bringing with it tendrils of things just out of reach at the edges of her mind.

"It is good, yes?"

"Mmm, delicious. Kaya used to pour guava syrup…" Tiponi gasped. "I remember her."

"Your memories are all there. You must allow them time to come back."

"It's nice here; must I leave?"

"No, child. Many are happy to stay here. Others, like yourself, have strong ties to the corporeal world and eventually find no peace here."

"Someone is calling me. How can I find them?"

"You must look into your heart and you will find them."

She savored the piki bread and turned her thoughts inward. It was difficult when she felt like an empty vessel. No memories rushed to her conscious thought.

"Ho, ho, Watanay." The woman sang softly as she bent to grind more corn.

The words were familiar to her, but she remembered a man's voice singing the tune.

Chills ran down her...body. She could actually see her body now.

"Ho, ho, Watanay, Ki-yo-ki-na." Her own voice joined the old woman's tune. Emotion filled her, and warmth seeped into her mind.

Come home to me, my love.

She heard the voice—the same one that had sung the lullaby to her.

The rhythmic scraping of stone against stone stopped. "The heart is a powerful thing, is it not? It can be broken, forgotten, and lost. Yet, it still sings."

"I heard him sing, and my heart answered. How can I speak to him?

"You must first search your heart. You will find the answer you seek."

When she looked up, the woman was gone. She picked up the mano, added more corn, and began the back and forth motion to grind the corn. Her hands and body were now fully formed. As her hands worked, she relaxed. Soon images skittered through her mind. A young girl in the desert, words spoken by a kind woman, and the mournful cry…of a wolf!

Chapter Thirty-Five

Spirits Return

Sam tossed a dry branch on the fire, and watched the sparks fly upward toward the starlit sky. He searched the heavens looking for signs, and finding none, returned to his contemplation of the hot coals within the circle of stones. Three long weeks had passed since her spirit left the Earth. At first, he had wandered aimlessly, howling his anger and grief. Still, she had not heard and had not come. His wolf form had grown weak with sorrow, and now he sat before the fire in his man form.

Tossing sweetgrass and cedar onto the coals, he inhaled the sacred herbs and let them cleanse his thoughts. He had to believe she would make it back. She had been a strong person and an even stronger Katsina. Spirits returned in their own time not his. Hadn't he taken almost a year to return? He had struggled with many things before deciding to fight to return. His search for his wife and child in the spirit world had been fruitless. Either he no longer could recognize them, or they had drifted away.

Grandfather's voice had called him in his despair, reassured and helped him. He would continue to do the same for Tiponi.

He stripped down to his breechcloth and picked up

the bowl of pigment he had prepared. To increase the potency of his prayers, he had mixed water with ash from the volcano to create a black pigment. With fingers that shook, he dipped them into the paint and drew vertical lines beneath each of his eyes. From the second bowl, he removed a handful of red clay. Spirits did not bleed, and this would represent his blood. Just as she had made a blood sacrifice for him, he would do the same for her now.

He placed his palm to his chest, leaving an imprint of his hand. The symbol was used by many tribes, including the Kahoti, to represent self. He had signed his body with his name and would offer it up to the Great Spirit. He knelt before the fire and threw his arms upward in supplication.

"Oh, Great Spirit, I have honorably served you these past centuries. You have blessed me with strength to fight many battles. Now I have become stricken with grief. Please help my beloved's spirit return to me. My heart bleeds for her. Without her, my strength will leave."

From the sky a mighty bolt of lightning arced across the desert and struck a boulder behind him. Thunder clapped in a deafening roar and echoed as it rolled across the landscape. The still air whipped into a frenzied storm, screeching in competition with the thunder. From the dryness of the air, rain miraculously poured in heavy sheets, washing the sand and him with its cleansing freshness. The red clay dissolved from his chest, ran down his body, and hissed as it touched the hot coals. His face upturned to the heavens ran with black tears until he no longer cried.

As quickly as it began, the storm was over. Sam

bowed his head in reverence of the mighty power of the Great Spirit. Around him, the desert had gone eerily quiet. He sat, crossed his legs, and breathed on the smoldering coals. The fire leaped to life and he looked around. His sensitive ears picked up a faint sound.

In the shadows just out of the glow of the fire, he saw a set of eyes. His muscles tightened, and he waited tensely.

"Tiponi?"

The eyes blinked at him but came no closer.

"Don't be afraid." He kept his voice velvet soft. The creature was timid, not an enemy. He could feel its heart beating rapidly. As he watched, one small paw, then another eased into the light. He held his breath. Next, a small black nose inched forward. He forced himself to stay still as the shy creature inched forward into the light.

Moments later, he sucked in his breath, awed as a beautiful red fox stepped into the light. "Tiponi, love. Please tell me it's you."

The fox avoided the fire but walked toward him. The creature approached him, moved behind him, allowing the long red tail to brush against his back.

"You vixen, it is you."

"You once told me how much you liked my red hair." Her hands ran down his shoulders and back.

"Tiponi, I—" His words died as he swiveled to see her face. "Didn't you forget something?"

"This is the first time I've changed forms. I haven't figured out how to materialize with clothes on yet."

He grabbed her and pulled her tightly against his chest. "I'm not complaining."

"Sam," she murmured against his neck. "It feels so

wonderful to have your arms around me. I love you so much."

He felt the wetness of her tears against his cheek. "No more tears. We will be together now and always."

"Always?"

"Yes, always." He pulled her face up to his and crushed her lips to his. He had waited so long to have her.

Tiponi pulled back from him and ran her fingers over his face. "I want to memorize every part of you."

"I'll start by kissing every part of you," he said. "I thought I would die if you didn't return."

"I had a few things to work out before I could come to you. But now I'm here, I'll never leave your side."

He lay back on the sand, pulling her with him. Her body covered his intimately, skin to skin.

"I have so many things to learn about being a spirit, Sam."

"Not now, love. I'm going to teach you about being my wife first."

She sat up in excitement. "Spirits can marry? I can't wait."

"Neither can I. So, bring that lovely body down here and let me show you how spirits make love."

Hours later, they lay, limbs entangled by the dying fire. Tiponi felt as if her heart would burst with love. Everything that she had endured had been worth it. Her people and her world had been saved. She had become a woman and had the love of the bravest, most handsome warrior ever.

"Sam, do wolves eat foxes?"

Several minutes passed before he answered.

"Only the gray ones. We just chase the red ones."

"Sam." Her voice was full of censure. "I don't know if I'll like being chased by a big wolf."

"Then don't run." His laughter made her punch his ribs.

"One last question, I promise. Then we can sleep."

Sam looked at her and sighed. "All right, one more."

Tiponi gave him a wicked smile. "Can spirits have babies?"